Flame of RETRIBUTION

written by

Amir Jamal Williams

publisher

Nation of Flame Publishing, LLC

www.class5incorporated.com

This book is a creative work. No parts of this book may be repro-
duced, stored in a retrieval system, or transmitted by any means
without the written permission of the author.

Cover Design: Deesignz Web & Graphics Studio

Edited by: Deneen G. Matthews

Categories: Fiction Based on True Story, Drama, Loss

ISBN: 978-0-692-89261-9

REVENGE NEVER DIES.

Amir Jamal Williams

Amir Jamal Williams is an actor, novelist, playwright, and lyricist. He was born on December 12th, 1981, in Harlem, New York, and raised in Washington Heights. At the age of two, he began his career in acting, appearing in numerous commercials and print. In 1988, at the age of six, he landed the role of J.T. Rallins in the first season of the hit show, A Different World. After a few years of theater, *Black Nativity, Betsey Brown,* he took over the role of Jamal Wilson-Cudahy on the soap opera, *All My Children*, where he remained for several years. He also appeared in numerous television movies, such as *Daybreak* (HBO, 1993), *Silent Witness: What a Child Saw* (USA, 1994), *The Anissa Ayala Story*, and *I'll Fly Away*. He also appeared on television shows, such as *New York Undercover* and *Law and Order.* After some more years in off-Broadway theater and opera, *Gianni Schicci, Different Fields,* he began the voice-over role of "Mack" *MacKenzie* in the MTV cartoon, Daria, where he remained until its end. He retired in the year 2000, at the age of eighteen, to pursue writing and other interests.

As a child, Amir always had a love for writing. He spent most of his free time reading books, and mysteries and thrillers held a special place in his heart. Authors such as Agatha Christie, Edgar Allan Poe, and R.L. Stein rank among his favorites. In addition to Flame of Retribution, he has completed another literary work, *The Blackbird Chronicles: Volume One*; a work of ten short stories, with more volumes to follow. He is currently directing two plays; *The Diary of a Mother*, a documentary-theater, which examines eight mothers suffering loss, and *Pretty BIG Monologues*, written by him, following the life and struggles of a group of plus-sized dancers – due out at a later date. While he has no formal training, he knows great writing, compelling stories, and memorable characters. They are his life. Amir now resides in New York State, with his wife and children.

Table of Contents

Dedication

To Sean Bell (R.I.P.) and Nicole Paultre-Bell

CHAPTER ONE

The Wedding

It was only a few hours after the ceremony, and they were already arguing. The wedding itself was beautiful, but that was really no surprise. It took them months to find the right church. The dress search consumed even more time and effort – nearly a year. Although he had nothing to do with that part, he heard all about the fabrics, the textures, and the endless combinations of bridesmaids' colors; not to mention the constant company of female relatives and friends who squawked and cackled over every detail. It was this highly stressful period, now so easily forgotten, that made the present argument nothing short of ironic.

"I can't believe you would spoil such a beautiful day – the most important day of our *lives!*" she exclaimed.

Eric kept his eyes on the road.

"That's *exactly* what I was trying to do – ruin our wedding day."

Sarcasm – the married man's first line of defense.

She didn't address it. "Well, that's what you're doing," she continued. "You're ruining it."

"You complain about everything!" Eric exclaimed. "Only you could be angry on the way to a party."

"Our *reception*, Eric! It's our reception! Who has their wedding reception at a nightclub?"

Her name was Joanna Mosley, and he knew her for most of his life. They grew up together in the same complex and attended the same elementary school on the west side of Harlem – a small section of New York City. She was quite a character, even then; more than a bit on the bossy side. He remembered vividly the times he witnessed her on the playground. She imposed her will upon the other kids and insisted on being the leader in some of the games they were playing. She *always* got her way. No one ever challenged her demands, and why was no secret – she had a furious temper. Joanna was always a small girl, but he witnessed more than a few examples of what happened when she became angry and what she did to the person responsible.

As a child, Eric couldn't stand her. She got on his last nerve. It wasn't only her behavior that annoyed him, but the way everybody seemed to bend to her will. She was pretty, though – dark brown skin, a bright smile, and shiny black hair – always pulled to the sides in two long pigtails. But he didn't like her. He couldn't. She was too skinny anyway, he thought, and way too bossy. He decided early on, as many young boys do with difficult girls, to ignore her. After all, there were plenty of other girls his age in the neighborhood.

The neighborhood soon proved to be too small for both of them. They were always running into each other. Even when they attended separate schools, they saw each other everywhere, all the time. Then suddenly, it was time for college. Joanna went off somewhere, but Eric stayed in the city. Even still, for some reason, he never forgot about her. Of course, there was never anything between them. How could there be? They hardly spoke a word in all these years. Besides, they hated each other. He thought she was obnoxious. She thought he was goofy. Even if there *was* something, Eric thought, it was too late. She was gone now – off to learn wonderful new things and meet all sorts of new people – especially boys. No, it was best to forget about her altogether, he reasoned, even if the familiar face that kept popping into his mind only reminded him of just how little he really knew about her and how much he wanted to know.

Then one day, he got a call from Joanna. Even now, he remembered that day so clearly. It was wintertime, and the trains that passed by on the el in front of his window looked as if they were covered in marshmallow fluff. He cleared his throat for an eternity and tried to make sure his voice didn't crack. She got his number from her mother, who obtained it from his grandmother. Joanna didn't make small talk. She was in town for the holidays and wanted to see him. She invited him to her family's house for dinner. As strange as it seemed, the invitation wasn't as ridiculous as it sounded at the time. Their families weren't completely ignorant of each other. Nevertheless, he made a conscious effort to sound vacant while he agreed, as if the offer was of no appeal to him one way or the other. Truthfully, he was unsure of how he felt.

When the day came for them to finally see each other, Eric was in a state of total disarray. He showered three times. He tried on six different pairs of shoes. He tore his room apart in search of the perfect shirt-and-pants combination. It was disgusting. He considered wearing a jacket or at least, a tie, but decided against it. After all, he didn't want to seem anxious, even though he was – as if he had never been to a girl's house for dinner before, although he had not. He assumed a lot of her family members would be there, and he wanted to look presentable. It was odd, for sure. He wasn't certain of Joanna's plan or what to expect.

Suddenly, he heard the dull sound of their worn-out doorbell. Before he could get to it, his grandmother – proving that she could move fast enough when she wanted to – was already there, and the door was opened. There were small flakes of white frost on the shoulders of her charcoal gray, wool coat that halted just above her knees. Her skirt, which was just a bit lighter than the coat, peeked out about an inch from beneath and gave way to black tights; but only long enough to reveal the top of her black leather boots that started just above the calf and displayed a small heel. Eric couldn't see her hair. It was covered by a matching, gray, wool hat. She didn't smile, well not exactly, but he sensed that she was pleased to see him. It was in her eyes.

"I was going to come to the house," Eric stated.

It echoed in his head with such banality, but he couldn't think of anything else to say.

Joanna rescued him. "I figured I would walk with you."

She glanced in his grandmother's direction. "Aren't you going to introduce us?" she demanded.

"Right. Nana, this is Joanna – Joanna Mosley. She's a friend of mine," Eric said.

Cora, his grandmother, never took her eyes off Joanna as she wiped her hands on her apron.

"I know you," she said with not much warmth. "You're Estelle's daughter, aren't you?"

"That's right. You know her?"

"Of course," she replied, almost sounding offended.

"I remember when you were born." She glanced at Eric as she shuffled back to the couch. The sound of her worn-out slippers dragged across the floor as she walked.

She continued, "I didn't know you and my grandson were friends. I've never seen you together."

"I've been away," Joanna replied.

"At college, Nana," Eric interjected.

Now it was his turn to save her. "She's back on winter break. We haven't seen each other for a long time."

His grandmother was already at her seat and exhaled deeply as she sat down. There was a large bowl of potatoes on the table that she was peeling before she was interrupted. She now resumed her task and sat with her back facing them. Eric turned his attention to his houseguest, whom he left standing in the same spot. He thought of asking her to sit down, but the sooner they left, the better. There was tension in the air. He had no idea why, and he didn't want to know.

"I wasn't expecting you to come here. I mean, I don't care," Eric stated matter-of-factly. "It's just…"

"I didn't mean to intrude, but I wanted to talk to you – before dinner, I mean. Could we take a walk?" Joanna asked.

A walk? He thought. It was thirty degrees outside, at best, and there was an inch of snow on the ground. On top of that, he hated the cold, but she wanted to talk.

"Of course, that's fine," Eric said. "Just let me get my coat."

As Eric left the two women alone, there was no sound other than the theme music of an old game show, where mostly overweight people failed miserably while they tried to guess the cost of various items, and the sound of the metal peeler methodically scraping potatoes. The radiator in the far corner hissed occasionally as the open window blew in gusts of cold wind, billowing the curtains – an odd combination to be sure, but not uncommon with steam-heated apartments – the kind that were ungodly hot when it was freezing outside.

The wind hit him violently as he opened the door to the building. He let Joanna out first. He figured he'd better be as chivalrous as possible. She didn't exactly seem like the fragile type, but a young man could never be too careful. Better safe than sorry, he thought. They walked out of the project complex, which was quite a ways, but she hadn't said a word. He just listened to the sound of their feet crunching in the snow that started to freeze overnight, and its whiteness covered everything. Eric shuddered and folded the collar of his coat in tighter. He should have worn the puffy one, he thought angrily. He chose the thinner, more stylish coat he owned, and he was paying for it.

"I love the cold," Joanna stated, finally breaking the silence. She took a deep breath, exhaled, and blew out a thin stream of white air. "Don't you?"

Eric jammed his hands deep into his pockets and simply stated, "No."

They both laughed.

"I'm really glad you decided to come, Eric. I know it must have been kind of a shock."

"I don't mind. In fact, it's great. Now, I don't have to help Nana peel those potatoes. Speaking of which, what was going on in there? It was like a Mexican standoff or something," he said, laughing.

Joanna didn't laugh. "I don't think your grandmother likes me."

"How? Why? She doesn't even know you."

"She does know me," Joanna replied. "Actually, it's really my mother she knows. There's some history there."

Eric's eyes widened. "Really? I've never heard of it. Do you know what it's about?"

She looked at him now.

"Yes, I do, but I don't want to talk about that," she stated firmly.

Eric just nodded. They walked for a little while longer, toward Broadway. They were getting close to her building, and he knew it. He became more and more nervous with every step. He thought to call it off and return home. He could say he was getting sick, but she wouldn't believe that. Why did she have to ask him to this stupid thing? He honestly didn't know what he was doing. He looked down at his feet and watched the penny loafers he usually reserved for church sink into the frozen snow with every step. He wanted to go home.

"You're probably wondering why I asked you to come with me," Joanna blurted.

Eric shrugged. "Why did you?"

She didn't answer right away. Instead, she stopped walking and paused at the corner. The wind blew past them furiously as people shuffled by, occasionally showing disgust on their faces for the two idiots who stood in their way.

"I think I'm in love with you."

"What?!" Eric said, almost shouting. He hadn't meant to, but this was crazy.

"Eric... I've thought about you a lot since I've been away. I mean, I know we weren't close, but..."

"Weren't close?" he exclaimed. "Joanna, we've only spoken once since you left, and before that, we were kids. I barely know you, Jo, and you don't know me."

"You're wrong. I *do* know you. Look at the way you call me Jo. Nobody calls me that. It's like you know me in a way nobody else does."

He shook his head. "We've never been on one date together. We've never kissed." He thought about that one. It sounded so wrong. "I don't mean that we should have... It's just..."

"You don't understand," she said sharply, cutting him off. "When I first wrote you, I wasn't interested in you. I just wanted to let you know how things were going. I guess I wanted somebody back home to know I was doing well. Even though you didn't like me, I knew you would at least be proud I was in college."

"I never *said* I didn't like you," Eric insisted.

Joanna smiled. "It's okay, Eric. I understand. I understand a lot of things." She paused for a moment, looked out into the street, and allowed herself be distracted by the passing cars.

"But you *don't* understand my family. You don't know them, but your grandmother does. That's why she hates me. When your grandmother was younger, she and my grandmother were like best friends, sisters even, but she got really sick – too sick to take care of my mother. So, your grandmother took her in."

Eric's eyes widened. "She never told me anything," he whispered.

"Things were good for a while," she continued. "She was like a second mother to her, but my grandmother just got sicker, and when she died, my mother went wild. She started drinking a lot and, eventually, started getting high. She got hooked on crack, Eric. Then she started stealing from your grandmother, sold her stuff, and then she had me."

Eric just looked at her. He thought maybe he should reach out and grab her hand, but he didn't.

"I'm sorry, Joanna," he said finally.

There were tears in her eyes now. "She wanted my mother to leave, but she wanted custody of me. She figured I wasn't safe with her, and she was right," Joanna added.

"Was there no one else who could take you until your mother got better?"

She shook her head. "I have uncles, her brothers, but they had their own families and were too busy, or worse. Nobody really cared what my mother was going through, and she didn't want to lose me, so she moved out of your grandmother's house," Joanna explained.

"Things were pretty terrible for a long time. They never spoke again after that. My mother tried to clean herself up and find my father, but she never pulled it together. Don't you understand, Eric? The *whole* neighborhood knows my mother – my family, and they think I'm just like them – your grandmother too! But I'm not, Eric! I'm nothing like her!" she cried.

That was all he could take. He grabbed her by her hands and pulled her close to him. She sobbed quietly as her body shook in his arms. She was so small, he thought.

"My mother's not a bad person," she whispered. "She's sick. She never got over grandma's death, and there was no one to support her. All of it was on me. I *had* to get away."

"Of course, Jo... of course," Eric nodded. "Anyone could understand that."

"But it was your letters that helped me," she said and pulled away slightly to look at him. "You made me feel that I wasn't forgotten. I felt proud that I was in college. You were there for me."

He sighed and watched the passing cars leave tire marks in the snow as they rumbled by. It was quiet now, and even though there was the occasional passerby, it felt as if they were all alone.

"Look, Jo – I want the chance to get to know you better, to get closer. I don't know about being in love and all of that. Let's just be cool for a while and take it from there," he said calmly.

As calm as he was, the foundation was already laid. He remembered that night, as if it just happened. The dinner was a disaster, but in a crazy sort of way, it was also endearing. The two spent the rest of the break on the phone and every waking moment together. When it was time for Joanna to return to school, they swore up and down that they would stay in touch. Joanna hinted that she wanted Eric to go with her, but he had his own schooling to continue. However, he promised to visit her as well.

The mood at home with his grandmother cooled off considerably since Joanna's first appearance. Even though he wanted to inquire about the past between them, he knew the subject matter was way too explosive. He spent most of his time out of the house and worked as a pharmacy clerk by day and took journalism classes at the community college at night. Words always fascinated him, and he aspired to write for a newspaper someday – maybe even become a field reporter, but that was a long way off. Joanna wrote to him every week, so he got plenty of chances to practice at his new career. He didn't want to take the chance of his grandmother picking up the phone and finding her on the other end, so he begged her not to call. He didn't want to phone her either, as a frequency of long distance calls would certainly give the old woman something new to complain about, on top of everything else.

Despite the obstacles, the romance blossomed through adversity, as it often does. Under scrutiny, their home lives seemed very different, but there was much that, paradoxically, bonded them together. One example of this was their mothers. Eric never had the chance to meet Joanna's mother. She made some excuse before the dinner and every time they were supposed to meet thereafter. Joanna, who apologized emphatically at every infraction of his trust, brokered all of the arrangements. Eric always assured her that it was no big deal, and even though the missed appointments were annoying, they weren't entirely impractical. They made it okay for *his* mother and father to be absent as well; the explanation for which he was unwilling to divulge, although she often inquired. He too understood what it meant to be disappointed by loved ones. The family he *did* meet was quite entertaining to him, although they embarrassed Joanna to no end. Her loud aunts and crazy uncles were more colorful than his own family, who barely spoke to each other at all. At least they talked, he thought to himself.

In any event, it became evident to them, and anyone else watching, that they were now in love, and they started making wedding plans. As he thought about it now, it took quite a bit of time to save the money and make all the necessary arrangements, but even more importantly, to win everyone over on the idea. The time went by so quickly. They considered running away, eloping, and doing it on their own, but Joanna said the wedding could be just the thing to bring the two families closer together. They already started to paw at each other. One family made inquiry of the other often with veiled questions. Before he knew it, the big day had arrived, and by that evening, Eric had a wife – Mrs. Joanna Harland.

Now they were arguing.

Eric slowed down the car as they approached the street to the nightclub. They were about two blocks away, but he saw all of the family gathered outside, awaiting their arrival. He wanted to make sure he said his peace before they got out.

"I know what this is about," Eric stated definitively. "This has nothing to do with a nightclub. It's because of Charles. You don't like him. His place is nice, which by the way, we couldn't afford if we tried to rent a place like it on our own. He's throwing us this reception as a gift and losing money tonight as a result, and you're complaining! You let your family help you with the dress and everything, and they were *all* kinds of annoying, but I can't accept help when Charles is *my* cousin."

He felt good. He let her have it, but it was bulletproof logic.

"I don't want to hear it," Joanna said dismissively as she waved her hand. "But, you *are* right about one thing – I *don't* like him. He may be your cousin, Eric, but he's a criminal. What kind of grown man calls himself 'C-Rock?'"

Eric had to laugh. They pulled up slowly in front of the large crowd of applauding family members, who were bathed in bright, red light every two seconds by the flashing sign that hung above them that shouted the name of the club into the night. Rock Steady was one of the most popular clubs in the city – the kind of place that was packed every night with wild, young women, shifty-eyed, young men, and local celebrities who loved to be seen there, even if it was by the same people every week, but it was no banquet hall. Eric didn't go to nightclubs, but he had been inside once before. Even though he knew little about receptions, he couldn't imagine that what he remembered about *this* establishment's interior matched up with the overall idea.

Nevertheless, he was assured months prior that everything was taken care of, and not to worry. He didn't except for one thing – Joanna. He kept the reception plans from her. First, because he knew she would go ballistic, and secondly, he really didn't know anything besides where it was taking place. All he did in the final months was pick her brain about exactly what she wanted to have at the reception, from the largest to the smallest of details and then relayed that information to his facilitator, who doubled as Master of Ceremonies.

Eric glanced over the group and picked out the family members he recognized. He then noticed that Joanna was doing the same thing, only much more intensely, for a much more important reason. She was looking for her mother. She was a no-show at the wedding, although she was invited (even if only by word-of-mouth). Joanna naturally assumed that she would do everything in her power to attend the most important day of her daughter's life. Eric never said anything at all on the subject, but he knew she would disappoint her. After all, they were engaged nearly a year, and he still had not met her. Joanna tried to hide her disappointment when she realized that her mother was not in the crowd, because she should have been right in front. Instead, that space was occupied by the photographer – an older gentleman of rather small stature, who appeared even smaller by the large leather case hanging off of his right shoulder, that caused him to hunch over slightly. Eric briefly wondered why he didn't have an assistant.

Suddenly, the crowd started to move and parted slowly as a large figure pushed his way through. The man was strikingly tall – at least 6'4" – and a little on the heavy side. He had light-brown skin and even lighter brown eyes which were set deep in his massive head. His head was clean-shaven, as always, and on this night, shined brightly under the streetlights, like a well-polished marble. He sported a thin, neatly-trimmed beard and a diamond in his left ear. The white pinstripe suit he wore resembled a gigantic gallon of milk pushing its way through the crowd. His pants flowed like curtains when he moved. He was holding a dark bottle in his hand – champagne – and was smiling from ear to ear. Whenever Eric saw him, he was smiling, which was unfamiliar to Eric. He never remembered him wearing that expression when they were kids. He doubted that it was an appetite for life that was responsible for the large grin, although it was true that he did enjoy himself. Eric suspected that it was simply the power he acquired at such a young age that pleased him so much. He was notorious, and he knew it. There wasn't a person in that neighborhood that hadn't heard of or had personal dealings with Charles Henry Wakefield. As he approached the car, Joanna shot him a look that could only be described as mildly homicidal, but Eric put on his best smile as he greeted his cousin.

"He's paying for our reception," he said through clenched teeth as he grabbed Joanna's hand and squeezed it tightly.

The man in the white suit leaned down; put his face to the glass on the passenger's side where Joanna was sitting, and grinned even wider. Then he stood up, turned away, and faced the waiting crowd.

"Ladies and Gentlemen – can I have your attention, please?" Charles shouted as he raised his humongous arms. "It's my pleasure to welcome you all to *my* club – The Rock Steady – for a very special night. It's my pleasure to introduce my baby cousin and his new bride – Mr. and Mrs. Eric Harland!"

With that, he pulled the cork off the champagne bottle, and the white suds shot up into the sky like fireworks. The crowd erupted, in like manner, with thunderous applause that filled the night air. Eric exited the car, checked his reflection in the window, and smoothed down his tuxedo. He walked around to the passenger's side, opened the door for Joanna, and held out his arm for her. The man in the white suit motioned for everyone to let them through, and they parted simultaneously. Though it wasn't the traditional way she would have liked, she had to admit to herself that it felt great. The man in the white suit ushered everyone inside and put his arm around the connubial couple, champagne bottle still in his hand.

"Wait 'til you see how it is inside," Charles exclaimed. "You're gonna love it."

CHAPTER TWO

Wakefield

"The man we are after tonight is a Mr. Charles Henry Wakefield, street name, C-Rock," the man at the front of the room stated firmly.

He had a gruff voice and a tone that resonated somewhere between a shout and a bellow. His spiky, light-grey hair was close shaven at the sides and contrasted heavily with his thick mustache. His complexion was almost red, and he peered around the room with serious, yet squinting eyes. His chest resembled a barrel that was turned on its side as it threatened to bust through the tight, black t-shirt he was wearing. Layered on top was a tightly strapped, bulletproof vest emblazoned with the bright yellow letters ATF (Alcohol, Tobacco, and Firearms). Sean noticed that his belly protruded out a little because the sergeant had a habit of pulling on his belt periodically as he spoke, but his pants never went anywhere.

The sergeant continued with his speech, but Sean allowed his mind to wander. He already knew all he needed to know about Charles Wakefield. His first run-in with him was a little over five years prior, when he was just a regular beat cop – or more accurately – a patrolman. He often reminisced about that day. He and his partner, Angelo Anderson, responded to a 'shots fired' call. As the car ascended up Polk Avenue, Sean saw a thin boy, not more than nineteen, sprawled out in the middle of the street. He writhed in agony, and dark red blood poured through his clutched fingers. His attention was quickly redirected to two figures on the right side of the street. The two men were about the same height, but one was considerably larger than the other. They wore dark clothing and stockings over their faces. Both of their arms were raised, and bright orange sparks spewed from their hands. Sean never witnessed a shooting before that day, and he was terrified. He exited the patrol car and kneeled down behind the open door, as he was taught. He pointed his weapon through the window of the door and aimed directly at the two suspects, but he didn't fire. He hesitated.

His partner, Angelo, shouted, "Freeze! Drop your weapons!"

The smaller one took off running, but the larger one turned and faced them. At that moment, Sean saw the automatic weapon in his hand. It all happened so fast. He couldn't tell how many shots were fired, but he knew his partner was hit. He was down. Sean crawled through the car, over the seats, and kept himself as low as possible. His partner was on the ground and unconscious. A few of the bullets struck him in the chest, but fortunately, he wore his vest. One of the bullets entered his neck, and the wound bled profusely. He heard the echo of the *ping* of metal hitting metal as more bullets struck the body of the car. Sean snatched off his tie, rolled it into a makeshift handkerchief, and kept it pressed down on his partner's neck. Out of the corner of his eye, he spotted a black man in his forties, facedown on the ground.

"Hey!" Sean yelled. "Help me! My partner's been shot!"

Brrraaapp, Brrap, Brrap!

The man turned his eyes toward him, but held his position. He tried to remain calm, but Sean saw that he was shaken.

"Please..." Sean pleaded. "He's gonna die if you don't."

Brraap. Brrrrrrrraaap!!!

The man's eyes moved back and forth between the wounded cop and the direction of the gunfire. Finally, he acquiesced and crawled over to them on his belly. The young officer handed him the rolled-up tie already soaked in blood.

"Keep this pressed down on his neck – right here." He guided the man's hand down to where he needed to apply pressure to the neck wound. Sean grabbed the radio from the dashboard and pressed hard on the red button.

"This is 115. Come in, Dispatch! My partner's been shot, and he's bleeding badly! Dispatch! Do you read me?" he yelled.

Almost immediately, the voice of a middle-aged woman came through the speakers, clear and calm. She displayed no indication that her emotions were moved by the call one way or the other.

"*115, this is Dispatch. What's your current location?*" she asked plainly.

"We're in the middle of Polk... Anderson's been shot in the neck! He's dying..."

***

Sean never caught the man who shot his partner. In fact, he never even saw his face, but he remembered his size, his build, his body language, how he held the gun, and the way he ran from the scene. His partner, Anderson, did not survive. He was pronounced dead at the scene. He lost too much blood too quickly. The truth was, Anderson never really had a chance, and somewhere in his heart, he knew that, yet he continued to blame himself. *He* hesitated. He delayed engaging the suspects in a chase because he didn't want to leave his partner. By the time he did, the two suspects were long gone and left their guns behind. They ran the weapons for prints, but of course, there was nothing. Sean knew who was responsible – Charles Wakefield. He just couldn't prove it. He also knew that it was no coincidence that after a few random shootings, a new group of young kids became more than visible in the neighborhood that he patrolled, and a big kid was always among them – one whose body type matched the suspect's frame embedded in his memory.

As a patrolman, there was nothing much he could do about the new direction of that neighborhood. What was obvious to him was that the shootings, and the new faces, had a lot to do with it. He recalled one encounter with the group after he completed his probationary period and psychiatric evaluation. He was with his new partner, Benny, who didn't stick around for long. While they were out on one of their routine patrols, they spotted a group of kids who always hung out in front of a small bodega on the corner of Cooper Street and Ridgewood Avenue. The problem was actually catching them doing something because they always scattered before he was in reaching distance. When they *were* caught, there was no evidence of drugs or guns, but that day was different. Sean was fired up. He hadn't said a word all day. Benny, who was a big guy, sat quietly in the passenger's seat as they rode around. Sean was not much of a talker – at least since Benny became his partner. Something was noticeably different. It was in his eyes. An aura of rage surrounded him.

When the patrol car came up Cooper, Sean stopped the car suddenly, pulled his gun, and got out of the car. Benny drew his weapon also and commanded the five or so teenagers in colorful hooded sweatshirts to stay exactly where they were. He tried to keep his eyes on all of them, but he was really concerned about Sean, who marched right up to the largest boy. Benny didn't know his name, but he was out there most of the time. Identification was a huge problem when they were young. They almost always gave fake names, and they never carried id. That was the least of his problems that particular day. He watched in amazement as Sean grabbed him by his white t-shirt and shoved the gun in his face.

"I know it was you who killed my partner," Sean hissed. "You know it, and I know it. I can't prove it now, but one day you're gonna make a mistake, and when you do, I'm gonna kill you."

Benny wondered whom he was going to have to stop in the next moment, but the kid never moved. Instead, he smiled and never took his eyes off Sean while he kept his hands at his sides. Benny looked at the guy. He was pretty big – almost six feet and husky. Sean was average size, so the kid could have definitely wrestled him for the gun – that is, if he didn't already have one. Sean had not searched him. Benny wasn't long acquainted with his partner, but he never knew him to be reckless. Sean told them to get off the street and that business was closed for today. The kids walked off slowly and spewed an array of colorful obscenities and racial slurs. The big one kept his eyes on Sean a little longer, then shifted his gaze to Benny. He grinned widely again before he did a short jog and caught up with the others. Sean never lowered his gun until the pack was about a block or so out of sight. Then he got in the car, put on his seatbelt, and started the engine. Benny checked his surroundings before he holstered his weapon and joined his partner, who was staring straight out of the window without saying a word. He thought about making a joke or even chastising him, but decided against it. He didn't believe in that kind of policing, so later on that week, he put in for a partner transfer.

Later on that day, Sean was called into Chief Lannom's office, accompanied by his shift commander, Sergeant Dierdorf. Lannom was okay, in his opinion, but Dierdorf was a jerk. He was a big, tall, burly guy. He kept his hair combed to the right side in an old-fashioned style with a thick mustache to match. As if all of these random features weren't 'rough' enough, he had a sour disposition to match. He rarely spoke, but when he did, he always folded his arms across his chest. He had a wrinkle above his nose – well, actually, it was more of a crease – and when combined with his low-set brows, gave the impression that he was always frowning, even when he wasn't. He stood by the window adjacent to the chief's desk. He made a rather magnanimous gesture with his hands and motioned for him to sit down in the chair in front of the desk. Sean liked the chief. He was the kind of guy with an even temperament – never too much one way or the other – and his face reflected that philosophy. He was also what Sean called a 'watcher.' He was always aware of what was going on around him and even things that were not, but he never let on. This was a quality that Sean himself aspired to imitate, but lacked know-how. Yet, he admired him.

Chief Lannom continued to stand for a while after Sean took his seat. He was average height with less than broad shoulders. His light blond hair was combed haphazardly, as if he barely had enough time to run his hand through it before he rushed out the door. This was not uncommon, especially when he wasn't wearing his hat, which was most of the time. He also wore glasses, the kind that made his eyes just a little bigger than they were supposed to be and gave him the appearance of being overly concerned. After shuffling a few papers, he sat down, loosened his tie, and took a long, hard look at the young officer.

"Joe," he said softly, "Would you please excuse us?"

It took the sergeant a moment to process the request. When it finally registered, he became aware of the expression on his face and abruptly tried to hide it. It was obvious that he relished in the young policeman's impending discipline, even if he had no idea what form of chastening would be implemented. He shot Sean a quick look, one that he was unable to read, and left promptly. The chief's gaze shifted momentarily to Dierdorf as he left the office, but once the door was shut, he diverted his attention right back to Sean. He couldn't help but be a little nervous. Besides, he knew why he was there. He already kicked himself mentally for his behavior while Benny was in the car. He just couldn't control himself that day. The truth was, he was spiraling out of control more and more each day.

"How long have you been with the department, Officer Coughlin?" the chief asked.

Sean cleared his throat. "Just over two years, sir," he replied.

"And in all that time, you've never used your gun?"

"No, sir."

"Never had to, huh? Well, except that one time with Anderson. You probably wish you could have that day back."

He walked over to the window and looked out, with his back facing Sean. There wasn't much by way of scenery, so it was probably more for effect. The window faced a scant parking lot that intersected onto the street and showcased nothing special at all.

"You know, Coughlin, I know how the men view me. I'm an outsider to start with, and they believe, as many do, that you can't be a real cop unless you were raised in a violent, dangerous city like this one, but... I'll tell you... I was raised in a small town. I would ask you if you've heard of it, but I'm pretty sure you haven't. Anyway, you learn a lot in a small town. You hear of every instance where a girl you went to school with was getting smacked around by her husband, or a guy you thought you knew was using drugs or drinking... or touching his daughter." Then he turned around to face Sean. "Do you know what you learned, Coughlin?" he asked.

"No, sir," he replied.

The chief came over to Sean's chair and stood by it.

"Nobody is who they seem to be. Take you, for instance. You're calm. You're quiet. You've got the clean face and the nice haircut, but you've got *rage* down on the inside. There's darkness and violence. Let me tell you something about rage, Sean. It will destroy you, if you don't learn how and when to use it."

Sean swallowed hard.

"Listen to me. Everybody feels bad about Angelo, but no matter how you feel, it wasn't your fault. Cops die. That can't be what drives you out there. Your focus should be your desire to clean up those streets and to protect people, but I know how it is. They're animals out there, aren't they; especially the kids?"

He paused for a brief moment. "Do you know how animals are caught in their world?" Lannom asked.

He didn't wait for a response. "By bigger, stronger animals. Not just stronger, but *smarter*," Lannom said, shaking his index finger and touching the side of his head.

"But, you're right. Stronger, bigger – wilder – that's the only way, but not in that uniform. The blues are for reassuring the public and keeping order. Detectives do the dirty work; at least, that's how it should be. So, why don't you try that for a while?"

Sean tried to contain himself as best he could, but couldn't stop his eyes from lighting up.

"Really, sir? I'm a detective now?" Sean asked.

Chief Lannom pulled something shiny out of the middle drawer in his desk and placed it on top. He then indicated with his finger that Sean should take it.

"You'll need that first. Go see Shelley in HR, and she'll get you straightened out. Don't worry, just do what I tell you, and you'll be fine."

Sean looked at his badge for a moment, turned it in all directions, and it kept shining. Then he put it in his pocket.

"Thank you, sir. I'm sorry about before, but I won't disappoint you," Sean said reassuringly.

He stuck out his hand, and the chief shook it calmly. He turned and walked toward the door, eager to get out, as if somehow his promotion might be rescinded. He halfway expected the chief to call him back and say it was a joke. As he turned the knob, Lannom made a gesture for him to wait.

"One more thing, Coughlin," he said firmly.

"What's that, sir?" Sean asked cautiously.

Chief Lannom took off his glasses, set them on top of his desk, and rubbed the space between his eyes. He exhaled briefly.

"Cut out the 'sir' crap. It's *chief*," he said, smiling slightly. "I'm not that old."

Sean nodded. "Sure, chief."

***

That was nearly five years ago, and he remained a detective, much to Dierdorf's chagrin and the surprise of others. He started out on the vice squad and then transferred over to homicide. He made his presence known in the neighborhood that Lannom assigned him to. However, it wasn't the neighborhood that Wakefield and his crew ran in. Nevertheless, he made plenty of arrests over the years, but he never forgot his man. He took Chief Lannom's advice and learned how to channel his rage into a determination to keep the streets safe. He made a strong effort to be polite and courteous – even with the people of this neighborhood. On those same blocks in the dark of the night, he unleashed his rage. Sometimes people got hurt and really badly. He wanted criminals to get the message that no violence was tolerated on his streets. It was hard to feel like you were really making an impact in the Gardens when you saw dead bodies all the time. There was always someone new dying before their time. Of course, much of it was drug-related. That really wasn't his department, but he couldn't help but get frustrated with the Narcotics Division. Sean failed to comprehend just *how* they were doing their jobs.

There was a bigger issue, however. It was the guns. There were just so *many* guns on the streets. So much of his time was spent circling off shell casings, attempting to lift finger-prints off of discarded weapons, and hoping to retrieve serial numbers that were long since filed away. There was one time, one case that really brought his mission to the fore; one he would always remember.

A shooting took place in front of one of the area's best West Indian restaurants about seven months prior. The incident resulted in the deaths of two men and critical injury of a third. The building itself took quite a beating, but the men were almost torn apart by the force of the large caliber ammunition that was used. Of course, being in a hurry, the shooters hardly had time to pick up the casings, and they told the story.

For the first time since he joined the force, Sean was really coming to grips with the kind of weaponry and firepower that was out there in the hands of criminals and psychopaths, when the department's meager budget couldn't even hope for those kinds of upgrades! It was frustrating, but more than that, it was quite alarming. Indeed, the weapons were a major problem, but there was an even larger one. It was the city itself. It had a spirit and a soul – a soul that was darkened. As much as he may have desired to, he was not the one to bring this to light, at least not from within. He had way too much darkness of his own. There was violence. There was rage. There was far too much whisky he ingested in an attempt to erase the images of Angelo's eyes and the replays of his neck wound out of his mind, but they never left. No, he could not be the light, but he was clean. He refused to take bribes, nor did he extort criminals. He never stole evidence, and he never planted any. Sometimes he hurt people – the ones that needed it, but he never killed anyone.

The shooting in front of the West Indian restaurant prompted Sean to ask the chief for a special task force aimed specifically at taking illegal guns out of the neighborhood. This was hardly the first time that the police department declared war on guns or instituted a program that exchanged them for cash or some other reward. They all fizzled out or failed altogether because, in Sean's opinion, there was no intelligence involved. What Sean proposed to the chief changed all of that. He requested resources to pool all information related to firearms or any crime that included them from the various departments throughout the precinct – from misdemeanor possessions to felony crimes like robbery and homicide. All information was to be examined and compiled and the actual weapons scrutinized as always, and fragments, fingerprints, as well as casings and serial numbers entered into the database and traced back to their original owners. The new element for suspects found with guns would include surveillance for the sole purpose of being led to their suppliers.

Chief Lannom liked the idea and agreed to a budget and a team, which Sean was allowed to select. He chose four team members – a 14-year veteran from Narcotics named Haines, Castobell and Velez, who were both from Robbery, and his partner from Homicide, Matthew Stone. Every one of them was fully devoted to getting as many guns off the street as possible. He informed them right off that they weren't in the business of charging suspects as of yet. Their main purpose was to gather intelligence.

Even the streets can give you a break sometimes. An anonymous tip alerted the team about a kid showing a gun, and Velez happened to be the closest to the scene. She called for backup, but by the time they got there (after only a few minutes), she had already disarmed the kid, had him cuffed, and on the ground. Sean never worked with Velez, but he knew her reputation from around the office. Her name was Rosemary, but everybody called her 'Rosie', though the name was hardly relevant. She was tough, but she was clean – at least as far as he knew. That's why he picked her for the team. The kid she collared was a 19-year-old from the Gardens named Tariq Marion, who had two prior gun possession charges and a pending aggravated assault charge. The victim in that case failed to show up to any of the status conferences, which meant, in all likelihood, that the case would be dropped soon, but they could squeeze him with this third gun charge.

Sean was gambling on the chance that he was not familiar with the 'trigger law' and that it did not apply to juvenile offenses. He was right. Scared to death of a long sentence, Tariq told them right away where he obtained the high caliber handgun – a black Heckler and Koch 40. Caliber with a thirty-round magazine. He also informed them that one man supplied nearly all of the guns in the borough, and although he never worked for him directly, everyone knew who he was. His name was C-Rock.

At the time, the name C-Rock meant nothing to Sean. It wasn't long before he discovered that he was none other than Charles Wakefield himself. Unfortunately, the young man he identified had no warrants. He didn't even have a record. However, Mr. Marion proved to be a valuable informant, and over the next few months, all of his friends were picked up for gun possession, and they turned over other criminal activity and developments to their appropriate departments for prosecution.

Every stash of weapons they found further legitimized and validated the task force in Chief Lannom's eyes. Not to mention that getting all of those guns off the streets made them appear like hometown heroes. Then, the case got a little more complicated. At a small buy of about a dozen machine guns and smaller arms, the task force picked up a short, dark-skinned man who was doing the selling. He said nothing, but seemed to be of South African descent. He possessed no identi-fication except for a small, white, business card that displayed a shield and was stamped with the letters ATF. There was also a number under the name, Sergeant Alfred York. Sean never got a chance to dial it because, at that very moment, the selfsame sergeant marched in with some very serious-looking cohorts and demanded to see the chief.

After a very strained introduction, Chief Lannom led the sergeant back to meet Sean, while his subordinates remained in the front area of the station. Sean wanted to laugh as they approached his desk. He thought amusing York's cartoonish looks that clashed with his serious nature, but also the scene of *both* men, who were rather rotund, side by side with their bellies jutting out, caught him off guard. However, his amusement was short-lived when Sergeant York suggested they speak in the chief's office and required the utmost discretion. As Sean followed the chief into the office, the sergeant separated from them momentarily.

"Chief, who is this guy?" Sean asked mockingly. "He looks like one of those fat southern sheriffs from the movies – or Yosemite Sam," he added.

Lannom didn't laugh, but rather let out an exasperated gasp, as if Sean was an overactive child he tried to correct all day.

"We may have a problem on our hands," Lannom explained. "Apparently, the perp you just picked up is an immigrant from South Africa – Joanna-something or other. Anyway, *that* sergeant is from the ATF and *that* guy is a part of his investigation."

"He's a little bit more than that," Sergeant York interrupted.

He entered the office rather noisily, carrying a thick, brown file in his hands. He thrust it into Sean's lap and plopped down in the chair next to him. Sean was already annoyed as he looked at him, and he did not attempt to hide his disgust. He wore a pair of tan khakis and a navy blue windbreaker jacket over a black polo shirt, both of them adorned with the ATF. logo. Sean noticed what looked like a class ring on his fat finger. The young detective had a habit of judging people rather quickly, which proved formidable in his career, but unfortunately, was a trait that he didn't know how to turn off. He had an instant dislike for York; not only because he sensed he was about to step all over his case, but because he was incredibly rude. Chief Lannom must have sensed the tension between the two men.

"This is Detective Sean Coughlin," he said as he gestured toward Sean with an outstretched hand. "He's the head of our Firearm Task Force responsible for cleaning up the guns in our city streets."

Sergeant York ignored the introduction. "The man in that file is Charles Henry Wakefield, but he goes by the name C-Rock. I'm sure you already know. He is one of the biggest arms dealers in this city – in fact, the only one in your borough, but here's the kicker. He's *only* twenty-four. Now, how on God's green earth did a kid that young get to be so powerful, you may ask? Well, we believe the son-of-a-gun has a connection in the armed forces, and we haven't been able to prove this yet. We believe that to be the source of his weaponry arsenal, as most of it is military-issued. Unfortunately, that's *not* his only source."

"What's our guy got to do with this?" Sean asked.

"That foreign fella you picked up today... His name is Sviala or something. I won't even try and pronounce his last name. In any case, he's an African fella who's been here a couple of years selling machine guns all over the country. Somewhere along the line, he connected with Wakefield's crew, and we caught him making a rather large sale one night, much like you did tonight."

"So, why's he still walking around?" Sean snorted as he flipped through the file.

"He was afraid of deportation, so he started giving us information right away. He's become one of Wakefield's best salesmen, but he's also a supplier in some cases. So, they're pretty close, and in the last few years, he's come to learn all the players. He's gonna be the one who helps us bring Wakefield in," York stated.

"Wakefield's mine," Sean said firmly.

"Detective ..."

"No, you listen to me, Sergeant," he yelled, interrupting the chief. "You don't understand. Not only is the scumbag responsible for almost all the stray bullets flying around these streets, but he also killed my partner – a clean, dedicated cop with a family, and he got away with it. He's going away *forever*, and I'm gonna be the one that puts him there."

Sergeant York turned to face him, and Sean noticed that his face turned red. He was angry, but so was Sean. He had a lot of nerve marching into their precinct, invalidating all of the work he and his team were doing. His whole career was leading to an arrest like Wakefield's, and now, it was about to be snatched out from under him, right before his eyes. He looked toward the chief periodically for support, but he displayed no expression one way or the other. He only moved his eyes back and forth between the two of them. Aside from this casual movement, Lannom remained calm.

"This is an interdepartmental investigation, son," York replied, trying to keep his cool. "There are a lot of cogs in this machine, and there's no room for any one man to be runnin' off playing cowboy. We'd be more than happy to involve you."

"If it's interdepartmental, like you say, then why isn't the NYPD involved already?" Sean asked.

"That's a good question," Chief Lannom added, making his first contribution to the conversation since they sat down. "The fact of the matter is, we're already involved. He's operating in our city, and we should have been informed."

"You got me there," York chuckled. "I got no excuse for that, but he is transporting firearms across state lines, some of which are being brought from overseas; only God knows where else. Not to mention in addition to assault rifles, there's ammo and explosives involved. This is a little bit bigger than *your city*," he added sarcastically.

"My team has done an extraordinary amount of work in the last couple of months," Sean remarked. He stood up, tossed the file back at the sergeant, and caused him to jump slightly. "This is the big fish, and we're *not* backing off." With that, he walked out.

He left feeling pretty riled up that day – so much so that he went outside to calm down. His first instinct was to let things go on the way York wanted, then grab Wakefield on his own, but he had no charges on him. The only person who could corroborate his crimes was Sviala, and he belonged to York. Besides, he didn't want to make Lannom look bad, like he couldn't control his men. After all, he put a lot of faith in him when he made him detective and gave him leave to create the task force. He couldn't embarrass him by going rogue. He was resigned to just let this play out.

In the coming weeks, he found that decision was the right one. Chief Lannom was able to sweet talk the sergeant into giving them some leeway. Not only would Sean and his team be present at the arrest, but Sean alone would have the privilege of putting the cuffs on Wakefield – *Angelo's* cuffs, which he was saving for just that occasion. As far as the murder charge, that was another story. Maybe the gun that Sean retrieved from the scene would match up with some of the other weapons seized by the ATF that York promised to make available to them at a later date.

Almost suddenly there was a major problem. Sviala, the informant who worked for Wakefield, heard about a really big deal going down that Wakefield was involved in. He didn't catch any details except for the date, November 18th, which was tonight. Unfortunately for the FBI, the NYPD, and the Bureau of Alcohol, Tobacco, and Firearms, Sviala disappeared after he provided his last statement, before he clarified what was going down, and who was going to be there. Sean knew what happened to Sviala. No one had to tell him. It was obvious that his arrest proved fatal. Wakefield in his paranoia probably had him eliminated. He may have even done it himself, Sean figured, especially if they were indeed as close as he led York to believe.

In any event, the FBI was no longer interested without a witness, but York, not unlike Sean, had invested too much time and manpower to let Wakefield go. If it was indeed Sviala's arrest that aroused his suspicion, chances are they would never be this close again. So, York's plan was to watch him and try to catch him in the act. Sviala wasn't supposed to be involved in whatever was going down tonight, so there was a chance that everything was still a-go according to plan. It was their only shot.

Sean processed all of this in his mind while he listened to Sergeant York go on, with Chief Lannom at his side, who validated him. He was a little more gracious than on his last meeting, now that he needed help. The good sergeant needed the NYPD to show him around and take point. Sean was happy. At least now, they both needed each other.

Just then, Sean's phone vibrated in his front pocket. When he looked at the display, he saw that it was Danielle, his wife. Normally, he was pleased to hear from her, but on a night like this, he didn't really want to think of his family. He needed to focus.

"What's up, honey?" Sean asked as he answered the phone. "I'm about to go out."

She said, *"Danny's been asking for you. He's been calling for you all day."*

"Now, how can he ask for me? He's only..."

"He's six, Sean. That's old enough to know your father's gone all the time," she replied.

"Come on, Dani – let's not start this again. I really can't do this now."

There was a brief pause.

"He wants to talk to you," Danielle stated firmly.

"Don't do that."

"Don't do what?" she exclaimed. *"Your son wants to talk to you."*

In the background, Sean heard Sergeant York introducing him to the men on his team. He remained seated at his desk and ducked his head down in order to conceal his phone.

"Danielle, I have to go. They're calling me. Look, just tell Danny I'll see him later on tonight. You too, but I really have to go."

"Sean, I really think you should come home. You should be with us tonight. I don't want you to go out," Danielle pleaded.

"Honey, I have to, but I'll call you later." With that, he hung up the phone and walked briskly to the front of the room where York and the chief waited for him. There were about a dozen or so ATF agents clad in their SWAT-like gear, seated in chairs at the front, whose eyes followed him. The three remaining members of his team, Castobell, Haines, and Velez, were standing to the right of the board that displayed everything they knew about Wakefield and his organization. One of the articles tacked to the board was a blueprint of Wakefield's nightclub. Sean pointed to it.

"This is Wakefield's club, the Rock Steady. The last piece of intel we have says that something is happening there tonight, and that's all we have to go on. From what I understand, we lost contact with our CI." York shot him a nervous look that he didn't return. It was their job to protect the witness – or at the very least, know where he was. "Now," Sean started again, "A member of my team is already stationed at the location – my partner, Detective Stone. He's inside now. If there is a buy or an exchange of money or weapons – *anything* – the ATF team will move in. I want *my* team – Velez, Castobell, Haines – I want you guys at the back of the club in the parking lot, just in case he tries to make a run for it."

The three members of his team nodded in agreement.

"Now, I want you to understand something. Charles, as we now know, has been flooding the streets of our city with guns for God knows how long, but he's never been caught, and he has no record. Take it from me – this is a dangerous man. There's no telling what he might do to avoid his first arrest. So stay sharp, and let's go get him.

CHAPTER THREE

A Noisy Reception

Mrs. Joanna Harland sat on the dais, with her new husband seated to her right. Her small, dainty fingers were clad in white, satin gloves that stopped just below her elbows. She lifted her champagne glass to her lips cautiously and very slowly. She was careful not to miss anything. Of course, Eric was oblivious. She watched him as he talked and gestured wildly with his hands. He really appeared to be having a good time. Joanna was focused intently upon his conversation with their benefactor, who was seated on the other side of him; who on top of everything else, assumed the role of best man. Eric was sweet, she thought, but she knew he failed to appreciate the elegance of the affair. For Joanna, it was all about the details.

Club Rock Steady was illuminated with a soft, white glow that replaced the customary sleazy, red lighting suitable for its questionable clientele. In fact, the décor itself was all white, in full compliance with Joanna's wishes. Everyone seemed to be enjoying the music, and the food was excellent. She still didn't care for the source of her splendor, but oddly enough, Joanna was satisfied. She was indeed queen for a day. Little did she know that her husband relayed all the pertinent information to their gracious host and was quite instrumental in bringing her vision to pass. Eric's incognizance wasn't feigned; he just did not share the same zeal as Joanna for all the fanfare.

They finished their first dance just moments before. Eric was a bit concerned beforehand, but realized how much he enjoyed it. He even found the cake-cutting tradition to be quite engaging. The cake was a white and golden frosted, multi-tiered cake, and each table was furnished with a white, linen tablecloth and a bottle of champagne for a centerpiece.

Eric was equally impressed at how everything turned out. He then realized that this occasion was as much for Charles as it was for Joanna.

"So, how do you like everything, Mrs. Harland?" Wakefield asked in a mock-fancy accent, leaning his head forward so Joanna could hear.

"Everything is lovely, Charles. Thank you," was her muted reply. "You really cleaned the place up."

"Well, I had to make everything special for my little cousin." With that statement, Wakefield grabbed Eric and pulled him in close with a one-armed bear hug. His girth made Eric appear tiny in comparison.

"Speaking of which, I almost forgot. I have a few more surprises."

He raised one of his hands and beckoned with a quick gesture. In that same instance, someone rushed over and immediately appeared at his side. He bent down only slightly as Wakefield whispered something in his ear, and he disappeared as quickly as he came. The man was small in stature, but had a terrifying face – scarred many different times in multiple places, as if he had been slashed with a straight razor.

"Eric, come outside with me," Wakefield said. "I got something to show you."

***

Detective Sean Coughlin rode in the car with Velez. His partner, Stone, drove their cruiser and was already at the scene. Velez talked his ear off, as usual. It wasn't often that they rode together, but when they did, it was always the same scenario, but he wasn't paying attention. Sean thought mostly about his conversation with Danielle. It wasn't a new one, but there was something about her tone that was different. She sounded more worried than angry. Sean's normal modus operandi was to refrain from taking personal stuff with him on a bust, but their relationship was complicated. They met as teenagers in high school, and their encounter proved to be a harbinger of difficulty to come.

Sean, with his pale skin and reddish-brown hair, fit in just fine in school of mostly Irish and Italians, but Danielle was black. Her dark skin stuck out like a sore thumb, and dating her in that environment bought him a little more attention than he wanted at age seventeen. There was no question that he would hide the relationship from his parents. Although he didn't like the idea, he took solace in the thought that Danielle probably did the same, but a union such as theirs would not stay secret for long. When his parents found out, he was presented with an ultimatum. Get rid of her or leave their home. He chose the latter, and soon after asked Danielle to marry him. She asked him to wait a little while, and he used that time to find work and save what little money he could. He stayed with friends and slept in parks and shelters. Sean worked in fast food joints and did odd jobs for families in the neighborhood who knew of his plight and tried to help as best they could, while they secretly hoped he would come to his senses and leave the girl. He never did. Danielle proved to be more industrious than he. It took him a little bit longer to find his niche, but he had to do something.

Sean came up with the idea to join the police force. He wasn't interested in anything else enough to attend college. Besides, he had neither the intelligence nor the finances. He knew the streets, and he knew cops. His family was full of them, and his new career choice became a family matter as soon as he hit the academy. His enrollment placed him and his father on uneasy speaking terms. His father was not only a veteran officer, but well-liked and respected, and his desire to see his youngest son join his two brothers on the force was stronger than any racial prejudice. The Coughlin Dynasty was now completed. Sean was fast-tracked in every way possible, and he was also mentored by his father – whether he wanted it or not.

His father extended himself with yet another gesture; he offered the Coughlin home for Sean and Danielle to have their wedding, but Sean refused. He was not about to give his family the opportunity to make his new bride feel uncomfortable. They married at the courthouse. He agreed to move back home for a while, however; at least, until he officially became a police officer. With his father's help, at the young age of nineteen, it was official, but it wasn't long before they were at odds again. His father arranged to be Sean's first partner, just to show him the ropes. The ropes turned out to be discriminatory behavior and taking of bribes – neither of which Sean believed in, even at his young age. After a rather huge fight, they separated for good and never spoke to each other again. Danielle was his support system, and he needed it. Not long after that incident, he lost his first partner and had his firstborn son, all in the same year. That alone was more than enough stress for a 21-year-old cop.

Danielle worked for the post office, and they could afford a small house, but the baby changed everything. Sean started drinking heavily, and his drinking was accompanied by outbursts and mood swings, but she put up with him. When the Firearm Task Force took shape and required more of his time, Danielle put up with that too. Earning a little more as a detective took some of the edge off, but recently, the fighting became more frequent. Sean made a decision that when the case was over, he was going to spend more time at home. He considered giving up his position as the head of the FTF altogether. Danielle was a good woman, and he wasn't going to risk losing her over the scum of this city – especially someone like Wakefield. That's why tonight's bust was so important. It was his chance to put him away and put his partner's death behind him once and for all. Besides, there *was* Danny to think about. He was six now and old enough to know what a cop was, and old enough to worry.

As Velez pulled up the street where the club, Rock Steady, was located, Sean saw the license plate to his unmarked car. It was strange that Stone parked it out front. That thought was interrupted by the even stranger realization that there was someone in the driver's seat. He saw that it was Stone, his partner, but what was he doing outside? He was supposed to be inside, keeping an eye on Wakefield's activities and reporting in with regular updates.

"Rosie, stop right here," Sean whispered. "I'm getting out. I want you to pull around to the parking lot and take your positions there. Haines and Cas will back you up, okay? I'm gonna go see why Matt is not inside."

"Okay, Sarge," Velez replied.

As he exited the car, he checked his surroundings and looked up and down each street. They were pretty dark, but he didn't see anything. The light from the club's neon sign was stretched in all directions and illuminated the black avenues in strips of stunning ruby. Sean walked slowly toward his car and kept his eyes on the entrance to the club the entire time. There were a few well-dressed people out front, blowing clouds of white smoke into the night from their cigarettes. God, he wanted one, but he was on the wagon for the past few months. Of even greater interest to Sean, however, were the two large men with stern faces and darting eyes on both sides of the door. Sean visited the club a few times, and from what he remembered, it was a sleazy place. The bouncers in tuxedos seemed a bit out of place to him. When Sean arrived at the driver's side door, he reached out and tapped on the glass twice with his knuckle. Stone was visibly startled, but offered a warm grin when he saw who it was. He slid over to the passenger's side and allowed Sean to get in behind the wheel.

"Why aren't you inside?" Sean demanded. He was discernibly annoyed. "We need every bit of intel we can get tonight."

Stone grinned. "Hello to you, too. That," he said and pointed toward the club with his finger, "is a wedding reception, and it's by invitation only, judging by the two gorillas posted out front. Being the obvious Irish cop that I am, I didn't want to try blending in, especially without a warrant, but Wakefield is definitely inside."

"How do you know?"

"He was outside earlier when the bride and groom arrived. You should have seen him. He was dressed in a milk-white suit and popping champagne – real flashy type. I'm surprised we haven't caught him yet," Stone sneered.

"The operative word is *yet*, Matt," Sean replied. "Who was the groom?"

"A nobody. I didn't recognize him, but it's definitely no one in his crew. We would have seen him before."

"He's definitely somebody important to Wakefield – a good friend, a family member, maybe even a major player we just aren't aware of yet," Sean suggested. "Somebody like him doesn't just throw a major reception in his club if you're a nobody."

Sean was pretty annoyed, but not really with Matt. He liked him a lot, in fact. He was one of the few people Sean actually trusted. Detective Matthew Stone was his partner, the first member he selected for the Firearm Task Force. He had one of those rash personalities – laughing, joking, and playing practical jokes. He took nothing in life too seriously except for his job. He was a good cop – clean and loyal, and Sean trusted him as much as the others, if not more.

"How come you didn't call me?" Sean asked.

Stone shrugged. "I got into a big fight with Erin and didn't bring the phone. I left it right in the house."

"I got into a little something with Dani, too. Not a fight really, but I don't know. She didn't want me to come tonight."

"Doesn't she know this is your big bust?" Stone exclaimed. "What's she talkin' about?"

"Danny was asking for me. That must have set her off. But she's been like this for a while now. After chasing Wakefield so long, I can't say that I blame her. I need to spend more time with her and Danny," Sean stated. "That much I know."

"So, what does that mean?" Stone asked.

Just then, Sean's radio broke in. Sergeant York's voice and his southern drawl spoke from the other end, just in time to distract them from his partner's question. He didn't have the heart to tell his partner that, for the past two years, he was thinking of leaving the force. He didn't want to repeat the same mistake his father made by not being around. He wasn't even sure he wanted to be a cop anymore. He owed Angelo, but after that, he was done.

"What's the sitcheation over there, Detective?" Sergeant York demanded. *"My men are waitin' to move in."*

Detective Stone chuckled at his accent and gestured with his hands an imaginary mustache as Sean motioned for him to be quiet.

"My team is here at the location. Our suspect is inside, but there's a problem," Sean said. "There's a wedding reception going on."

"Coughlin, do you mean to tell me that after all this waitin', nothin' has gone down? We're sittin' here waitin' to move in, and you're at a dang wedding?" York shouted. *"What kind of intelligence do you call yourself gathering up there?"*

"I should be asking you that. He's *your* witness!" Sean shot back into the radio. "Who you can't even find, by the way. We're following the lead."

"Well, what else has happened?"

"Nothing – at the moment, but something will," Sean added. "I'm sure of it."

A loud breath came from the microphone. *"I'm pullin' the men out,"* York replied.

"Sergeant, with all due respect, Wakefield probably set up this reception as a cover for whatever's going down tonight. He's figuring we won't move in."

"And he's right!" York barked. "The CI probably got it wrong. In any case, I'm not riskin' dozens of lives for your hunches. Bring it in, Detective," York said with finality. "Operation's over."

Now Sean was angry.

"Your CI's probably dead," Sean shouted back. "Either that or he fled the country. Good luck finding him. Whatever the case, this is the last bit of intel he left before he disappeared. It might be my only chance to arrest him, and I'm going to arrest him."

As his response tried to transmit through the radio's speakers, Sean turned the knob to off, and he and Stone sat silently for a moment. Stone thought about making a joke, but before he thought of one, the club's glass doors opened, and out came two men. The shorter one was wearing a black tuxedo with a red rose in the lapel, but the other man was much taller, larger, and sported a garish suit as white as new snow.

"That's Wakefield," Stone said.

Sean turned on his radio and switched the channel from 3 to 4.

"108 – 108, come in," Sean said.

A gruff voice came crackling through the speaker. "This is 108. Go ahead."

"This is 43, Coughlin. I've got Stone with me, and we've got a visual on the suspect," Sean replied. "He just exited the club with someone. Black male, 20 to 25; about 5'8". There are also a pair of bouncers out front. They might be packing. How you guys looking?"

"There's one guard at the back door – nothin' we can't handle. Other than that, everything is clear. No movement yet."

"Hey, Castobell – what's shakin'?" Stone yelled in the background.

Sean shot him a look of sharp disapproval.

"Alright, Cas, listen up. Wakefield is dangerous, and we can only assume he'll do anything not to be caught. We also have to assume his boys are armed. We don't have the ATF's support tonight. I just got off the wire with York. He's pulling his men out."

"What did the chief say?" Castobell replied.

"Never mind that. This is our bust. We're gonna make sure all of our work amounts to something tonight. When Wakefield makes the trade off, Stone and I will move in," Sean stated. "When that happens, you keep the parking lot covered, you hear? And call for backup."

"Copy that," the radio answered.

"Stay sharp," Sean said.

***

The cool night air hit Eric as soon as he stepped outside the club, and he knew instantly that he had too much to drink. It was a rare occasion that he drank champagne, and the truth was, he was having fun. His cousin really came through for him, everyone was having a good time, and the place looked great. Wakefield pointed to a black SUV with one hand as he supported Eric's stumbling frame with the other. He opened the driver's side and let Eric in.

"Slide over," Wakefield said.

"This is your truck?" Eric asked.

"Nope. It's yours." He handed Eric the keys, climbed into the passenger's seat, and closed the door behind him. "It's a wedding present. It's bangin', right?"

Eric nodded and grinned as he turned the keys in the ignition. The gear was in park, but he revved the engine anyway. He pressed the buttons and turned the dials on the SUV's various gizmos. He switched on the radio and filled the vehicle with a thunderous drum beat, but Wakefield turned it down almost immediately.

"Hold up, E. We gon' take a ride in a minute, but I gotta talk to you first," he said.

"What's up?" Eric leaned back in his seat, trying to keep his eyes open.

"You still in school?"

"Yeah. Studying journalism," Eric replied. "I wanna write for a newspaper."

"But are you making money?" Wakefield asked, although it sounded more like a statement than a question. "You got a wife now, kid. You gotta take care of her."

"I got a job," Eric said defiantly. "I can take care of Jo."

"What I'm saying is," Wakefield stated seriously, "You can come work for me. I've got stuff you can do – nothing crazy, but things I need done. Who better to trust than my cousin?" he added.

Eric shook his head emphatically while his inebriation made the action even more intense.

"Can't do it, C," he explained. "I really want to finish school. I can't let myself get sidetracked." He exhaled slowly and leaned back in the seat, closing his eyes momentarily. "Besides, that's not really for me."

Suddenly, their conversation was interrupted by sharp tapping on the glass. Eric looked over toward the passenger's side and instantly noticed the short, dark-skinned man standing outside of the SUV, dressed in a black tuxedo with a white carnation stuck in his lapel. His arms were filled with a moderately-sized, black case that seemed to take all of his effort to carry. A larger man could have carried the case effortlessly with one hand. Even in the dark, Eric saw that his face was horribly disfigured, like a surviving veteran from the front lines of some long since forgotten war, but he seemed too young for that. It took a minute for him to realize that this was the same man he saw inside only moments ago, who whispered into his cousin's ear. Wakefield gestured with his head toward the back of the vehicle, and the man promptly left the window.

"Pop the trunk," Wakefield said. Eric bent down and fished around under the seat for a lever. He found one on the left side and lifted it cautiously. The back of the truck lifted up, and the man immediately deposited the case inside. He disappeared into the club as quickly as he came, and the two mammoth-sized men out front followed close behind. Eric followed them with his eyes. He was just a little frightened, and that feeling sobered him up a bit and made him more aware.

"Who was that?" Eric asked, his eyes wide with wonder.

"That's my man," Wakefield replied calmly as he turned around and climbed slightly over the backseat to retrieve the case. "We call him 'Chance.'"

"Chance? Why?"

"Well... really, it's two things. When the old heads see him, they always say, "He never had a chance." He was taken from his parents when he was real little 'cause they were gettin' high. Every foster home they sent him to, he was abused. Nothing funny-style, but they would beat him. One of his foster parents cut him up bad one night. They ended up dead, though." He paused for a moment. "After that, he went to a group home."

"He works for you now?" Eric asked, trying not to react.

Wakefield nodded. "Yeah, but we been cool a long time. We met in the group home back in the day. When we aged out, we stuck together on the street. I made him part of the team. He's a stand-up guy; a real official dude."

They both sat there while the tragic story sank in. All sorts of scenarios ran through Eric's head, and he kept looking at the black case on his cousin's lap, wondering if there was a gun inside. Then he thought of Joanna. He had been outside for a while now, and left her alone on their wedding day. He figured he'd better get back before she got too upset.

"What's the other reason?" Eric blurted out suddenly, as if he just remembered. "The other reason they call him Chance?"

Wakefield laughed and rubbed his chin in a thoughtful manner.

"Sometimes, before he shoots people... He gives them a chance to draw."

***

Detective Sean Coughlin's eyes remained intent on the black SUV. With one hand, he took his gun out of its holster, and the other was on the radio.

"108, come in.108, come in," Sean whispered. "It's 43."

"Go ahead, 43," the radio responded.

"Change of plans. Black male, about five feet tall, just deposited a black case in the back of our guy's SUV. He just went back into the club. Dark-skinned, face heavily scarred, and wearing a tuxedo. Cas, Haines – go in and arrest him."

"What about Wakefield?" Castobell answered.

"We got him. Velez, you come around front and back us up."

"I'm on it," replied Velez. The sweet voice that vibrated through the radio's speaker starkly contrasted with the appearance of the woman from which it originated. "But you are going to call it in, aren't you, Sean?"

"If you ever get off the channel, I will," Sean laughed.

It wasn't a genuine laugh, and Stone sensed it. He took his weapon out of its holster and looked at his partner with concern.

"You're not calling it in, are you?" Stone said knowingly.

Sean kept his eyes focused on the SUV, which was parked about six car lengths ahead, right in front of the club.

"This is ours," he replied steadily. "And we're bringing him in alone." He looked at Stone. "You with me?"

Detective Matthew Stone nodded his head. "All the way," he said.

$$***$$

"I hope you like this," Wakefield said as he patted the large, black case on his lap with affectionate satisfaction. "But, I also want you to know how hard it was to find."

"What is it?" Eric asked while he tried, unsuccessfully, not to sound nervous.

Wakefield smiled.

"You mentioned wanting this a couple of years back, and you specified a particular type and model. It's not really a wedding present, though..."

Instantly, Wakefield whipped his head around at the sight of a flashing, red light in the rearview mirror. He saw the dark-colored sedan that was parked right behind them, and the siren on top flashed methodically in the night. It was joined by a bright beam of white light shining from the right hand of the driver. The man on the passenger's side, with arm out of the window, pointed a gun at them.

"Driver!" Sean shouted authoritatively. His already stern voice was amplified by a loud speaker. "Put your hands on the dashboard. Do it now! Charles Wakefield – let me see your hands!"

It would have been laughable seeing a 300-pound man twisting around to put his arms out of the window, if it wasn't such a serious situation. He almost looked as if he was showing off his bracelet and rings, which sparkled under the flashlight's beam. Eric was frozen as he kept his eyes on the rearview mirror and stretched his arms out straight in front of him.

Detective Stone nodded toward the car's exhaust pipe.

"The engine's on," he stated matter-of-factly.

Sean nodded. "Driver!" he yelled again into the speaker. "Take the key out of the ignition, and place it on the dashboard. Put the car in park, and turn it off!"

Eric Harland was rarely scared of anything, but at that particular moment, he was genuinely frightened. He looked over at his cousin for some measure of moral support, but found none. Charles was imperturbable. Perhaps it was the streets or his disdain for the police, but more than likely, it was his own inflated sense of self that left him unmoved by their plight. Eric's mind, however, was racing. He thought about the fact that he was drunk and sitting behind the wheel of a running vehicle. He thought about whether or not his cousin had a gun on him. He wondered what was in that box. He considered the prospect of spending his first night as a married man in the bullpens at central booking, staring at gray stone walls instead of a hotel room, gazing into the eyes of his loving wife. Eric was a pretty bright kid, but bright people make dumb decisions all the time that tend to be magnified even more by their intelligence. Eric grabbed the gear shaft, put the truck in gear, and pressed down on the accelerator. In his haste and slight drunkenness, he put the gear in reverse. The heavy SUV shot backward with a growl of the engine. The bumper made a short crunching sound as it made contact with the police cruiser's headlights.

The first shot hit the back windshield of the SUV, shattered the glass, but landed harmlessly in the brightly-lit dashboard. The second shot struck Eric in the back of the head and sent his body careening forward onto the steering wheel. He was dead instantly. Several more bullets entered his body and the body of his cousin, who mustered enough strength to open his door while trying to show his hands to prove that he wasn't armed. The gunfire was intensified as Stone and Coughlin's 9mm semi-automatics were joined by a third. Velez just arrived from around the corner to meet them. At that moment, the door to the club suddenly flung open, and out rushed Castobell with his gun drawn. The detective was a rather large man, so his movement was a bit burdensome, but that didn't stop him from adding his own rounds to the volley; a dozen or so more shots were fired at the vehicle and at Wakefield before he went down.

His flashing, white suit was now forever corrupted by the dark red entry wounds and crimson-stained liquid that flowed out of him and onto the cement, mixed with the shards of broken glass. Wakefield laid as quiet as the night, and the shooting had stopped. The air was filled with a ringing silence that usually preceded an uproar. The air was also clouded with gun smoke – white, wafting up, spreading out wider – until it disappeared into the infinite blackness up above.

Out next was the one called Chance, whose hands were cuffed behind his back. He was brought out of the club by Haines, who made him look like a small child by comparison. The detective's massive frame was shoved aside by a much smaller one. A blur of white, flowing fabric blew past them all. Joanna rushed toward the tattered SUV, leaped over Wakefield's bleeding body, and grabbed Eric's body with both arms. She was instantly soiled with his blood as she pulled him close and gently tried to shake him awake.

"Grab her," Sean said softly.

Detective Stone holstered his gun, confident that his fellow officers had his back. It was pretty obvious that the woman was his wife. He took hold of her as firmly and as gently as he could manage, but she wouldn't let go. She didn't fight or resist, she just held on to Eric as tightly as she could. After a while, Velez came over to give him a hand and took a stunned Joanna off the immediate scene, further into the background. Castobell and Haines kept one eye on Chance as they tried to contain the ever-increasing number of people who tried to get outside and have a look. Detective Coughlin came around to the passenger's side and shined his flashlight around the inside of the vehicle. When the beam of light found the black case, he grabbed it and almost dropped it because he under-estimated its weight. It was unusually heavy for a gun. Stone gave him a hand, and they set it down atop the hood of their cruiser. Both of their eyes widened when they opened it. They glanced at each other and shared a look of dread and worry. Inside of the black case was an old-fashioned typewriter.

Joanna screamed Eric's name toward the heavens. Every syllable was filled with anguish and pain, but the sound was quickly drowned out by the blazing sirens of dozens of police cruisers who arrived on the scene.

It was a sound Sean Coughlin would never forget.

CHAPTER FOUR

The Aftermath

The black asphalt shined like expensive jewelry in the night; the result of the reflection cast from the dozens of brass shell casings that covered the ground. Miscellaneous cries emitted from the group of onlookers, mixed with devoted family members and curious passersby. The crowd grew larger, but the police managed to at least keep them restrained and under control. Dozens more police, patrol cars arrived on the scene in addition to the unmarked Impalas that belonged to the detectives. Bright yellow 'caution' tape stretched from one side of the street clear to the other. Many looked on with pity at the young detective whose duty was to circle and number all of those discarded shells.

Detective Sean Coughlin ran over to the bleeding body of Charles Wakefield, who lay facedown on the pavement. He patted around his clothing and lifted the blood-soaked jacket that revealed an even bloodier shirt underneath; but there was no gun. He cupped his hands under his massive body. It took all of his strength to turn him over. Blood ran from the opened mouth of Wakefield, but he remained unconscious.

"Where is it, you son of a bitch?" Sean hissed.

There was no response. Sean got up quickly and walked over to the bullet-riddled SUV. He pointed menacingly toward his fellow officers.

"Don't let *anybody* near here! Understand me? *Nobody* comes near this car!"

Sean went over to the trunk, which was still open, lifted the heavy typewriter out of its case and tossed it to the ground.

The clanging of the metal from the impact of the heavy object made such a racket. He ran his hand skillfully along the inside of the case lined with felt, but there was no false bottom, and there was nothing else in the case. He turned it upside down; then tossed it in the same direction as its counterpart. Detective Matthew Stone watched solemnly from a few feet away as he climbed into the trunk and felt around inside. The color drained from his face as his eyes went from his partner to the body of 21-year-old Eric Harland, whose eyes were still opened and stared back at him. There he lay, motionless on the steering wheel, with a gaping head wound.

As Sean searched furiously through the leather seats, he realized the SUV was brand new and void of any personal effects. He peered out of the window briefly. When he veered to his left, his eyes met with Joanna's. The purity of her white dress stained with her husband's blood gave the appearance of a murdered bride come back to life. Her eyes locked onto his, but she did not move, nor did she say a word. She was still held in restraint by his partner, but her eyes, and the intensity of her stare, burned with hatred. Sean stopped what he was doing and promptly climbed out of the car. He kept his eyes on her and walked over to where she stood with Detective Stone who took her from Velez after being properly searched.

"Who was your husband to Charles?" Sean demanded.

"Sean..." Stone said softly and put up his hands in protest.

"What was he doing here with him?" He came closer.

"Tell me..."

Joanna maintained her silence; she didn't respond. The tears streamed down her face and created wild, black streaks as they mixed with her mascara. Her eyes left his only momentarily as she looked intently into the eyes of her beloved; her now departed Eric.

"Sean – *back off!*" Stone reprimanded. He turned away slowly and took Joanna with him. When they disappeared, Sean went over to inspect the body of Eric Harland. He seemed so young. Sean witnessed death and dying before, but he never killed anyone himself – not even a suspect. This was his first time. He thought he was adequately prepared for this moment – that it would feel right and the end would somehow justify the means, but it did not. He felt as if his soul was torn from his body; he was nauseated and his heart was empty, but the deed was done. He knew it was useless, but he felt at the boy's neck for a pulse – an act he performed hundreds of times before – and just like most of those occasions, there was no pulse.

He thought to himself, "There has to be a gun. There *has* to be. Why else would they try to run?"

He felt around Eric's waistband and unbuckled his seatbelt slowly. The body began to fall under its own weight, but Sean caught him and laid him gently onto the passenger's seat. He opened the glove compartment, which was unlocked, but found nothing but the driver's manual.

"*Leave him alone, you bastard!*" someone shouted from the crowd. "*Respect the dead!*"

Another voice yelled, "*He's planting something – he's planting something in there! That's what they always do...*"

"*Pig!*"

An ambulance arrived on the scene; blaring its sirens and cutting through the ruckus. As detectives and officers made way, the ambulance pulled up to the yellow tape and stopped just short of the makeshift barricade. Three EMS workers exited the vehicle. On duty were two stocky-looking women and a slightly overweight male. Immediately, one of the women made her way over to the SUV where Sean was standing, while the other two went over to Wakefield's body.

"They're both dead," Sean said to the worker. "This one looks about twenty, twenty-two at the most. He has an entry wound..."

"Sara! Sara! We got a pulse over here!" the male EMS worker shouted. "It's weak, though. We gotta get him up, now!"

The woman promptly left Sean and walked over to Wakefield's body while the other young woman ran to the ambulance and retrieved a stretcher. She wheeled it over near Wakefield's body. The male grabbed Wakefield under his arms and the women grabbed him on each side.

"One...two...three..."

All three EMS workers grunted loudly as they lifted the gargantuan Charles Wakefield with great difficulty. One of the workers fitted him with an oxygen mask as they rushed him into the ambulance, started the sirens once again, and pulled off into the night. Sean turned his attention to his team and some of the other detectives who joined them in their efforts to keep the perimeter and guests under control.

Sean instructed, "I want everybody back in that club, understand? No one leaves. If they try, arrest them. Have them form a line and search them. If they're clean, then they can go."

Haines nodded as he and Castobell ushered the guests who were outside back through the club doors. This request prompted a slew of obscenities, protests and racial slurs from the crowd, but no one ran or resisted.

Sean returned his focus once again to his weapons hunt. As he bent under the car and resumed his search efforts, a pair of well-shined, black wingtips approached him. He arose and found himself staring into the face of the imposing Sergeant Dierdorf. He was in full uniform. His hands looked like hairy catcher's mitts as they jutted out from the sleeves of his navy blue uniform. His hair was swept to the side in a boyish fashion that was incompatible with his stern demeanor. His eyes were serious as always, yet he displayed the slightest of smiles under his push broom mustache.

"Well, well, Detective," said Dierdorf. "What the hell happened here? That truck looks like it just came back from Afghanistan."

Sean sighed. He hated levity in intense situations and the sergeant's least of all.

"The two perps inside backed up on us, then tried to get away..."

The sergeant ignored him. Instead, he looked to his left at the club's blinking, neon sign.

"I heard over the radio. You disobeyed a direct order and moved without backup or authorization." He paused for a moment. "The Rock Steady, huh? That's Wakefield's club." He looked at Sean. "I see you're still chasing ghosts."

"Well, at least I'm chasing *something,* Sarge." Sean said defiantly.

Dierdorf came close to him and pointed one of his huge fingers at his chest, like a native's spear warning of oncoming danger.

"You know, I never approved of you leading the FTF. A leader needs confidence, decisiveness – you don't have it. First, you don't shoot when you should and let your partner get killed; then you can't even follow protocols," he mocked. "And now, you'll never have what you wanted so badly. Now, you'll never become a sergeant."

Sean stared him down and retorted, "Better than being a washed-up, drunken son of a..."

"You're finished, Coughlin!" screamed Dierdorf. "I'm not letting your insubordination affect the rest of the men any longer. I don't give a crap that your Daddy was a legend. You're nothing like him, and you've got no place on this force."

Sean's fists were clenched now. He knew it would cost him his entire career, but at that moment, it was worth it. He moved toward Dierdorf...

Suddenly, a hand gripped him firmly on his shoulder.

"Stop – the *both* of you," said Chief Lannom calmly. He was also in full uniform – a thin jacket over his departmental white shirt. His badge and bars sparkled in the city's nightlights as if they were just polished. He turned his eyes to the sergeant. "Joseph, Coughlin may be under your command, but you're under *mine*, and no one under my command disciplines officers in public. I don't care what he's done." He looked around cautiously and checked to see if anyone overheard him. "Go secure that club. The press will be here any minute. I'll handle this."

Sergeant Dierdorf gave Sean a look that burned with defiance, nodded his head to Lannom and responded, "Yes sir, Chief." He then turned around and walked in the direction of the club. The chief took a moment to inspect the SUV, and then turned his attention to the gathering crowd. Finally, he set his eyes on Sean.

"Dammit Coughlin," Chief Lannom whispered.

"I'm still looking..."

Lannom peered at him through his glasses. "I told you that this was their operation," he said through his teeth. "You and your team were to take point, but this was *their* operation. What didn't you understand? If they had done this, it would be all on them. Now, it's all on you!"

"The CI was in the wind, Chief," Sean explained. "He said something big was happening tonight. We didn't have time..."

"Have time for what?" Lannom yelled. "To get a warrant? To follow proper procedure? To stand down when the ranking officer tells you? Now, we've killed an unarmed man in front of a hundred people. I know there are no guns in that car because you would've already been waving 'em at me." He pointed a firm finger at Sean. "You better hope we find something in that club. Stay put and wait for the investigative officer and your reps to get here. My men will assume the search. FTF is done for tonight."

"Chief..."

"Just stay in the car 'til we find someplace to do this, Coughlin," Lannom said firmly as he turned away. "End of story."

Sean stood alone as the chief walked into the Rock Steady. He stood there for a long time. Finally, he walked over to his car, where Stone was already waiting. The bride – or more accurately, the widow, Joanna Harland, was in the backseat. He didn't look at Stone or her. He just kept looking at the SUV with the dozens of nine-millimeter holes in it and the dead body of another unarmed African-American man.

"Did you cuff her?" he asked.

"Yeah," Stone replied. "But I don't know what for." He nodded his head in the direction of Sean's waistband. "Did you call Danielle? I gotta call Erin. She'll kill me if she finds out about this on the news before I tell her."

"You know the deal – we gotta wait for the reps," Sean added.

He finally mustered the courage to look at Joanna as he thought about staying in the car to watch her. She finally turned to him, and her eyes met his again. It wasn't only hatred in the young woman's eyes, but a determination, and Sean felt something he hadn't felt in a long time – even in all his years on the street. It was fear.

"I'll go get the rest of the team. You stay here and watch her."

"Sure thing," Stone said half-heartedly as he dialed his mobile phone. He watched as Sean walked under the blood red neon sign and back into the club. In a haunting kind of way, it seemed fitting.

"The people of New York search for answers this evening as another shooting involving the NYPD and two unarmed men unfolded in Harlem; in front of the popular Rock Steady nightclub. 21-year-old Eric Harland, who was here celebrating

his wedding that took place only hours before, was shot several times along with another man. The second victim of the shooting is 24-year-old Charles Henry Wakefield, who was rushed to Harlem General and remains in critical condition.

Allegedly, Harland refused to turn off the engine and exit the vehicle. When officers approached and identified themselves, he rammed one of the cars, and that's when members of the 25th precinct's Firearm Task Force Unit opened fire on the vehicle, killing Harland and wounding Wakefield. At this time, members of the wedding party; including guests, are being detained inside for questioning. Details are still being pieced together, but the unit is headed by Detective Sean Coughlin, whose former partner, Angelo Anderson, was murdered when they responded to an ill-fated robbery five years earlier..."

Danielle Coughlin sat on the soft, leather couch with her arms folded and her legs crossed as she stared into the eyes of the female reporter on her television screen. She had difficulty believing what she just heard and failed to process her own feelings at that moment. A part of her loathed him, and she hated herself for it. It must have been an accident – a terrible, horrible accident. She asked herself, "How *could* he? Didn't he realize the implications of such an act before he did it? What was he thinking about?" It even made her question the very foundations of their relationship. Because Sean showed so much love for her, she took for granted that he was above any prejudice or racism of any kind – especially toward her people.

Even though he was a police officer, which in the neighborhood she came from and amidst family and friends for that matter, meant he was the enemy. He suffered great pains and personal loss to be with her, but did she *really* know? She heard his car pull up into the driveway, and she knew she had to make a decision. The way she responded to him tonight would set the tone for the rest of the relationship. She turned off the television and got off the couch. She decided not to talk about it. She saw no harm if she pretended not to know. She still couldn't face him – not that night. So, she walked up the stairs to Danny's room, went inside, and closed the door. She began to cry as she lay on the bed next to their son.

***

He sat outside in his car for quite some time. He finished up a long-forgotten pack of stale cigarettes he found in the glove box. Danielle hated cigarettes. She was the one who pushed him to kick the habit he picked up at the tender age of fourteen.

He was also going out of his mind. His only ray of hope was that the chief or one of the other officers found a gun in that club. Somewhere deep in his heart he knew they wouldn't. He asked himself, "How did things go so wrong tonight?" *Angelo.*

Sean looked at the house and noticed that all of the lights were off. Danielle must have decided not to talk to him. That was the usual routine when he got home really late. He looked at the display on the dashboard – just after 3 am; it was a long night. They met with investigators and his rep and then gave their statements. He had to see the doctor and then consult with his attorney. He tried to call Danielle, but she did not answer. Was it possible that she already knew? Was it? His mind was racing. He wanted a chance to explain the circumstances himself before she heard any other version. Maybe she watched the news or spoke to Erin, but that was unlikely. Sean remembered that they fought earlier. He figured she was probably still mad. Maybe it was better that they didn't see each other, at least for the night. He wasn't really up to it. He constantly thought about that kid's face and how his eyes looked.

He took another drag of his cigarette, which was almost gone. There were only three in the pack. They were stale, but they did the trick. He finished up the last of it, blew the smoke out of the window, took a deep breath, and went inside.

***

"Daddy...wake up, I'm hungry," Danny said flatly, while shaking him with his small hands.

Sean stretched out his body and wiggled his toes under the sheets. His eyes were barely opened, and it took him a moment to register that it was his son who was speaking. He wondered, "What time was it?"

He reached over with his left hand, grabbed the small alarm clock on the nightstand and brought it close to his face. The display read 10:17 am. If it were a regular workday, he would have been more than two hours late. He doubted very seriously that the chief wanted him in today. He sat up on his hands and stretched again. Danielle left without waking him up, without saying hello or goodbye. That wasn't like her. She also forgot to take Danny to daycare, or she deliberately left him. That wasn't like her either. He looked at his little boy, and for a brief moment, he forgot about all of the trouble that was headed his way.

"How you doin', Champ?" he asked.

Daniel Shane Coughlin smiled at his father. He had his mother's eyes, and his other features resembled hers as well. He was very light – a little too fair-skinned to be solely African-American. Besides, he had freckles and they were complimented by a shock of dark red hair that stood up all over his head in dire need of taming. His white undershirt stopped just short of his underwear, which were decorated with superheroes. Sean scooped him up with one arm and carried him on his waist.

"What are we doing today, Daddy? Are you staying with me?" Danny asked.

"You hungry yet? Did Mommy feed you?" Sean asked, changing the subject.

"Yeah," he said. "I ate cereal."

Sean carried him to the kitchen and sat him on the counter. He thought about Danielle. He knew he would really score points if he stayed with Danny. Besides, it would be nice to spend quality time with his son, but he knew he couldn't sit at home – not after last night. He wanted to follow up on the shooting, find out who that kid was in the front seat and maybe even get a lead on the CI, Sviala. In any case, he wanted to have something to present before he went in front of the firing squad. He knew what was coming and wanted to get out in front of it – if at all possible. Sean grabbed a package of bagels out of the cabinet, took out two, and placed them in the toaster.

"I can't stay home with you today, little buddy," Sean said calmly. "Daddy's got to work, but I'll take you to the park or something tomorrow, alright?" He took Danny off of the counter and placed him in his favorite chair at the table. The bagels popped out of the toaster, and he was just about to grab them when the phone rang.

"Hello?" Sean said gruffly.

"Hey, *Coughlin*," the voice replied softly through the receiver. It was Chief Lannom. *"Could you come in as soon as possible? We need to talk."*

"Okay," Sean replied. "I'll be in as soon as I drop my son off."

As he hung up the phone, he tried to gauge what the call meant, but Lannom was famous for being difficult to read. Was it possible that they found something at Wakefield's club or was Internal Affairs already in the mix? He couldn't tell.

"Let's go Buddy," Sean said as he grabbed Danny in his arms, leaving the uneaten bagels standing upright in the toaster. "Daddy has to go. Let's find you something to wear."

Danny didn't respond as they ascended up the stairs to the second landing. He didn't even protest the uneaten bagels in the toaster. He had no idea what the phone call entailed, but for him it was a repeat of the very thing he experienced a thousand times over – he was being left alone again. He hated kindergarten and wished he could spend all of his time at home with his dad. Sean never saw the tears that welled up in his son's eyes.

∗∗∗

"Come on in, Sean," Lannom said. "Have a seat."

The chief's office was a bit of a mess. Sean hated when he had to come in there. Not that he was a neat freak, but he did like everything in its place – at least he believed that it should be. He sat in front of the desk, looking uncomfortably at the papers scattered about. The walls were a cluttered array of awards and achievements, with awkward lines of dark shadows cast from the reflection of the sunrays that peeked through the blinds. However, the chief's appearance was in stark contrast to his unkempt office. Some days he wore his crisp, white, departmental shirt and bars, but today, he sported a sharp, navy blue suit. He sat down and appeared particularly grim, although he wasn't known for cheerfulness.

"There was nothing in that club, Coughlin," Lannom said abruptly. "No guns, no ammunition; not even the bouncers were carrying guns. What possessed you to go in there, even after York told you to stand down? He was letting the FTF tag along as a courtesy."

"Chief, I didn't have much of a choice. The last bit of intel from Sviala said something major was going down last night at the Rock Steady. That was all we had. I didn't want to let him go. It's bad enough we gotta let them piss all over us. Were we supposed to stand down on our guy because they didn't wanna move in?" Sean argued.

"Well, Sviala's still missing... and that's *their* problem, but officers under *my* command, who discard direct orders are my problem. You and your team managed to kill an unarmed man on his wedding night and almost killed Wakefield. All of this and you didn't even have a warrant on him."

"Wakefield's not dead?" Sean asked.

Lannom shook his head. "No, he's not, but not for lack of trying. He's over at Harlem General. The word is, he's gonna pull through. Most of the shots that made contact were in and outs, but they're still operating."

Sean shook his head. The one bright spot about this was that Wakefield was finally gone and that chapter in his life would be closed. Now, that was not the case.

"Look, Sean. The NYPD, especially Harlem, have already been going through a tough time. Louima, Diallo, and the last few incidents this year have the city screaming for blood, and now this?" The chief shook his head. There was a mixture of dread and fatigue in his eyes. He continued, "The wake for Eric Harland is tomorrow, and the funeral is Tuesday. We're gonna be out in full force because we're expecting it to get really ugly. The widow, Mrs. Harland, has already retained Albert Sampson as legal counsel. He offered to represent her pro bono, and she accepted."

That last tidbit of information made Sean's head ache. Albert Sampson was well-known and respected; the go-to guy for these types of cases. Sampson was a former DA and a long-time champion for civil rights. He was always at the forefront, leading the charge in press conferences. Sean saw him a few times, but never met the man personally. He had no love for him, though. As far as he was concerned, all he wanted to do was bury cops. Ironically, Danielle loved him.

"Legal counsel?" Sean exclaimed. "For what?"

"They are entering a charge of murder in the first degree against you and your entire team for the murder of Eric Harland and the attempted murder of Charles Wakefield. They are also suing for damages," Lannom said soberly.

"*Murder?!*" Sean howled. "Chief, that's a bunch of BS. The kid rammed the car!"

Lannom held up a hand in protest.

"Coughlin, you know what comes next. I gotta put you and the whole team on modified duty until the trial's over. Right now, I need your piece and your shield," Chief Lannom added.

"Seriously, Chief?" Sean cried. "You think I *killed* that kid?"

Lannom shook his head. "Of course not, but I gotta do something. We've been looking bad for a long time, and this department is not gonna look like it condones police brutality, excessive force, or any misconduct – not while I'm running it. Until everything gets hashed out, that's the way it's gotta be. Forensics is going to examine the guns to see whose bullet actually killed the kid. After that, you'll get it back."

Sean sat silently, looking down at the floor. He reached into the back pocket of his jeans and pulled out the leather case that contained his badge. Then he grabbed his holster and unstrapped his weapon and placed them both on the chief's desk. He wasn't exactly angry. He expected something like this, but he also hoped the chief would be able to fight for him. After all, it was he who promoted him, made him a detective and gave him his own squad. Everything was politics now, he thought to himself. Everything had to look good. The pressure came from everywhere, and Sean knew this was only the beginning. It was about to get a lot worse.

"Go see the psych," Lannom ordered. "Right now. You see the shooting board tomorrow. I'll be there to support you, but don't lie and *don't* make anything up. I'm behind you, Coughlin," he said reassuringly.

Sean nodded silently. He got up and exited the chief's office. As he opened the door and entered the squad room, he saw the faces of his fellow officers in what appeared to be slow motion. There were mixed emotions; some seemed to feel sorry for him, while others appeared to be angry. Some even looked disgusted. He walked past them all without a single word, headed toward the elevator, and pressed the button.

He kept his eyes on the door as his muscles tensed, seethed with rage as the reality of what was happening set in. All he wanted was to go where no one could see him. Sean silently hoped that his elevator ride to the floor where the psych was afforded him some privacy. After what seemed like an eternity, the doors opened...

... And there was his partner, Matthew Stone.

He looked exactly like Sean felt – beaten. Matt was always good for a smile and a joke, but Sean doubted he would get either.

"How you feelin', Sean?" he asked.

"Won't know 'til I see the psych," Sean replied. "How goes it, Matty? What'd they ask you?"

"What happened last night. No big deal."

Sean raised his eyebrow. "And what'd you tell 'em?"

Detective Matthew Stone looked his partner straight in the eye.

"Eric Harland rammed us, and we had reason to believe there was a gun inside. We had no choice but to fire," he explained.

Sean smiled. "I'll see you at Mike's later," he said.

He watched his friend walk off as the elevator doors closed, and Sean Coughlin felt a little better. Everything was going to be all right.

***

"We are gathered here today to celebrate the life of Eric Maurice Harland, who was taken from us way too soon," the pastor explained.

The church was packed to capacity. Every pew was filled, and every space along the wall was occupied. There were some family members present, but many in attendance were just folks from around the way; young ones who were familiar with Eric by face or in passing, who not only wanted to show their respect, but their solidarity against the racist and trigger-happy police in their neighborhood. The old ones shook their heads in shame and disgust and remembered how hard they fought to keep this from happening, while they recalled a time when it happened far too often. Now, it was happening again.

The dark, wooden coffin containing Eric's body was placed in the center at the front of the sanctuary, but it was closed. The pastor stood behind it, elevated by the pulpit, draped in flowing robes of white and gold satin. There was a Bible on top, but it was also closed. To the left of the church, seated in the front row was Eric's widow, Joanna. Shockingly, her mother attended the services and sat beside her. Joanna wore an elegant black dress beneath a sweeping, black cloak, and a wide-brimmed hat with a veil. Her mother appeared frail, attired in a worn, rumpled, imitation leather jacket. She held her daughter around the shoulders and rubbed them mechanically as her eyes stared into some faraway place.

"Our young brother's life was ended, when it was just about to begin... a new wife and a promising new career..." the pastor continued. "We have with us today his grandmother, Cora Jackson, who has always been a loyal member of this church. We know little Eric was like a son to her. Would you like to stand up and say a few words, sister Cora?" he prompted.

Eric's grandmother, Cora Jackson, was seated on the other side of the church with Eric's parents and other family members. She looked over at Joanna with utter disdain, but Joanna didn't see her. She was in her own world. Cora was dressed in all black as well, with a hat somewhat like Joanna's, but adorned with a lavender band that matched the flower on its side. She had some difficulty getting up out of her seat, but some of the men in the pew helped her stand up. She made her way toward the three steps that led to the pulpit. As she caught sight of the casket, she imagined his body inside and remembered how he looked just two days prior – smiling, happy, and full of promise. She thought back to when he was small and how he ran around her house naked when she tried to wash him up. She recalled a few of the arguments they had only weeks before, when it became evident that he was definitely going to marry that girl and there was no changing his mind. Now he was dead.

"Oh my Godddd!!!" she screamed, raising her hands into the air as she collapsed on the red carpet. Members of Eric's family immediately rushed to her aid and escorted her off to the side, then into a back room. At this point, Joanna stood up erect, and the entire room was silent as they watched her ascend the steps to the pulpit. The pastor moved aside and Joanna took her place at the microphone. She didn't remove her veil, but spoke through it instead.

"I've known Eric for most of my life. He was always sweet, even when we were younger. I never saw him do anything bad. He never really hung out with the neighborhood kids, and he always did well in school. When I went away to college, Eric was the only one in the neighborhood that I kept in touch with. Somehow, I knew that I could trust him, and he was so proud that I had gone away, that I had left this place. When

I came home, and he proposed, he made me the happiest I'd ever been. He told me we would be together forever..."

She began to cry and the pastor placed a consoling arm around her shoulder, but it was Albert Sampson who came to guide Joanna down the steps and back to her seat. He was a stout man with a thick, black mustache and a flattop haircut, both of which he colored. He wore a jet-black suit with pinstripes and a golden-yellow tie against a white shirt, accessorized with a matching handkerchief. The hanky was folded into five points like tiny golden spears, and was stuck in the front pocket of his suit jacket, and his shoes shined almost offensively. With just the right amount of empathy and in just the right manner, he guided Joanna Harland back to her seat. He sat on the side opposite her mother, as if he was a family member. He was just legal counsel, and even though there were no court proceedings this morning, he was more than ready to perform one of his other functions – handling the television cameras.

Albert Chandler Sampson was a native New Yorker. His mother moved him and his two brothers from their hometown of Mississippi in an effort to escape the climate of racial violence in the south. Ironically, what they discovered when they arrived was racism of a different kind. By the time Albert was ten, on the cusp of the end of the civil rights movement, he witnessed more than a fair share of young black men who died at the hands of the police. His mother was a strong, devout Baptist and she believed that Jesus would come soon and rescue black people. She was a devout member in their church back home, and when she moved to New York, she found another church right away for her and the boys.

Albert was the oldest sibling and followed his mother's faithful example. He joined the choir and participated in other church activities. In his late teens, he became a minister and preached the word of God to the young ones in his neighborhood. He encouraged many, old and young alike. After he witnessed many shocking examples of police brutality, he decided he would be more effective as an attorney, fighting for the rights of his fellow brothers and sisters. After he graduated from high school in Harlem, he attended community college in the Bronx and studied law and civil rights. After Albert worked as a law clerk for a few years and was assigned to some landmark cases, he became a defense lawyer for the wrongfully convicted and defended a few celebrities along the way. This thrust him into the limelight and gained the attention of the press, and he never looked back. He understood early on that the court of public opinion was just as powerful as the actual court – if not more so. At age 60, he was one of the most popular and most visibly recognizable attorneys in the city; maybe even the country. He was known for getting large settlements for his clients, and over a period of twenty years, he made quite a bit of money himself. Over the last fifteen years, he made it his personal cause to defend the people or families who were victims of excessive force and/or police brutality. He made speeches. He organized and led marches and non-violent protests. He even raised legal fees. Most importantly, he was a voice for the black community, who had no voice and no recourse against the blue wall of silence.

This day, he planned to be the voice for Mrs. Joanna Harland, in the wake of her husband's murder. There was no doubt in Sampson's mind that it was anything less than that. Some shadow of a doubt may have been attributed to other cases, but this time, he was sure they would get a conviction. Little did he know, the last thing Joanna needed was a mouthpiece.

Service was over, and throngs of onlookers came up, placed flowers near the casket, said their final goodbyes to Eric and paid their respects to Joanna. As they formed a line, Sampson guided Joanna swiftly through the sea of black coats and white tissues.

He whispered softly in her ear. "Now listen to me, Mrs. Harland. There are gonna be plenty of T.V. cameras outside, and they're all waiting to see one thing – your reaction. There are gonna be plenty of cops, too. You should appear to be grieving, but not weak – firm, but not angry. Now, if you want me to make a statement..."

Joanna turned on him.

"Mr. Sampson, I agreed to let you represent me because I know you can get the job done and because you're coming to Mr. Wakefield's aid. Please let me be clear. I don't need anyone to speak for me. As Eric's widow, it's my voice they should hear, anyway. The loss is mine."

Sampson remained silent. He had done this a hundred times. What did this woman know about what she was about to face? Like a lamb to the slaughter, he thought. If she wanted to make a speech, who was he to stop her?

They continued through the crowd of mourners and Joanna stopped periodically and received condolences. Her interaction was quite graceful; like a queen receiving her subjects. Her mother faded into the background. Even though Joanna conversed with many other family members and some strangers, Sampson noticed that she had not spoken to her mother the entire time. No one acknowledged her in any way. He wondered what that was all about. Finally, Joanna was done with the meet and greets. She walked toward the heavy wooden doors of the church and pushed them open herself.

"Mrs. Harland! Mrs. Harland! Do you have anything to say to the officers that killed your husband?" one reporter asked, pointing his microphone at Joanna.

"What was Eric doing with Charles Wakefield?" another shouted.

"Do you know Mr. Wakefield's condition?"

Joanna stopped at the third step and looked over the crowd. Only a few mornings ago, her new life was just beginning, and now, it was all over. When she awakened to the realization that this day was designated for Eric's burial, she had no desire to continue; she no longer wanted to live. Now, as she stood before this multitude of mourners, reporters and police officers, she felt empowered. No, she did not want to die. She wanted to live, so that Eric Harland's death was not in vain. She would make sure the officers that killed him were brought to justice and that everyone remembered his name.

Joanna stepped forward confidently and lifted the veil from her face. "Tell the mourners, mourn in red... 'cause there ain't no sense in me bein' dead."

With that, Joanna Harland walked down the steps, made her way through the crowd, and got into the black limo that waited at the curb. Sampson watched thoughtfully as it pulled off.

"What the heck did that mean?" the first reporter asked, leaning toward Sampson.

"It's Hughes," replied Sampson. "Langston Hughes."

"What do you think it meant?" another reporter asked.

"Mrs. Harland is obviously quite distraught," Sampson said quickly and turned his body toward the rest of the crowd so that he would be in full view of the cameras. "This is a trying day, as you can imagine. Mrs. Harland grieves for the loss of her husband – her true love – cut down in the prime of his life by four reckless officers who were supposed to be our protectors..."

***

Sean watched the scene covered by the local news unfold on television. The bottle of Jamison was nearly empty now. Danielle wasn't at home, so he could drink in peace. He didn't bother the cigarettes, though. She would smell them the moment she walked in the door. His plan was to go out to the car for a smoke in a moment. Danny was in his room. He knew he needed to spend some time with him, but didn't feel he would make for such great company considering the circumstances. The psych kind of pissed him off, and almost immediately they arrived at the topic of his late partner, which he still hated to talk about. Remembering the incident wasn't the problem. The memory of that day was constantly with him, but he hated where this was going. They were going to try and make him appear unstable – as if his partner's death somehow drove him to murder. He had no intent to murder Harland or Wakefield. He just wanted to finally bring him to justice and get all those guns off the streets. Nobody thought about that. Even though he couldn't prove it, everyone in that neighborhood knew what Wakefield was about, and if Harland knew, it was careless for him to have been with him. Sean shook his head with disdain. When little kids get shot in the head, everyone is heartbroken, but nobody wants to talk. Nobody wants to get the drug and gun dealers out of their neighborhoods until it's their child. "*Then* everybody understands," Sean murmured to himself. His thoughts turned to Danny and how when those guys started shooting at each other, that Danny could be laid out on television; or him for that matter. He could not afford to take that chance.

His fight was just beginning. It wouldn't be long until the actual charges were filed and the department was hit with a lawsuit. He still had to meet with Internal Affairs and that was an entirely different problem. He hated them. They were like a whole separate police force. Even though he dreaded seeing them, he felt confident that he was okay. The kid had clearly charged at them when he backed up the vehicle. They identified themselves as police officers and he had reason to believe there might have been a weapon in the car. Sean saw no reason why IA would give him a hard time.

Even still, he needed a smoke. He changed the channel periodically to see if they were running the story on other networks. Tensions were really high the past few days after the shooting, and the evidence of that became apparent. Uprisings broke out all over the city. Some conducted simple, peaceful demonstrations – while others spun out of control. Young people were throwing things at police cars and spitting at them. What was that going to resolve? He already knew how some of the officers would react. These things only made matters worse. He bent down, grabbed his sneakers, put them on and then went outside into the night. It was still relatively warm, but there was a cool breeze blowing.

Although they still lived in the city, the Coughlins had a nice home in a quiet section of Queens. It was a modest home with two bedrooms and one and a half baths, but it was their own. Danielle was still employed at the post office. When Sean got his promotion and was assigned to head up the squad, things really turned around for them financially, but they weren't exactly rolling in dough. He worked like a dog, and they cut Danielle's hours all the time. On top of that, daycare took a huge bite out of his take-home pay. At age six, young Daniel should have been in elementary school already – first grade – but there was a problem.

They noticed for quite some time that Danny wasn't talking. For a while, they thought he was just shy. Upon further observation, some of his interactions with the kids at daycare revealed that he needed to be evaluated. He was diagnosed with autism. Sean put on a brave face, but he was heartbroken. Danny was such a sweet boy, and now he had to deal with such a challenging illness. Of course he loved him. He loved him more than anything and tried his best not to treat him differently, but Danielle sensed what he was feeling; at the very least, that he was feeling *differently*. She attributed it to his inability to cope with Danny's disease, and that was the beginning of the tension between them. Nothing was farthest from the truth. He blamed himself, not her, but this diagnosis affected them all. Danny needed special treatment to ensure that he could function socially in a school environment. The staff at the daycare he attended was equipped for his special needs. He had to remain there until his communication and comprehension skills improved. For the last two years or so, Sean's workload increased as a result of the FTF and he threw himself into his work. He was running. He was afraid – afraid to iron things out with Danielle, afraid to spend more time with Danny. He realized that those were additional contributors to why he felt so guilty as of late. It even explained that nagging urge to slow down or even quit. He needed to take care of his family before he lost them.

He stood in the driveway of his house for a few moments and admired his car. He named it *Sherona* – a shiny, black Corvette he began restoring a couple years prior. He named it after a popular song he liked growing up, and it was his great love. He always wanted one. Well, to be totally honest, he really wanted a Ferrari, but that was just a bit unrealistic on a detective's salary, so Sherona would suffice. When he bought the rusty old clinker for a few thousand dollars, it became one more thing he and Danielle fought about. Look at her now, he thought. Even Danielle had to admit that she enjoyed when he took out in it. He still had a few things he wanted to do, but they were all internal. He took care of the cosmetic particulars first so he was able to drive around as soon as possible. Matt had a similar scenario going on over at his house. His was a blue and white Shelby. It was a little more stylish, but Sean doubted it was as fast. He opened the door and sat behind the wheel with his feet out in the driveway as he dug in the glove compartment for that old pack of cigarettes. Funny thing was, he agreed with Dani about his need to quit. He reached into his pocket for the old purple BIC lighter and lit one up. As he watched the smoke fill the car, he turned on the ignition and filled the quiet street with a roar of the motor. Then he closed the door and turned on the radio. He closed his eyes for a moment and let the sound of smooth, classic rock take him away.

Almost immediately, his cell phone rang. He looked at the display. It was Desmond from the lab. Sean asked him to call as soon as he got the results. This was not exactly standard procedure, but with the way things were developing, he needed as much of a head start as he could get. He felt a little uncomfortable as he talked to Desmond. He wasn't exactly black, but he was from one of the islands. Besides, in light of the shooting, everything was different.

"Hey Desmond," Sean answered cautiously. "What's up?"

"How ya doing, Sean?" he answered with a mild accent. *"How you holding up?"*

"Just taking it easy...what you find out?"

"Well...it's not good. Eric was hit eight times and four of the eight were from your gun. The shot that killed him was the one that struck him in the head and the bullet was fired from your weapon," Desmond said softly.

Sean ran his hands through his hair and banged his head against the seat cushion. Stupid! Why did he have to shoot that kid? He didn't exactly know, but he was hoping that maybe one of the other guys on the squad... They exchanged a couple formalities and ended the call. He didn't want Desmond to hear how much the news affected him.

The feelings of dread began to surmount. Even though he never experienced this type of scenario himself, he saw plenty of officers who had. There would be harassment. There would be marches, and the lawsuit would be multifaceted. Not only would the Harland family sue him and the rest of the squad, but when Wakefield woke up, if he ever woke up, he could also sue the department. They searched his club without a warrant and left them open for attacks. If York hadn't backed out on them, the whole ATF would be on their side, but they removed themselves from this case completely. His thoughts then moved to the walks back and forth to the courtroom with the family. Not to mention the demonstrations and crowds with signs outside of the police department. He couldn't estimate how long it would last, but one thing was certain – it would be brutal. This whole thing presented him with some questions; questions he fought not to think about just now.

"Sean?" his wife's voice shouted through the glass. "What are you doing?"

He was so deep in thought that he did not hear her pull up nor did he see the lights. He turned off the ignition and waved his hands around in a futile attempt to rid the air of the cigarette smoke. Then he opened the door. His wife, Danielle stood before him in her powder blue postal uniform and hands filled with plastic grocery bags. In haste, Sean relieved her of the groceries and gave her a kiss on the cheek.

"How was your day?" he asked.

"You're smoking?" was Danielle's reply. "*Really?* You better not be doing that around Danny."

"I'm not." He followed her into the house, hoping she wouldn't harp on the cigarettes. He walked into the kitchen and put the bags on the counter. He felt a twinge of guilt because he could have gone to the store.

"Danny's sleeping. I didn't really think about dinner..." he offered uncomfortably.

She stood there silently with her hands on the counter, facing the wall.

"What's wrong?" he asked. "What happened?"

"I don't understand, Sean. How could you? I mean, did you really murder that boy?" she asked.

"Wow. What the hell are you talking about, Dani?"

"Why did you have to kill him?"

"First off," Sean said angrily, "I didn't *kill* anybody. We were after somebody, and he was in the car with them..."

"But why'd you have to shoot him, Sean? Why'd you have to kill him?" Danielle pleaded.

"What are you even asking me that for?" Sean shook his head. "Everybody thinks they know what it's like to be a cop. Everybody thinks they would have reacted better. Nobody would dare put themselves on the line every night. You people make me sick."

"*You people?*" Danielle repeated. Her eyebrows were now raised in shock and anger. "That's what you call your wife now – you people?" Tears welled up in her eyes as she looked into his. "Wow. It's taken this long, but your true colors are finally starting to show."

He reached out for her, but she pulled away.

"I did *not* mean it like that, and you know it."

"Mmmhmm."

She turned and headed up the stairs to the second landing, and Sean exhaled as he heard the door to their bedroom close and lock. He stood there for a moment. He was a bit stunned. How did they get there so quickly? All he wanted to do was make dinner for her. Now, he wasn't even hungry. He walked back into the living room, flopped down on the couch and kicked off his sneakers.

"You're a real genius, Sean," he said to himself. "Real smooth."

He finished off the Jamison and fell asleep in front of the television, failing to hear his name repeated over and over in the news coverage of the Eric Harland shooting.

***

Sean woke up the next morning and found himself alone on the couch, but at least there was a note. It merely stated that Danielle had taken Danny to daycare, but nothing more. None of this was getting any better. He had to do something special for her and set aside some time alone for them; a nice dinner – maybe. It had been so long since they had a nice dinner. He worked so hard and so much, and now with this shooting, he felt beat up. He was also scheduled to see the shooting board today. He stood up, stretched himself out, and turned the television back on. Danielle shut it off before she left. He always fell asleep with it on. He really had no intention of listening to it, so he walked over to the stereo and popped in one of his cassettes. Sean knew it was old-fashioned, but there were mixtapes he made when he was a teenager he continued to play to this day – especially when he was getting ready for work.

He went upstairs to the bedroom and searched through his closet. It wasn't often that he wore a suit or a tie, so it was odd when he couldn't find it right away. He finally came upon his navy blue suit and grabbed an off-white shirt and a navy and red striped tie to go with it. He danced to the music; something he only did when he was alone. He never considered himself much of a dancer, but that was all right. He gave the clothing a once over and determined that ironing was not required. The last time he wore that suit was for a policeman's function, and it hadn't been disturbed since. He thought to buy more suits, but every time he thought about it, he became uncomfortable. Walking into one of those classy places made him aware of how little he knew about it and just how much class he was lacking.

He stepped into the shower, closed his eyes and let the hot water rush all over him. At that moment he realized he hadn't showered the day before. This shooting incident was governing over his life already... and the worse was just about to begin. He got dressed quickly and wished he had time to eat, but he was already late. He thought if he ran the siren, maybe he could make it on time. Out of habit, he almost grabbed his spare gun – a nickel-plated 1911 Colt, but he decided against it. It was a present from his father when he joined the force. He never actually fired it or used it in the field. How appropriate, Sean thought to himself – carrying a gun into the shooting board while on modified duty. He ran down the stairs and grabbed his keys off the kitchen counter. As he locked the door, he turned around and caught a glimpse of his car in the dull sunlight that shone through the clouds. Scratched across his hood in gigantic letters was one word.

Murderer.

***

Joanna Harland strode confidently into the lobby of Harlem General Hospital. Her black cloak flowed behind her paired with matching wide-brimmed black hat. Her black high heels clicked rhythmically on the glossy floor tiles. They made such a distinct sound that those waiting in the lobby turned to see who was approaching. Those that recognized her from the news reports whispered among themselves, which gave her a degree of satisfaction. She was a bit of a celebrity now, and she knew it. She intended to use that celebrity status for good – to keep her husband's name in the public eye and to make sure that those responsible for his murder would never get away with it. They would pay.

She approached the large, circular desk marked "Reception." A young nurse, about twenty-five years of age sat behind the desk. To her left was a security guard who also appeared to be in his twenties. He looked up briefly as Joanna approached, then turned his attention back to his phone. Joanna looked at his uniform and badge and felt an instant hatred for the young man.

"Hello ma'am?" said the nurse. "How can I help you?"

"I'm sorry – I'm here to see Charles Wakefield," Joanna replied.

"Okay... let me look for him..."

"The one the cops shot up?" he asked rhetorically. "He's in Recovery," the security guard stated half-heartedly.

Joanna glared at him, then her eyes moved downward to the gun on his hip. She contemplated taking it off his hip and shooting him with it. That image brought her momentary pleasure, but he still never looked up.

"Oh," the young nurse responded softly and retrieved an orange-colored badge from a drawer. She handed it to Joanna. "He's in 318 – third floor, to your left."

"Thank you," Joanna responded. She made ready to leave, but the young woman stood up and motioned for her to come closer. Joanna hesitated momentarily, but she turned back toward the desk and the nurse leaned in.

"I'm so sorry about your husband. When I saw it on the news, I was so sad. I kept thinking, what if that was me? It's really a shame. These cops think they can just kill whomever they want," she said, shaking her head. "But I'm proud of you – standing up to them and taking them to court. I hope they get life in prison."

Joanna nodded and smiled.

"Thank you for your kind words... Cherise," she said, after looking at the young woman's nametag. "I hope so too."

She walked down the hallway, turned to the right and arrived at the elevators.

When she got off on the third floor, she was suddenly bombarded with the overwhelming smell of antiseptic synonymous with hospitals and she felt instant dread and sadness. They reminded her of a vague memory of long ago when she was taken to a similar place with a similar smell. The floor was a light, speckled pea green color with a high gloss shine. She walked a little slower now and shied away slightly from the elderly man in a gown who sauntered along; attached loosely to an IV and a pulley. She turned left at the end of the hall and entered through a pair of double doors marked "Recovery" overhead. Joanna came to another desk occupied by an elderly, pale-looking nurse. Joanna decided to continue past her; the nurse looked like she would give her a hard time. She looked along the door frames until she found room number 318. Joanna stood in the doorway and dared not to venture inside.

Charles Wakefield laid there. His massive frame was completely still except for the steady rise and fall of his chest. There was a hiss followed by a beep as the respirator moved along with his breathing. Her attention was drawn to the long clear tube flowing from his mouth. A little stubble began to grow around his otherwise neatly-trimmed beard. A few tiny, black hairs peeked from his oft-shaved scalp. The bottom half of his body was covered by a white sheet, while his midsection was swaddled in white bandages stained in various sections with bright red blotches where blood set in. There were bandages around his right arm as well. His left arm was hooked to an IV that hung just overhead. His left leg, however, was suspended above him in a pulley and covered with a cast. He looked so helpless – silenced. His larger-than-life personality and self-aggrandizing speech was now reduced to the buzzes and beeps of the machines around him.

Joanna looked upon him and felt regret for all the things she said against him. Then, she began to cry. Not for Charles in his present state, but for her memory of her dearly beloved who suffered a similar outcome, only his proved most fatal. She imagined what if he was there, like Charles, and hooked up to those machines. She pictured him in that bed. Now, she experienced a different feeling.

"Excuse me... are you a relative?" a gentleman with an Indian accent inquired.

Joanna looked around and discovered a slightly smaller man behind her. His hair was jet black and swept across his forehead. His beady eyes hid behind old-fashioned frames. A thick mustache covered his upper lip and gave him the look of a dog in desperate need of grooming. He wore a checkered brown and tan shirt with a woven brown tie under a white lab coat. Joanna took him to be the doctor.

"I'm Joanna Harland," she offered. "I'm his cousin."

"I'm Doctor Neebat." He held out his hand in an official manner, but not at all friendly.

"How is he?" she asked.

He went into the room, checked his IV and gave the other machines a once over. Joanna followed behind gingerly and kept her eyes on him cautiously as if she expected him to leap up.

"He suffered twelve gunshot wounds. Some of them went straight through, leaving only blood loss to be dealt with. Four of them hit his left leg. A few of them are still in there because they are too dangerous to remove."

He checked on the bandages and examined them with a keen eye.

"His middle took the worst of it; hit seven times. He has a collapsed lung. That's why we have him on the respirator. The last bullet went through his right arm – but because of the nerves that were struck, I'm not sure he'll ever use it again."

Joanna was silent for a moment as she watched him. She made her way over to the bed and touched him slightly on his uninjured arm. "Will he wake up?" she asked.

"Yes," Doctor Neebat nodded and replied. "We have him in an induced coma. He will wake up, but he won't walk so well. He will need therapy. When he no longer needs the respirator, we will put him on morphine. He will be in a great deal of pain." He looked directly at Joanna with an insincere expression of regret. "I am sorry. "

He walked past her and out the door. Joanna remained still for a moment while she continued to observe the immobilized Charles, but her mind was a million miles away. She pulled up one of the chairs that was off in a corner, and with a loud screech, she dragged it in front of the bed. She sat down and grabbed one of his hands and placed it in hers.

"I'm so sorry this happened to you, Charles. I was never all that nice to you because I didn't agree with your lifestyle, but now Eric is gone," she said somberly. "You were his favorite cousin – he loved you so much. All he talked about was how he would do anything for you and how you always looked out for him. So now, I will help you. Cora hates me, and his parents don't know me. You are all I have left of him. We are his legacy... we have to keep going. We have to make his name live on, and we have to make sure those bastards don't get away with this, like they get away with everything else."

There was no reply; only the beeping and hissing of the respirator as its sound filled the room.

Joanna sat there silently for a long while; drowning in her thoughts. For the past few days, she felt so weak. All she felt was numbness. When she first saw the image of her Eric slumped over the steering wheel of that car and realized he would never wake up, she too felt that death had come for her at that moment. She literally *wanted* to die. At Eric's funeral, as she stared at the closed casket and the family members, she realized something – that she was all that remained. *She* was Eric's legacy. *She* was his voice. His would never be heard again. It was that realization that now motivated her and was only confirmed and reinforced by what she witnessed today. She took out her mobile phone and dialed a few numbers.

"Yes, may I speak with Albert Sampson?" Joanna said firmly. "Tell him it's Joanna Harland."

After a few moments, Albert came to the phone and he seemed slightly annoyed.

"Yes, Joanna? How can I help you?"

"Come down to Harlem General and call a press conference. I want the world to see the NYPD's work in person," she insisted.

***

Sean was visibly flustered as he walked into the building. His skin was flushed and his hair a frizzy mess. He tried to get extra fancy for the occasion and put gel in it, but he forgot and rode to work with the top down. As he passed by, he saw some looks of solidarity from those who knew him, whose silent glances whispered, Keep your head up, but there were also looks of shame. It was the message on his car that had him out of sorts. Sherona was his baby, and the sheer audacity of the message shook him to the core – the accusation itself – *Murderer?* He never murdered anybody in his life, and on this job, he came across more than a few who deserved it.

Now, it was time to see the shooting board. Despite his long career, this was the first time he ever saw them. None of the suspects were injured during the shooting incident where his partner Angelo was killed. In all of the busts in his role as lead over the FTF, they either took fire or were drawn upon, so there was never a question about the validity of the shooting. Today, he was on mini-trial. He thought to himself sarcastically, I better get used to it, as he pressed the button for the elevator. He got a break. When the elevator arrived, it was empty. He really didn't feel like being close to anybody at that moment. All he wanted to do was get this over with. Even though he was placed on modified duty until this thing was over, at least he was in the beginning stages of getting this thing behind him. In some strange way, he felt like he was making progress.

When the doors opened, he instantly felt a sense of comfort when he saw his team. The entire gang was present – Matthew Stone, Donnell Haines, Rosemary Velez, and Frederick Castobell. He loved these guys like his own family – hell, they *were* family. As he looked over their faces, he realized that their expressions were indicative of who they were; Castobell was pissed as usual, Haines was unmoved, and Rosie had on her best tough face and looked a bit too muscular for the black pantsuit she was wearing. Matthew came up to him with a big smile and arms outstretched. He was wearing a tan jacket over a white, striped shirt and a maroon tie, which appeared to have been purchased together, but he was also wearing jeans. Stone was never one for dressing up.

What happened to your hair?" he pointed and inquired jovially. "You and Danielle make up yet?"

Sean shook his head shamefully. "I don't think I'll be gettin' any of that any time soon. I didn't even see her this morning – woke up on the couch."

Stone patted him on the shoulder and consoled him mockingly. "Can't say I can relate, buddy," he laughed. "Me and Erin have been at it like rabbits. Must be 'cause I'm home more. I certainly haven't gotten sexier."

"What do they say in there?" Sean asked.

"We went already. I went last – probably because we're partners. They wanted to ask me about Wakefield; how much you talked about him, were you obsessive... you know," Stone offered.

"What did you say?" Sean inquired, trying his best not to sound nervous.

"Come on Sean," Stone said reassuringly. "Everybody knows you're no murderer. Go ahead. They're waiting for you."

"Wait for me," Sean said. "We'll go to Shirley's after."

Stone nodded affirmatively. "I'll be downstairs. Lie good," he said, laughing.

Sean continued down the hall and stopped in front of the benches where the rest of his team sat.

"Hiya boss," Castobell said.

"I'm not your boss, Freddy," Sean replied. "Not anymore." He looked at the rest of them. "What are you guys still doing here? Matt said you went in already."

"They want to see some of us again," Velez said softly.

"They're a bunch of pricks – investigating boys just doing their job," Castobell added.

"What did they ask you?" Sean asked.

"How many times we fired, stuff like that," Castobell spat. "But mostly, they wanted to know about you. What you had to say about Harland and Wakefield."

Sean wanted to inquire further. He thought about probing for their responses, but he didn't – for a few reasons. He just nodded thoughtfully and turned his attention to Rosemary, whose eyes appeared a little sad despite her expression.

"Que pasa, Rosie?" Sean asked. "What's wrong?"

Velez shook her head and looked down at the floor.

"I shot him in the neck... they told me. It was probably me who killed him," she said.

"Take it easy," Sean responded. He patted her on the shoulder and bent down to make eye contact. "You didn't kill him. I did. I... found out yesterday. He took a round in the back of the head from my piece. You guys did your jobs. So you see," he added while standing up, "The captain always pays, not the soldiers."

He turned his attention to Haines now, who seemed more detached than the rest, and he guessed why. It wasn't exactly like he could celebrate, even if he was exonerated. He was black and he had the added pressure in his community of killing one of his own. He extended his hand, and Haines took it. Sean pulled him up for a bear hug and patted him on the back.

"This is our job," Sean whispered. "To protect the public from the bad guys. Wakefield is a *bad* guy, Donnie."

"*I know,*" Haines said, matching his tone. "But the other kid? He was innocent, Sean. A good kid, and we took his life…"

"Coughlin!" yelled a heavy voice from a nearby doorway. "We're waiting on you!"

Sean didn't recognize the face, but he figured he'd better get inside. His appointment was scheduled for 8:30 am and it was already way after nine; he ran the siren but it was a failed attempt. He was still late. He gave Haines another quick embrace and let go.

"Keep it together, you guys. We'll be back to work in no time."

With that, he walked through the doors and into the room.

***

Two men and a woman were seated behind a long, wooden table facing the door with microphones in front of each of them. Two pitchers of water sat on both sides along with some glasses. On the far left sat Danny Gallagher, bald-headed with tufts of gray on each side. His navy blue suit looked a little too big for him, even though he was quite overweight. He was a member of the force for more than thirty years and for nearly twenty of them he served on the shooting board. He worked his way through the ranks into that position after he witnessed his partner fatally shoot a young teen. He had a lazy look about him as he stared through his glasses, but Sean remembered that behind that vacant expression was a keen mind. He was the one who questioned him years ago about *not* firing his weapon when his partner, Angelo, was shot. This was his first encounter with him since that incident, but boy, did he hate him. It really annoyed him that he and his son had the same name. Danny asked a lot of questions and seemingly went out of his way to upset you. Sean got the impression that he was living out his fantasy of being a trial lawyer through his participation on this panel.

Curtis Henson was in the middle, another veteran of the force, but new to the panel. He was a small, wiry man who was balding as well. However, his gray pinstripe suit seemed to fit him just fine and went along well with his neatly-trimmed mustache. At 51, he was almost ten years younger than Gallagher and not quite as grumpy. Sean didn't know him that well, but he seemed pretty even-keeled. In recent years, it helped the image of the NYPD to have an African-American on the board. It made them appear unbiased. The real story, Sean assessed, was quite another matter.

On the end sat Esmerelda Diaz, and at age 43, she was the youngest on the committee. A woman, a Latina, and a mother – she was the "Holy Grail" for this panel. She represented the voices of wives and mothers who lost their children. He had never met her before, but he heard plenty about her in the precinct, and the consensus was that she was a beast. She was an attractive woman; her tan business suit and matching high heels went well with her skin, and her dark brown hair was pulled back into a bun. Sean gave her legs a quick glance as she shuffled through papers, then watched the others to see if they had noticed. Facing them was a chair and a smaller table with a microphone, just a few feet in front.

"Have a seat, Detective," Henson said smoothly.

Sean sat down and straightened his tie. He didn't realize he would be so nervous. Now, as he was seated there in front of them, he started to question whether he had actually done something wrong.

"State your name and badge number, please," Diaz said.

"Sean Coughlin, badge number 8004."

"And what is your rank?" Diaz continued.

"Detective," Sean said, clearing his throat. "I'm head of the Firearm Task Force."

"But not a sergeant?" Gallagher asked snidely.

Sean remained calm, forcing a smile. "No... not yet."

Gallagher leaned forward. "And where were you before?"

"Homicide."

Gallagher nodded and continued. "We've already spoken to the other officers in your FTF unit. Their accounts match up for the most part. Your purpose here today, Detective, is to fill in the blanks."

"Did you know, Detective Coughlin, that the SUV that Eric Harland and Charles Wakefield were in was struck over fifty times?" Henson asked.

This hit Sean. As he envisioned the SUV, his mind instantly flashed back to that night. He closed his eyes momentarily and heard the gunshots and he saw young Eric's face.

"No," he responded softly.

"Almost thirty of those bullets were yours," Henson continued. "We've determined from the lab analysis that a bullet from your gun struck Mr. Harland in the head and killed him. Oddly enough, although he was the driver, he wasn't the one who received most of your rounds."

Sean raised an eyebrow. "I'm sorry? I don't understand."

Gallagher rifled through an open folder and settled on a particular piece of paper.

"You carry a Glock nine-millimeter, which is standard issue now. It holds seventeen rounds. That means that you emptied one magazine, reloaded, and almost emptied another one." He paused and read more from that paper. "Twenty-nine of your rounds entered that vehicle. Four of them hit Eric Harland, and *seven* of them hit Charles Wakefield. *Seven.* Were you trying to kill him?"

"We had cause to believe that a gun was in the car. Mr. Wakefield is a suspected arms dealer. When I ordered them to get out of the car, they rammed *our* car and attempted to flee the scene." Sean said.

"But there *was* no gun," Henson stated. "Forensics went through that car and searched that street thoroughly."

"What were you doing there in the first place, Detective?" Gallagher spat. "Why don't we start there?"

Sean took a deep breath. "Wakefield was already under investigation by the ATF. Their sergeant, York, came down to see us. They had a CI that told them that something big was going down that night, at that location..."

"Excuse me," Diaz chimed in. "*Going down?* Please explain exactly what that means for this panel."

"A sale of guns most likely, Ms. Diaz. We didn't know for sure. The CI went missing before we could confirm. He was probably murdered," Sean added.

"Please refrain from speculating, Detective," Gallagher interjected. "Just stick to the facts."

"We didn't know for sure. That was our last bit of information, and we decided to go with it."

"You mean *you* decided to go with it," Diaz said, pointing her finger for emphasis. "We spoke to Sergeant York of the ATF, and he's provided a full written statement. He informed us that even though it was his operation, he allowed you to tag along. He decided that there was not enough information to proceed and called off the operation, but you moved in anyway – without sufficient backup. Now, a young man is dead, a young woman is now a widow, and another man is in a coma. No arrests, no drugs, no guns. Nothing."

Sean took a deep breath and looked in his lap.

"What was *really* motivating you that day?" Gallagher asked. "Because it sure wasn't intelligence."

Sean was silent. Where was his lawyer? He asked himself. His insight was much needed at that moment. He looked at the three inquisitive faces in front of him, staring. What did they want to hear? He didn't have any other reason to go there that night except to get Wakefield.

Gallagher exhaled. "Why don't we begin with *your* theory about who killed your partner, Angelo Anderson, five years ago."

***

When Sean got outside to his car, his head was spinning. He hated to revisit the day his partner got killed, but it seemed as if the world was not willing to let him forget, no matter how hard he tried. Detective Stone was leaning against the door, smoking a cigarette, and Sean wanted one instantly. Under normal circumstances, he wouldn't have wanted Matthew to know he had fallen off the wagon, but today was an exception. As he approached the car, Stone smiled as usual. Sean reached out toward his cigarette, and he gave it to him.

"Don't think for one second I didn't know you were smoking again," he said. "I *am* your partner, but I can see why you want one." He gestured toward the hood of the car. "Geesh."

"Freakin' animals," Sean replied, taking a long drag of the half-finished cigarette.

"What happened in there?"

"Well, for one thing my lawyer didn't show up, so who knows if I said something I should not have said. Second," he said exhaling, "They wanted to know about Angelo. They didn't say it, but I think they're trying to make the case that I was obsessed with Wakefield because of Angelo and that I wanted to kill him."

Stone shook his head. "That's absolutely ridiculous. If you wanted to kill him, you could have walked up to him at any time and blown his brains out. He ain't that hard to find. You would have hardly waited for all of those witnesses."

"Exactly."

Stone waved his hand dismissively. "You'll be alright," he said. "Chief loves you. Worse comes to worse, he's got your back."

He got into the car, and Stone got in the passenger's seat. "Shirley's, right?"

The tires on Sherona, his black Corvette, spun for a full minute before they pulled off. The engine roared thunderously before they shot down the street.

***

Danielle sat at her desk, scrolling through her phone as she waited for her shift to end. According to the clock, she had a little over two hours. She waited to hear from Sean to find out if she had to pick up Danny or not. She knew he had his hearing, but she hadn't heard from Sean all day. Danielle was still curious. She closed her eyes momentarily and thought of how much they argued lately. In fact, she couldn't remember the last time they had a pleasant conversation. She had to admit that it wasn't entirely his fault. She loved him – she *loved* Sean. From the day they decided to be together, she never looked back and never once doubted that love, not once. She realized, even in the wake of the shooting, that it wasn't Sean she resented. It was the *job*. It was the job she hated. She reminded herself that she knew he was from a family of police when they met, and even then he talked about joining the force; it wasn't like he sprung it on her. When he finally joined, she wasn't pleased, but secretly hoped it would be temporary. Somewhere in the back of her mind she always thought he would get tired of it and settle into something a little more family-friendly. The danger that he could be killed was always present – especially after he lost Angelo. That really changed things. Danielle's heart sank when she traveled back to that time in her mind. At first, it was bittersweet because she thought he might actually quit; that she would get her wish. However, his subsequent depression and drinking transformed him into a different person, and he never came back.

Danielle Nubia Smalls was the third of five children. Her parents moved to the lower-class Queens neighborhood she grew up in when she was seven years old. The Smalls family, originally from Marietta Georgia, came to New York in search of a new opportunity for her father after the cannery where he was employed closed down. Danielle's father, Orrin, was a very quiet man, and a hard worker. It took some time for him to find his niche in the big city, but Danielle remembered this time with fondness because he was able to spend more time at home and a lot of it with her. They had picnics in the backyard, took walks through the park and talked for hours about all sorts of things, but she especially missed the fishing trips from back home. Once he went to work, things changed for Danielle. Her mother, Lou Anne, was not a sensitive soul like her father and wasn't much of a talker either. Her life revolved around her duties as a cleaning lady, which was the same work she did back home, and her duties as a mother. As Danielle got older, she helped where she could, but always begrudgingly. Her contributions never seemed to be appreciated. Her oldest sister went off to college and left her with two brothers, a baby sister and no one to talk to. The diversity of their neighborhood, mostly Irish with a few Pakistani and Indian families mixed in, made Danielle nervous rather than comforted, and school proved no better for making friends. Her naturally cautious manner, coupled with being black, made her an easier target for teasing by bullies. She was always a bright child, but in this new environment she realized her light was a liability and not an asset. So, she hid. Her teen years, however, transformed her from a skinny, shy girl to a brown-skinned beauty, complete with soft, brown eyes and the wide hips she inherited from her mother's side of the family. She had more attention than ever now from the young boys, and the girls hated her even more for her unique assets.

Danielle was a virtuous girl, partially due to her deeply ingrained church background and partly because there were very few boys of her skin color around, and her origins from the south forbade interracial dating – especially in her family, who took much pride in being black. In her junior year, she ended up in a Humanities class with a skinny, redheaded kid everyone called "Mad Sean." Although he ran with a little group of hell raisers and got into more than a few fights, he was quite passionate and very insightful in that Humanities class. She didn't know if he was a great student at first, but there was something different about him – and more than a few times, she caught him staring at her. It was a little disturbing at first, she thought, but it was also cute, but he never said anything, of course. It became clear that if they were going to find out about each other, Danielle had to make the first move. That's exactly what she did. She had no idea what came over her that day, but it changed her life forever. She marched right up to him while he was in the hallway with his rough-looking friends – a bunch of smug-faced Irish and Italian boys – and asked to speak to him alone. She remembered the look on their faces; some of them were quite arrogant, as if she had no right to approach them, and some were shocked by her audacity, wondering what she wanted with Sean. A few even made some remarks that alluded to the possibility of something tawdry between them. *That* she resented, but she had other pressing business that day. Sean displayed a look of shock, but he played along, as if Danielle was a movie and he just had to see it to the end. She never forgot that look on his face; in fact, she saw it pretty often.

"So why are you always staring at me?" she asked. "Do I look weird or something? Is it your first time seeing a black girl?"

Sean's expression never changed. "Yeah, actually – it is. There's not too many of you in the neighborhood," he said.

He had a little attitude about him, but he seemed sincere. He didn't appear to want anything from her. Maybe it was telling that the first words between them began on a racial note, but they kept speaking and met each other in the staircase during class, just to talk. Neither one of them were ready for the politics of being seen together. It wasn't long before they kissed. Once that happened, they had to decide whether or not to go public. Surprisingly, Sean turned out to be the one who advocated that course. Even though she wasn't quite ready for that, she thought he was brave, and he proved to be. Later on, when the relationship went public and he received heat from his family, he stood by her. She really needed that. Her parents were less than pleased. Where they came from and all they witnessed in the south, they saw whites as the devil – to say nothing of cops. Sean was Irish and from a family of cops. Ironically, it was her relationship with her father that suffered the most. They talked less and less. After things died down, they accepted her relationship with Sean – from afar. Sean wasn't welcomed in their home. Danielle didn't know to what extent, but she knew he had a tough time of it on his side. Sean was so closed off about his family, but they shared everything.

The point was that they were by each other's side for nearly ten years, and now it seemed they were farther apart than ever. She thought about her decision to pursue her own career when he got the promotion and she realized that she was really going to be a cop's wife. Her decision was predicated on the fact that rather than waiting at home every night worried sick about him, work provided her with something to help pass that time away. That's how she ended up at the post office. She got pregnant with Danny almost immediately after they were married, and that sort of sidetracked her from going to college for finance as she intended. So, she took a job at the post office, where she remained til that day. She was great at her job, well-liked, and had a good rapport with her co-workers – at least, until now. The publicity of the case made Sean's name, and subsequently hers infamous. She had a picture of them both on her desk. Besides, he had been by her job on plenty occasions and those who worked with her for quite a while knew him well. After the shooting of Eric Harland, her black co-workers started to be a little standoffish, while the white ones overcompensated with tremendous support. Of course, over the last week it was all anyone talked about and prompted people to change the subject or stop their conversations altogether. Danielle heard more than a few unpleasant comments about her husband and the police force as a whole. She came to near blows with someone. The funny thing was, she agreed with most of the comments about the police.

"Hey Danielle," a voice startled her out of her daydreaming. "I'm going to the store for some chocolate. You want something?"

That was Jean, a skinny, little thing whose shaggy blond hair looked like a mop atop her head, and her makeup resembled a fifties waitress. She was in her mid-forties and one of the post office veterans. She had a real easy-going attitude and didn't give a crap about anyone's opinion on anything. Jean was one of those rare people that treated everyone the same. When the case went public, she was the only person that Danielle felt didn't have something against her, and right now, she was the only person she spoke to.

"No, I'm okay," Danielle replied. "Thanks for asking."

She stopped at the door, holding it open halfway. "Come on honey, you gotta eat. Did you even take lunch today?" Jean asked.

"I did, but I only had half a sandwich; I haven't had much of an appetite," she said. "Okay, maybe a Hershey's."

Jean smiled. "Okay, I got you." As she proceeded through the doors, a tall man holding a garment bag and some flowers walked in. Danielle's heart leapt instantly.

"Sean!" she exclaimed and maintained a whisper. "What are you doing here?"

He smiled as he leaned over the counter and kissed her on the cheek. He handed her the flowers and rubbed his hair sheepishly.

"I wanted to come by and surprise you," he explained. "I figured we'd go out for dinner."

Danielle did her best to contain her pleasure. She looked at him standing there, with his curly red hair and navy blue suit. He was more handsome then when they were back in school. At that moment she realized that she never told him that. "Really?" she exclaimed. "And what brought this on?"

"I know we haven't really been speaking, Dani. I know how upset you've been over everything, and I thought tonight would give us a chance to talk. Besides," he added, "we haven't done this in a long time." He held up the garment bag. "I went home, got the black dress I like and some shoes. I even threw in a purse."

Danielle made a face. "Which shoes?"

"I don't know. Black?"

A short woman in a uniform passed behind her and shot Sean a dirty look. Danielle wasn't aware and he ignored it.

She shook her head. "Which purse then?"

"Now you *know* I don't know that," Sean said decidedly and handed her the bag. "I just grabbed something. Go and change!"

"Sean, I don't have any pantyhose."

He sighed. "We'll pick some up on the way. It's still early and we have time."

Danielle leaned over and gave him an affectionate kiss. "I'll be right back." She walked into the back toward the staff bathroom with garment bag in hand. Sean stood there and surveyed the room. There was a dull, off-white color on the walls and a couple of other desks in the room along with Danielle's. He noticed that hers was always the most tidy.

He had not been to her job in quite some time. He let work get in their way for far too long, but that's what tonight was all about.

The short woman that passed by them returned. Sean recognized her immediately when he first saw her. Her name was Dawn. She had been around for a few years; he met her at one of their parties some time ago. Based on the look she gave him moments before, he figured she would not say hello. Instead, the woman marched right up to him. She got pretty close as a matter of fact and whispered, "Well, hello, officer. Did you kill anybody today?"

He looked at her for a long time and just shook his head.

***

La Cantina was one of their favorite seafood restaurants. Sean and Danielle visited frequently while they were dating and periodically throughout their relationship. It had definitely been a long time. When they walked in, Sean was disappointed by all of the staff's unfamiliar faces. They always chose the same waitress. The place also now resembled a diner, where in days past, the atmosphere was relatively quiet. Considering current circumstances, Sean had no desire to be around crowds. A young girl of about twenty, with a bright smile; dressed in a black dress shirt and tight black pants, approached them.

"Hello! Two for dinner?" she said brightly.

Sean nodded, "Yes."

The young girl grabbed two menus from the wooden podium and with a slight gesture, beckoned them to follow.

She led them to a booth in the back, and they were seated on forest green leather chairs with cracked upholstery.

"I remember it being a lot fancier," Sean said, looking around. "Do you want to go someplace else?"

"No, this is nice," Danielle replied. "It's been a long time."

A short man dressed in black came to the table with a pitcher of water and displayed a wide, pleasant smile. He filled their glasses without saying a word and disappeared as quickly as he came.

"It's a younger crowd now. They've gotten more popular than they used to be."

She nodded. "So, what did you want to talk about?"

"Listen," Sean began. "I know things have been crazy with us. You've been upset about the shooting..."

"You haven't even spoken to me about it, Sean," Danielle interrupted. "You never speak to me about anything anymore. How do you expect to carry on a relationship like that?"

"I know... I..."

"I don't even know what to say about the shooting itself," she continued. "But I know how I feel. I feel sick. I mean... you *killed* that poor boy! You took him from his wife, his mother – you took his whole future for nothing! Have you even thought about that?"

Sean was quiet. He really had little time to think about it. The honest truth was, he avoided thinking about those things. He just kept seeing his face and hearing the shots. He never recalled reloading as many times as he did. He decided not to share that little detail with Danielle just yet. It would only make things worse, and besides, she would find out sooner or later from the news. He thought about what she said – about carrying on a relationship. Sean also thought about his parents. He didn't remember his dad telling his mother a whole lot of anything, especially about what he was feeling. Danielle didn't understand that it just never occurred to him to share certain things with her.

"I've got people giving me dirty looks at work and in the neighborhood, Sean, or they try not to look at me at all." Danielle shook her head. "Do you have any idea how that feels?"

At that moment, another young waitress came to the table. Her hair was pinned up. It was a bit messy and held in place with a hair clamp of some sort. The look on her face was as if she had seen it all before. As Sean turned to look at her, he noticed a young kid in the background who seemed to be watching him.

"Hello guys! Welcome to La Cantina. My name is Tracee and I'll be your waitress. Would you like to start with some drinks?"

"I'll have a glass of Merlot," Danielle said.

"Ginger ale," Sean added. The young waitress smiled halfheartedly, then turned and disappeared. Sean took a deep breath.

"Look, Danielle. I don't want to keep talking about this. It was an accident. I'm sorry that the girls are being a little mean to you at work, but I've got a lot on my plate as well. We have this lawsuit. I don't even know what the shooting board is gonna say or what the future plans are for my unit. On top of that, I have neighbors carving up my car and calling me a murderer."

"They didn't tell you anything today?" she asked, genuinely concerned.

"No." Sean looked around, as he often did, to check his surroundings. Again, his eyes fell upon the younger guy at a table with three of his friends. The man looked to be no more than twenty-five in the face, but he had quite a bit of weight on him and his muscles were bulging out of his checkered blue shirt. At first, he tried to avoid Sean's gaze, as if he hadn't been looking at him. He whispered something to the man seated next to him, who then turned around quickly to look at Sean as well. Sean felt rage boil up inside of him. He thought to the events of the day: his face plastered all over the television, his car, and the way the shooting board treated him. Now to be stared down by some young thug in a restaurant – that was the last straw.

"Dani," Sean whispered and kept his eyes on her. "Don't look hard. You see the guys behind me? At the table with the girls?"

Danielle's eyes shifted to them for a split second and then back to her husband.

"Yes. What's wrong?"

"They keep looking. I don't know what they're gonna do. I'm gonna get up. When I do, you go outside and head to the car."

"Sean..."

"Do it, Danielle."

Danielle grabbed her purse, got up slowly and gave Sean a look he was all-too familiar with. He kept his eyes on her until she was out the door. Then he stood up and walked over to the table. He put his hand on the back of his belt and felt for his gun. He cursed under his breath when he was immediately reminded that he didn't have one and left the backup piece at home. There was really no harm done. He just wanted to humiliate these punks a little bit for staring him down. He walked up to the kid in blue, who looked at him from under his royal blue cap, pulled down and slightly covering his eyes.

"You got a problem?" Sean said.

The kid looked at his dinner companions, as if to confirm what was actually happening, then back to Sean. The girls, who looked like teenage prostitutes, kept their eyes on their plates of shrimp. The other young man was dressed in black fatigue pants and a black hooded sweatshirt.

"Nah," replied the kid.

"Stand up and put your hands on your head," Sean continued. "Do it slowly."

"He didn't even do nothin'!" one of the girls shouted.

"Keep your mouth shut," Sean replied.

He grabbed the boy by his armpits, hoisted him up, and placed his hands behind his head. He was taller than Sean estimated – about six feet. He kicked his feet apart, spread his legs and began to pat him down.

"You got anything on you?"

"Nah man... I ain't got nothin' on me."

The kid wasn't lying. He was clean. Sean saw that some of the patrons started to get antsy, so he pulled out his badge and waved it quickly around the room.

"NYPD. You," he said, pointing at the other man at the table. "Get up. Join your buddy. Put your hands on your head."

"This is some B.S.!" the other man said. "I'm sick of you racist pigs, man! What, you gon' murder me too?"

"Shut up!" Sean yelled.

He felt around the man's waist and checked his pockets. There's got to be something, he thought to himself. These kids always carried some sort of weapon nowadays. He went down to his ankles and kept his eyes on him. He knew he shouldn't be doing this without backup, but he had already gone this far.

Damn, he thought. This kid was clean too.

Sean stood up, breathing hard. He came over ready to fight and now had to calm himself down.

"You guys enjoy your evening," he said calmly as he turned to walk away. "Stay out of trouble."

"Coward," the man in the blue muttered under his breath.

Sean turned around and punched the kid square in the mouth. He fell hard, backward onto the table. This resulted in the table turning over with a loud clatter of dishes and silverware. The other man jumped back quickly to avoid the spray of food particles. The kid was still conscious and laid there with his hands up. His eyes burned with hatred and humiliation. Sean looked at him, almost with shock; then he turned and quickly walked out of the restaurant.

Danielle was waiting in the car a few blocks away. She was sitting in the passenger's seat. Sean came to the car and opened the door. As he sat down, he looked at his wife. He was about to ask if he she wanted to go to another place, but he didn't. Tonight was his night to make it up to her, and he messed it up. He turned the key in the ignition, started the car, and drove off.

***

Julie Hernandez stood before the steps of the courthouse with a microphone clutched tightly in her hand as the wind whipped through her coat. She was more than excited to have the opportunity to cover this trial. She'd been waiting for something like this for quite some time. She looked at the crowd as they came alive just a few feet from where she stood behind the steel barricade. They all awaited the verdict from inside the courthouse. There were more than a few uniformed officers on duty in case trouble broke out. She smoothed down the few wispy strands of her hair as the cameraman counted her in. She cleared her throat and put on her most serious expression.

"Today marks the end of a case that has been tried in the court for nearly two months. After six days of deliberation, the jury is finally ready to render a verdict. It's been a little over three months since the tragic shooting of Eric Harland, a twenty-one-year-old college student. He was shot eight times by police officers outside of a nightclub on November 18th, after officers fired close to fifty shots at his SUV, killing him and wounding his cousin, 24-year-old Charles Wakefield. The FTF, a unit out of the 15th precinct, was there; apparently investigating Wakefield on suspected gun trafficking charges. Eric was celebrating his wedding of only hours earlier to his wife, 23-year-old Joanna Mosley-Harland, who has been a champion for her husband since his death.

Today marks the end of the murder trial against the five officers involved – Detective Frederick Castobell, Detective Donnell Haines, Detective Rosemary Velez, Detective Matthew Stone all from the 15th precinct, and Detective Sean Coughlin, who headed up the FTF unit.

Unfortunately, this fatal incident wasn't the last involving officers and the use of deadly force. Just a few weeks ago, police officers fired on and killed a fourteen-year-old mentally impaired boy who reached for his phone in front of his grandmother's building in the Bedford-Stuyvesant section of Brooklyn.

Mrs. Joanna Harland has also filed a civil suit against the department for her husband's murder..."

Sean sat in the courtroom looking at the yellow notepad in front of him. There was nothing on it. He took notes at certain points throughout the trial, but today was verdict day – judgment day. As he looked to his left, he saw his team members and read fear on all of their faces. They all sat together at the same table and were represented by the same attorney, which they agreed would be best. As they all waited for the jury to come back in, Sean silently wished he had taken the stand in his own defense, but the lawyer advised against it. He did not want to give Sampson an opportunity to introduce his past feelings about his partner, although Sampson tried when he was called. Sean did his best to remain calm, but he really hated that man's whole persona – never mind the fact that he could put him away on murder charges. Haines looked the most despondent out of them all, and Sean understood why. None of them meant to kill anybody that night. So far, Marty Chastin, their lawyer, had done an excellent job. He painted Charles Wakefield as a former drug dealer and a crooked gunrunner who eluded the police for years as the reason they were even there that night. He explained that they knew nothing of Eric Harland or his reception. All they saw was someone in the driver's seat talking to Wakefield when another man placed a large, black case in the trunk. One of the big points of the trial was whether or not they identified themselves as police officers. Unfortunately for Sean and the rest of the team, there was no one else outside at that time. There was only Sean's testimony and the word of his fellow officers. The biggest point of concern for them was Coughlin's disregard for procedure and policy. Technically, he didn't have an arrest warrant for Wakefield. York and the ATF secured the warrant.

Sean still held to his claim that they were pansies and didn't want to go ahead without Sviala, who was still amongst the missing. So Sean had to take the blame because he gave the order to go after Wakefield. Of course, Chastin brought up the question – if they were innocent, then why did they attempt to flee? It certainly seemed as if they had something to hide. Sean didn't mind that his lawyer raised the element of reasonable doubt, but he *did* mind that Castobell put his extra little spin on it when he was called to the stand. He said that he *heard* that a gun was in the car. No one else included that in their statements, and no one else corroborated it, simply because it wasn't true. Sampson made that painfully clear. It made them all look bad. They all agreed that they would not lie. There was no need to. Castobell was the most unapologetic about that night, and Sean couldn't help but remember that he fired his weapon even after it was clear that the threat was over. He turned around, very briefly, to look at the crowded courtroom behind him. It was packed. He didn't want to be met with the stares of angry, black faces who surrounded him and waited to see him condemned, but he did want to catch a glimpse of his wife. She was there every day of the trial and agreed to stand by him.

Home was another story, however. They barely spoke after the restaurant fiasco and drew even farther away from each other. Danny sensed the tension and withdrew further into himself as well. He spoke less and spent more time locked in his room or playing in the backyard by himself. The teachers at the daycare reported that his behavior was a bit violent as of late. Sean sighed to himself. Maybe it was time for another one-on-one session with a caregiver. They seemed to work.

One good thing was that the department showed great support and made a show of force in the courtroom. Many officers from the 15th were there as well as officers from other precincts. The visual of all those blue uniforms and white shirts of high-ranking officers was really prevalent, Sean thought. Even Robert Kavanaugh was here. He looked back to catch a quick glimpse of him – the man that led their army – the commissioner. He was in his mid-sixties and had a war-torn look about him. He looked like a colonel. His gray hair was in a severe buzz cut and his dress blues and the stripes under his badge enhanced his military edge. He had met the man only once before at some policeman's ball with his father. His demeanor was very serious, but he loved the men that served under him and respected what they did. For that, he had Sean's admiration.

He told himself not to, but something made him look over to the right side of the courtroom where Joanna Harland was seated. She wore a modest navy blue suit and her hair was straight down, about shoulder length and parted on the right side. She stared intensely to her right and kept her eyes fixed on the door where the jury would return. A nervous, thin-looking woman, whom she favored, sat beside her. Numerous members of the Harland family were present, but Sean noticed that his parents were not in sight. He did recognize Cora, however, his grandmother, who identified the body. She wore a lavender dress with a matching hat – a little ostentatious for a courtroom, he thought, but what did he know? Her expression seemed numb. A twinge of guilt shot through him and his stomach knotted up. He knew in his heart that he had no intention to kill Eric, but maybe he did want to kill Wakefield – but he survived. That was life. In the subsequent months, they hadn't found a cause for arrest. Now that he knew they were onto him, he would either shut down or find a new way to accomplish whatever he was doing.

Sean looked over his shoulder, and there he sat – the man who started this whole hellish chain of events. Wakefield looked a little thinner now. His stint in the hospital with a steady diet of intravenous fluid gave him that deflated look of a person on one of those shock diets, but his gray, pinstripe suit fit perfectly. It was obviously a custom job. Sean grimaced as the thought of that scumbag standing in front of a tailor getting fitted, crossed his mind. He would probably never wear a custom tailored suit in his entire life. Not that he wanted to, but it still pissed him off. At first, Wakefield supported himself with crutches, but the last few days he made due with only a cane. Dark tinted shades hid his expressions from the courtroom, but he was forced to take them off when he took the stand. He really tried to milk it. He testified that they were only there to have a good time and celebrate his cousin's wedding, and being shot 12 times didn't make them look great.

Sean's heart was pounding. For the first time in his life, he knew what criminals felt like. He now knew what it was to fear prison if they were convicted of murder or even manslaughter – jail was the definite outcome of such a conviction. He turned back to his team and watched their expressions. Castobell appeared confident, but the rest looked like they had food poisoning.

Suddenly, the jury began to file back into the courtroom by way of the small wooden door on the right. A short, Caucasian man took the lead. He was the jury foreman. He handed the bailiff a small piece of white paper, and the bailiff took a few steps and handed it to the judge. She unfolded it calmly, read it, and handed it back to the bailiff, who then in turn, returned it to the foreman. Judge Wojack was a woman of about sixty with an emotionless expression. She listened to all the evidence and never became outraged or uttered many directives, but she was sharp. Sean visited dozens of courtrooms throughout his career, and there was usually a point that revealed which way the judge was leaning, but in this case, his own, he could not discern. The next moment revealed that outcome.

The judge called their names. "Rosemary Velez, Matthew Stone, Donnell Haines, Frederick Castobell, Sean Coughlin. Please rise."

All of them stood on their feet.

"On the charge of murder in the second degree, how do you find?"

"We the jury find the defendants... Not guilty," the foreman responded.

The courtroom erupted into an explosion of gasps and countless vulgarities. Castobell made a small celebratory gesture. Velez and Haines hugged each other, and Matthew put his hand on Sean's shoulder and squeezed it firmly. Sean tried to keep his eyes forward, but he couldn't help but look at Joanna. She went limp. Sampson had his arms wrapped around her and pulled her close. Sean's mind immediately recognized that same dazed look as he recalled the image of her in that bloody wedding dress. She looked down into her lap, and quiet tears began to fall.

"Quiet in this court!" Judge Wojack stated firmly.

"I told you Bro," Matthew whispered into his ear. "We did our job. There was nothing to worry about."

Sean's jaw tightened. "It's not over yet," he replied.

"And on the charge of manslaughter, how do you find?"

This time, the foreman looked directly at Sean, and he felt his heart stop. This was it. He was going away. He could kiss Danielle goodbye. There was no way she would wait for him. All their chances of reconciling would go straight out of the window. What about Danny? Who knows how this would affect him. He was already so troubled. A cop in jail for murdering a black man... Dear God. His mind raced as he felt a lump well up in his throat. Why was he taking so long? He wondered. Would he just say it already, so it would be over? He loosened his tie.

"We find the defendants... Not guilty."

The left side of the courtroom exploded once again as dozens of police officers cheered and leaned over the courtroom's railing to pat the team on the back. A swarm of navy blue and white converged on the group. The wives of the men pushed through and tears of joy fell from their faces. The sound of their celebration quickly drowned out the cries of disappointment from the other side of the courtroom. Danielle pushed through the bodies, grabbed Sean and pulled him close.

"Oh baby," she whispered. "Thank God."

"Yeah…" he said. He looked over at his partner, Matthew, who had his arms wrapped around his sweetheart, Erin. He always liked Erin – very supportive girl, but something drew his attention in the opposite direction, toward the woman who lost the most today. At first he didn't see her. There were too many people standing and the bailiff and other officers tried their best to keep them calm. Then, her eyes met his. They cut through the crowd like lasers and burned with hatred and despair. The courtroom seemed to slow down, almost as if time had no bearing on them. Everyone faded away except Sean and Joanna as they shared an intimate moment – a moment they both understood. This verdict bonded them. They would be in each other's lives forever. Danielle grabbed his hand and pulled him toward the door. As they exited the courtroom, the press immediately bombarded them with microphones and flashing cameras. They walked as fast as they could through the crowd and along the glossy corridors. The echo of the cameras' shutters, the soles of hard-bottomed wingtips, the clicking of high heels and the various voices that clamored together bounced off of the high ceilings and created what was best described as a lonely ruckus.

"Detective… Detective Coughlin!" one of them yelled. "Are you relieved about the verdict?"

"What will happen now?" asked another eager young woman. "Will you be reinstated?"

"What about the rest of your unit?"

At first, Sean hadn't planned on stopping, but just before he reached the door, he realized there was something he needed to say. He stopped and momentarily silenced the rambunctious group of reporters who hung desperately onto this next valuable sound bite. Danielle looked up at him with surprise and wondered what had gotten into him. He was never one for the press and never considered himself an eloquent speaker by any means, but Sean felt strongly about what he was about to say – maybe more strongly than he ever felt in his life. He cleared his throat and leaned in ever so slightly toward one of the microphones.

"I'm not a murderer," he said soberly.

Then he grabbed Danielle by the shoulders tightly and walked out.

***

"I'm so sorry, Mrs. Harland," Sampson said as he stood up and smoothed down the front of his suit. He reached into his jacket, pulled out a crisp, white handkerchief, and handed it to her. "I'm sure there were more than a few families with cops in 'em on that jury."

Joanna stood up and her mother, who assumed the role of protector, appeared immediately by her side. She composed herself after the moment of the verdict and her demeanor seemed a bit more controlled now. Her mother looked thin, but more alert than she was at the funeral, but Sampson still noticed that she wore the same worn, imitation leather jacket.

"You know, I'm really sorry for my daughter," her mother announced. "But this don't surprise me one bit. The po-lice always gettin' away with killin' our young men. It's never gonna stop..."

"Mother," Joanna interrupted, "That's enough."

"But she's right, though." Wakefield agreed as he stood up. He winced as he leaned heavily on the crutches. His height made everyone turn their attention to him at that moment. "Something's gotta be done. That Coughlin dude has been after me half my life, but Eric didn't even do nothing. He was a good brother."

"We'll get them on the civil suit. They have to shine up their public image… The only question is what to ask for," Sampson continued.

"It's not about the money," Joanna stated. "I just want them to pay somehow. People should know that they can't just get away."

"You know, I remember E always talked about Martin Luther King back in the day," Wakefield said. His deep voice filled the now empty courtroom with its vibrations. "He believed in peaceful demonstrations, protesting and crap like that. Maybe we should do one for him."

Joanna smiled as she remembered some of their discussions about racism, black power, and demonstrations in their letters and phone calls from college. Eric was excited by many of the concepts he learned in one of his classes, and he often shared them with Joanna. She never had much of an interest in those things, but was always captivated by the passion with which Eric spoke of them. In fact, it was one of the reasons he wanted to become a journalist. It was ironic that his knucklehead cousin was the one who jarred her memory, but he had a point.

"Let's go," Joanna said. "I'm ready to leave."

"They're all out there," Sampson said cautiously. "Are you okay?"

"I'm fine," she said in a stronger tone. "Let's go."

***

"What do we want?"

"JUSTICE!"

"When do we want it?"

"NOW!!"

Police Commissioner Robert Kavanaugh stood at the top of the courtroom steps with a bank of microphones in front of him and two officers stood a few feet behind. He didn't like to give speeches, but this occasion forced duty to the forefront. He spent most of his life on the force, and he really believed in what the shield represented – to protect and serve the people. However, life wasn't always that simple. More often than not, you had to protect your own first. Of course he knew that there were those under his command who craved the power and authority that the uniform and badge offered. He knew there were those with serious baggage behind some of those guns and when he found them, he sought to get rid of them. Some days, like today, it was difficult to prove and in those cases he stood by his men. That's exactly what he was prepared to do.

"You know that in a situation like this, nobody wins. A family lost somebody very dear to them to a terrible, tragic accident. But that's all it was – an accident. For people to insinuate anything else is like throwing fuel on an already aging fire. It's irresponsible and reckless. Now, as commissioner I am prepared to implement necessary programs such as sensitivity training and more rigorous shooting drills to better prepare

our officers to meet the needs of the community. We will do everything in our power to make sure something like this doesn't happen again."

One of the reporters, a young man in his late twenties came forward and the commissioner gave him an affirmative nod.

"What will happen to Detective Sean Coughlin and the rest of the officers who were on trial now that they have been exonerated?" he asked.

"All of those officers remain on administrative leave, but will return to work as soon as possible," he replied sternly. *"However, the unit that they were a part of, the Firearm Task Force, will be temporarily disbanded as we investigate possible lapses in procedure with that particular division."*

He made the slightest gesture with his hand, signifying that the question and answer period was over, and made his way down the steps with the two officers in tow. He disappeared into a black Yukon with tinted glass and left promptly. There was a slight uproar as a small group of citizens debated the merit of what the commissioner just stated, but their argument was drowned out by the voices of the crowd who gathered across the street. An older white man in a black t-shirt with Eric's face on it marched back and forth behind the barricades with a bullhorn, leading the crowd. There were so many people of various ethnicities: White, Black, Hispanic and Asian. Every age group was out there as well – from infants in the arms of their parents to teenagers to the elderly. Almost all of them had on a t-shirt bearing Eric's name or face. If not, they carried a sign with a less than flattering statement about the NYPD. An older black man with khaki pants and a t-shirt bearing the face of another young black boy walked up, and the man who lead the crowd handed him the bullhorn.

"My son was just like this young man – innocent! He wasn't carrying no gun, and he had committed no crime!" he yelled. His voice ascended at the end of his sentences and resounded like the voice of a Baptist preacher. "But he was shot down two years ago in the street by the biggest gang in the world – the NYPD! How long are we gonna let these thugs in blue keep killin' our children..."

The roar of the crowd hit them with as much force as the stiff November wind when they opened the doors to the courthouse. The news reporters rushed up the stone steps to meet them with their microphones pointed out in front of their bodies like the bayonets of soldiers on the bloody battlefield. Albert Sampson moved quickly out front to meet them before they got to Joanna, who pulled the collar of her dark coat close to her neck. She tapped him on the shoulder and gestured for him to step aside. She then stepped down to meet the microphones thrust out in front of her. Charles Wakefield stood right behind her with her mother on the left. There was another cheer of support as Joanna hit the steps, and then everything went quiet.

"Of course I'm saddened to see the officers of the NYPD get away with murdering my husband – walking out of this courtroom free and returning to their jobs as protectors of our great city," she mocked. "But I am so happy to see all you who came out to support us and Eric's memory. Eric and his cousin, Charles, were shot while they were sitting in a car outside our reception. Charles had just given him a present, and do you know what it was? A typewriter! Eric wanted to be a journalist."

Joanna continued, "Eric wanted to give a voice to those without one," her voice elevated slightly. "And even though his voice has been silenced, we can help it to live on. Let's show this city that we have a voice – that they can't get away with murdering us! Let us march through the streets – peacefully – in a show of solidarity. We'll shut the city down..."

"*Yeah!*" someone yelled from the crowd.

"Maybe then they will take notice!" she continued. "This was an innocent man, and they took him from me! He would have wanted us to stand up for him and for ourselves! We are *all* Eric Harland!!"

"*WE ARE ALL ERIC HARLAND!!*"

"*WE ARE ALL ERIC HARLAND!!*"

As the crowd exploded in cheers once more, the plain-clothes officers, who were joking and laughing amongst themselves, stood at attention and braced themselves for a riot or a fight, but the large crowd marched as one and yelled and chanted in unison as they walked down Centre Street. Joanna continued down the steps after them, with Sampson closely behind her.

"You know we're gonna get arrested, right?" Sampson warned her. "It's called civil disobedience..."

"I don't care. We have to do something," Joanna interjected. "But it has to be peaceful. The media loves to portray us as out of control and violent. This is our chance to do something that matters and send a powerful message. That's what Eric would have done," she added.

"So be it," Sampson said, nodding his head. Wakefield limped slowly behind them, but then he put his hand on Joanna's shoulder and made her turn around.

"Jo, I can't. My leg is killing me already," he said. "But check it – I've got my phone. Call me if you get locked up," he said with a wide grin. He hobbled off, pushed through the reporters and made his way to a white Escalade, where Chance waited behind the wheel. Wakefield looked around cautiously as they pulled off. Joanna joined the crowd. Someone handed her one of their signs with her late husband's face on it. The crowd converged onto the streets and patrolmen struggled with stragglers. From above, they resembled the Praetorian army of old. Massive, marble pillars and the Roman architecture of the court district surrounded them. As they reached the intersection, they stopped and continued chanting Eric's name. The television news vans followed as their respective reporters ran and picked out a few stray demonstrators for comment. One reporter caught a young girl with curly hair of about twenty and asked her why she was here.

"They gotta know that they can't do this to us. I'm not black," she stated, "But that doesn't matter. Eric could be anyone of us or one of our brothers, fathers, cousins, uncles or sons. Maybe something like this will get the whole city to see that they need to be held accountable."

"We will all hold hands and form a line," Sampson shouted to the crowd. "We will slow up traffic. We will make the city stop and recognize the life of a young man taken from us too soon."

The crowd moved as one, grabbed hands, spread out in all directions, and all of the cars on the street came to a halt. Almost immediately, the air turned into pandemonium and was filled with the sound of a thousand different horns blowing at once and various languages and accents hurling curses. A few honked their horns in support of Joanna and her cause. The blue and white cruisers that followed emptied themselves of their officers whose hands were filled with plastic zip ties. A few seconds later, SWAT vans pulled up, and more heavily armored men climbed out, dressed in black and armed with plastic handcuffs. They promptly made a line of their own in front of Joanna and the rest of the protestors. A captain stepped forward and placed a blue and white bullhorn to his mouth. He spoke in a moderate tone – not yelling, but forceful.

"Ladies and gentlemen, you are holding up traffic and creating a disturbance. Please disburse right now. If you leave now and you do so voluntarily, there will be no charges filed against you."

"NO JUSTICE – NO PEACE!"

"WE ARE ALL ERIC HARLAND!"

"If you don't," the captain continued, his voice a little louder to compensate for the uproar, "You will be arrested for disorderly conduct. If you do not wish to be arrested, please leave now!"

The crowd only got louder and repeated the chants.

"I'm saying this one more time – if you don't leave here right now, you will all be arrested for disorderly conduct!"

But the crowd did not move. They only chanted with increased determination and added to the deafening noise of all the car horns as they thrust signs of Eric's face into the air. The officers converged on them. They grabbed Sampson first, who put his hands behind his head slowly and quietly. Joanna was next. She thought of saying something profound, something that would be remembered and quoted later, but she decided wisely that this was a time for silence. Her hands were placed behind her back, brought together tightly, and secured by the zip tie. One by one members of the crowd were subdued, and nobody resisted. Without consorting, everyone seemed to understand the importance of the demonstration, and that it remained peaceful. As buses pulled up and citizens were gently pushed into them, something occurred to Joanna. As the patrolman, who looked all of twenty-one, helped her into the bus, she stopped at the doors and turned around. The cameramen and news reporters all turned their attention to see what the brave widow had to say this time. She took a deep breath and looked over all the faces of those who waited to be arrested in her husband's honor and on her orders – and she smiled.

"Gather quickly out of darkness all the songs you know…"

"…and throw them at the sun before they melt like snow."

The silence remained uninterrupted as she disappeared inside the bus.

∗∗∗

A few hours later, Joanna was helped into the back of Wakefield's white SUV by a short, horrible looking man that she saw milling around their reception. He looked a little different with his black baseball cap pulled down on his head and his black hooded sweatshirt and jeans, but she never forgot a face, especially one like his. She couldn't forget anything about that night and doubted that she ever would. She was placed in a large bullpen with Sampson and as many of the protestors who accompanied her they could fit, but that short visit taught her a lot, and she had a newfound respect for those who went to jail and for what they went through. She noticed her mother hadn't come down – even when she got arrested, which Joanna was almost positive was public knowledge by now. It had only been a few hours, but Wakefield came and bailed her out, as promised. Now he sat in the backseat of the truck grinning. His tie was loosened and he looked relaxed, but periodically he flinched from the pain in his leg while bent from his seated position. The disfigured driver closed the door behind her, went around to the front and took his seat behind the wheel.

"You good, Joanna?" Wakefield asked nonchalantly. "They didn't hurt you or nothing, did they?"

Joanna shook her head. "No – I'm fine. Thank you for coming to get me, Charles. There is really nobody else I could call."

"Don't worry about that. I told you I got you. You like my sister now," he said assuredly. "E loved you to death, so that means you family."

Just then, his phone rang and blasted some current hip-hop song with the most annoying female voice ever heard. He took it out of his pocket and made a slightly displeased face when he saw the number. "My fault, Jo – I gotta take this." He put the phone to his ear. "Yo! This ain't even the number I told you to hit me on... What happened? Nah... I'm good. I'm in the car right now, but we'll talk in a minute. Yeah. Yeah... alright. Be easy."

Joanna looked around the car. The interior was honey color leather and it was immaculate. So were his suit and his watch – an expensive Patek Phillipe in white gold. He had good taste for such a young man. He was only a year older than Joanna herself.

"What do you do, Charles?" she asked.

Chance glanced into the rearview mirror at them, but only for a second.

Wakefield looked her up and down. His face totally transformed into a mask of seriousness. Then he smiled.

"Since when do you ask so many questions? What'd you do – make a deal in there?" he said, laughing. "That's only a misdemeanor."

"I'm serious, but you don't have to tell me if you don't want," Joanna said dismissively.

"I know!" Wakefield laughed.

"Because, what I really want to know is if Eric got killed because of something you were into," she said, looking straight at him.

"Nah, nah," Wakefield said, shaking his head. "Listen, Jo. The boys been after me for a long time 'cause I'm doing well, and I don't hide it. They don't like that. But *that* night? Nothing was going down that wasn't supposed to. Look at me!" he said excitedly as he gestured to his body. "They could have killed me too."

They rode in silence for a while and Joanna looked out of her window at the East River as they rode up the highway.

"Where do you want me to take you?" Wakefield finally asked.

"My mother's house. It's in Taft."

It didn't take long for them to arrive at her mother's apartment in the projects. Chance parked right in front of the complex entrance.

"I just want to get some of my clothes. I want to get out of the city for a while," Joanna said.

"Where you wanna go?"

"I don't know," she replied, shaking her head. "Just out of here – out of New York."

He looked at Chance and nodded toward her direction

"Go with her. Make sure she's good," Wakefield ordered.

Joanna raised her hand. "I'm fine, Charles. This is my building. I'm plenty safe."

"You with me. Chance goes with you."

Joanna snorted. "So who's gonna watch you then?" she said.

Wakefield reached up toward the dashboard and pressed the windshield wiper fluid button, the radio's tuning knob, and another button in quick succession. Suddenly, there was a whirring noise as the whole panel shifted and extended outward, revealing a compartment about half the size of a safety deposit box. Inside was a chrome and black automatic – a Walther p99 and a fully loaded magazine. He took it out of the box, pushed the magazine inside, cocked it once, and his hand – now armed – rested in his lap.

"I'm good," he said as he looked out the window.

Joanna took a quick look at the gun, then turned and walked into the complex, with Chance following a few steps behind her. He never said a word, but peered out from under his black cap like some predator. They passed a few buildings on the way to the one that her mother lived in; where she resided when she was on break from college. This was probably the most she stayed there her entire life. Her mother was always in and out of the hospital, sick – or as she later learned, in and out of detox. As she entered the building, a few of the tough-looking characters softened themselves and offered their greetings and condolences. She met them all with gracious acceptance. Joanna had to admit she was surprised. She used to disdain seedy characters who always hung outside of the building, getting drunk, smoking weed, and getting into God knows what else. Since the shooting, many of them showed so much support and gave of their efforts and resources. It was then that Joanna realized the value of all sorts of friendships.

She and Chance rode the elevator to the eighth floor in silence. She tried not to react to the scars on his face, but honestly, she couldn't tell if she had or not. He seemed indifferent. He made her terribly nervous. For some reason she had the idea that he had killed a bunch of people. Her mother's door was the third – apartment 8C. She gestured Chance to wait outside, which he readily understood. She somehow felt that speaking might make him uncomfortable. Joanna silently hoped that her mother wasn't there. She hardly felt like dealing with questions today, but when she opened the door, her heart sank.

Estelle was on the couch, leaning over to her right side, but not quite falling – as if she was suspended in mid-air. The left sleeve on her baggy and rumpled sweater was rolled all the way up, and a belt was tied tightly around her thin bicep. Just under that, a needle hung loosely from her arm with the entry point surrounded by marks on the skin, the evidence of a few failed attempts. Her eyes rolled around in her head as a thin line of drool escaped from her mouth and found its way onto the faded red couch. On the small, glass coffee table in front of her, was a small plastic bag about the size of a fifty-cent piece, and remnants of an off-white powder leaked from it.

"Mama!" Joanna yelled. She rushed over to her mother, grabbed her by the shoulders and shook her. "What the hell are you doing in here? Getting *high?!*" She snatched the needle out of her arm and threw it to the side of the room. "I thought you were done with this crap!"

Her mother barely responded. She slowly focused her eyes on her daughter and managed a wide, shabby-toothed smile.

"Hey baby," she said in a slow drawl. "How did things go?"

"I can't – I can't do this anymore!" Joanna shouted.

"Everything has been so sad, baby... Today was so sad..."

Joanna went into a back room and grabbed her bag. She stuffed her clothes in it and yelled to her mother from inside.

"I'm going back to school, Estelle!" she shouted. "I need to get away from here. Too much has happened." Joanna only called her mother by her given name when she was really upset and there was way too much stress. She really believed they had a chance today. She felt herself about to cry, but she fought against it. She knew she needed to be strong. Today she experienced a big loss, but Eric would have wanted her to keep going. She went back into the living room to give her a bigger piece of her mind, but found her mother on her side and passed out on the couch. Joanna knelt down beside her and kissed her forehead.

"I'm sorry Mama," she whispered.

***

The window rolled down slowly as Chance and Joanna approached the SUV. The thumping of the bass in the stereo system was instantly heard. Joanna rolled her eyes as Chance walked around to the driver's side. Some bodyguard, she thought – nothing like what she saw on television. He watched her lug the heavy suitcase all the way from the building while he looked around and never said a word the entire time. So much for chivalry, but at least he was serious about his job. The trunk opened slowly, and she saw Wakefield nodding his head vigorously to the beat while rapping – terribly. She thought about giving him hell for not helping, but she realized something. It was time to get used to doing things by herself now. She closed the trunk as hard as she could in a futile attempt to show them that she was angry, but it failed to provide the satisfaction she hoped for. She climbed into the back seat with a huff and folded her arms.

"What's the matter, Ma?" Wakefield asked as smoked escaped from his mouth.

Joanna didn't look. "Nothing," she replied.

He looked down at the marijuana cigarette in his hand and made an offering gesture. "This don't bother you, do it?"

Joanna thought about making some comment. Instead, she just grabbed it out of his hand and took a long pull. Oddly enough, she wasn't a regular user despite her college attendance, but it had been one hell of a day.

"So where you wanna go now?" he added.

She closed her eyes and laid her head back. "I'm hungry. I haven't eaten all day. You know a good place?"

The place was a soul food restaurant on the East Side of Harlem called Sandie's – the kind of place where you instantly felt comfortable as soon as you stepped through the door, and you *knew* the food was going to be good. Joanna's heart smiled inside when the smell of sweet yams and southern fried chicken filled her nostrils. It was still early, but it began to turn dark, and the place was jumping. As soon as Wakefield entered, limping on his crutches, the short, chubby woman dressed in all black ran toward him with open arms. Her head barely came past his stomach as they embraced. He flinched slightly, but quickly composed himself.

"Oh sweetie, how you been?! I'm sorry," she exclaimed, touching him carefully. "You alright, baby?"

Wakefield smiled and threw on the charm. "Yeah, I'm good Donna. Got a couple holes, but you know me. I'ma always be alright." He gestured back toward them. "Three for dinner."

She looked at Joanna with empathy and nodded ever so slightly.

"Come on. There's a booth in the back," Donna said as she waved them along.

Many of the patrons patted Wakefield on the back and gave her somber nods as they made their way to their seats. Joanna thought it was a little small inside, but she was surprised she had never come there. Besides, the food smelled magnificent. After they sat down, Chance immediately found an adjacent table not too far away, sat down and kept his eyes on them. Joanna figured this must be normal procedure, and she was relieved. She carried a great deal of anxiety wondering what dinner would be like with the dead-eyed, deaf-mute bodyguard sitting across from her. The prospect of eating with Charles himself was only slightly less unnerving. He was up and around as of late and just recently graduated from the confines of the wheelchair. Maybe it was seeing him in that weakened state that made him more palatable. His eyes also reminded her of Eric, but she would never tell him that.

"I'll be right back. Let me get you some bread," Donna said.

Wakefield nodded as he picked up a menu. "Don't forget my man over there," he added and gestured in Chance's direction.

"I got him, honey. Gimme a minute."

Donna placed a hand on Joanna's shoulder. "I am so sorry for you and that boy. I just don't understand how they could let them off. Somebody needs to make them pay."

"Thank you," Joanna said softly.

As Donna sauntered off toward the kitchen, Wakefield picked up a menu and thumbed through it.

"The swordfish is bangin' here," he said suddenly. "And the mac and cheese is crazy."

Joanna nodded. She never had swordfish, but she didn't want to admit it. She was so hungry that she wasn't in the mood to be disappointed. She looked through her own menu and then put it down quickly.

"Okay. I wasn't going to say anything, but I have to ask," she said.

Wakefield's mood instantly turned serious. His eyes narrowed at her.

"What is the deal with Chance? Why is he so creepy?"

Even though it was already loud inside, Wakefield's laugh was so boisterous that a few of the patrons turned around.

"Why don't you ask him?" he replied.

"I'm serious, Charles. What are you doing with a guy like that? I mean, he looks crazy."

"Maybe he is, but you shouldn't judge people, Jo. I mean, no disrespect, but you come from a different life. Silver spoon, college and stuff. A lot of stuff you just can't relate to."

Joanna laughed. "What different life? I'm from the same projects that Eric came from. Did you know that?"

He shook his head. "Nah, I didn't know that."

"See?" Joanna pointed a knowing finger and smiled. "You shouldn't judge."

Donna returned carrying a basket of bread as promised. As she set it down, she pulled a small notepad from her back pocket.

"You guys know what you want?"

"Yeah," Wakefield started. "I'll have the honey-dipped fried chicken with mash and greens. You still got some greens, don't you?"

"We got enough," she said, smiling.

"Cool, and um...a lemonade," he added.

Donna made a few scribbles then turned to her. "And you, honey?"

She knew what she wanted, but she waited a few seconds and appeared indecisive. She didn't want to seem greedy.

"The barbeque spare ribs, baked potato with a little sour cream, and a salad. Garden."

Donna nodded. "Anything to drink?"

"Sprite."

Donna promptly picked up the menus. "I'll be back with the drinks."

Joanna waited for her to leave, then turned her attention back on Wakefield. "So what exactly is it that you think I can't relate to?"

"Huh?" Wakefield said, genuinely startled.

"What you said before. What can't I relate to?"

"You know...street stuff," he replied, shifting uncomfortably. "You're a college girl."

"You got something against college?"

"Not at all." He reached into the basket of bread filled with all different kinds of rolls. "So what you in college for?"

"It was biology. I was always interested in how the body worked – particularly the brain," Joanna explained. "But I put everything on hold when we started to make plans... Now, I don't know."

"But you said you going back, right?" Wakefield said through a mouthful of biscuit. "What you gonna study now?"

Joanna was quiet for a long time. "Maybe law," she said finally. "Or business. I don't know."

Wakefield quickly glanced over at Chance, who was engrossed in a plate of shrimp, but kept his eyes on the door. He wondered how he got his food first, but more importantly, he wondered if he could hear them. The place was pretty loud, but he was only a few feet away.

"I never met any girls like you, Jo. You're really focused on what you want. You're determined. I can see it in your eyes. And the way you've been going hard for my cousin?" He paused for a moment, thinking about Eric. "I know why he loved you so much."

Joanna shifted a little in her seat. "And what about your business?" she asked. "You still haven't told me what you're into. You can save the suspense, though. I know it's illegal."

Wakefield smiled and shrugged his shoulders.

"It must be dangerous if you have to have bodyguards and guns."

"To be honest with you, I don't feel like what I do is illegal at all. I provide a service and a product that people need." He leaned forward. "The streets is no joke. If you walkin' around without a gun, you stupid – point blank. Now, with the police bugging like this – dudes need 'em even more. I know people that'll shoot a cop anytime they get a chance to. Why not? They'd do it to us."

Joanna thought about his statement for a long time. Donna came back with two steaming plates in her hands. She set them down in front of them.

"That's what I'm talking about," Wakefield shouted, rubbing his hands together. "Where's my lemonade, though?"

"Boy, you better shut up," Donna shot back playfully. "I'll be right back."

As she left, Joanna looked down at her plate. The salad was missing. She always started with her salad first. She would wait.

"You know," she said tentatively. "I've never even shot a gun before. Maybe you could teach me."

Wakefield smiled. "I got you," he said.

***

28-year-old Adrian Gates grabbed his coat out of the closet hurriedly and then stuck his head out of the door to his room.

"What kind of milk do you get again?" he shouted.

"The *ProSobee!*" shouted the voice from the other room. "The one in the blue can!"

He really loved Simone, but he hated when she did this. His girlfriend just came in from outside, but forgot her daughter's milk. Now he had to go outside and get it. True, he thought, he had to go out anyway, but the store was out of his way. Not to mention he was on his way to the studio tonight, and he didn't want to be late. He was finally ready to record the song he worked on for weeks; the one the label was asking about for quite some time. He was a fledgling R&B singer on his way to moving out of the terrible neighborhood of Brownsville in Brooklyn. He felt if he could just get this song on the radio, it would be the answer to all his prayers.

He grabbed his keys off the dresser and went out the door. He hummed the tune to his song as he walked down the long hallway and pressed the button to the elevator. Yeah, he really had to make this happen. He was employed as a manager in a chain superstore, but the hours were brutal and of course, there was no real money in it. Adrian had one daughter with his girlfriend – and one on the way. He pressed the button again. The elevator was taking forever. He very rarely took the stairs, but his ride was on its way, and he wasn't going to make them late. He pushed open the rusty door to the stairway, covered with graffiti and chipping turquoise paint, and was instantly hit with the pungent smell of urine. Disgusting. He never understood why people defecated where they lived. As he walked down the concrete steps, he heard voices a flight or so beneath him. This was another reason he didn't like taking the stairs. The lights were off in half the stairwells, and you never knew who was around the next corner – a crackhead or some stick-up kid – ready to rob you. Around every corner was a potential hazard.

The voices came closer as Adrian sped up. He still had a few flights to go. He reached the third floor and descended that flight. He hit the last step and turned the corner.

BANG! The gunshot echoed loudly. The sound of the blast blared against the tight, stone walls of the stairway and reverberated almost endlessly throughout the building.

Adrian fell back hard onto the concrete steps and clutched his chest tightly as the blood pooled beneath his hands. He choked and gasped for air. Blood came up into his throat and the burning in his chest intensified. As his eyes began to close, the last vision he saw was the faces of two police officers standing over him.

"What the hell did you do?" Officer Tron yelled. "Why did you shoot him?"

The officer who fired the fatal shot was still shaking with the smoking gun still in hand.

"It just went off..." He looked down at the man on the floor and bent down slowly to check his pulse. He was dead. "I hope I don't get fired," the officer said.

***

Officer Paul Lao was almost finished with his patrol. Before he went home for the day, he stopped to get his customary beef patty with cheese from the local Jamaican store. He loved them and now they became a habit – the something to take the edge off at the end of the day. In uniform, he resembled a teenager; he wasn't a tall guy and his department-issued jacket was a little too big for him. Even his hat fell down onto his face, threatening to cover his eyes. People showed him respect when he passed by, and he enjoyed it. Things were rough for a few months after the shooting, and since he was rookie, he was fortunate to still have his job. The department had his back. He admitted to himself that he was more than a little scared when he first got on the job. Afterward, well... it was different. He never admitted this to anyone else of course, but he felt *powerful*. He knew he could kill someone if he had to.

He was a few steps away from the store when a blur caught his eye – a dark, shadowy figure moved rapidly to his left side. He placed his hand on his holster, but it was too late. The bullet tore through the right side of his temple and exploded through the left side of his skull, and the glass of his favorite fast food restaurant was splattered with his brains. The man inside who sat at a nearby table jumped back from his plate of curry goat as Officer Lao's body collapsed on the concrete. The blood that dripped down on the glass thoroughly ruined his appetite.

"OH MY GOD!!" a nearby woman squealed.

The figure dressed in all black with a hood pulled down and tightly cinched over its head, quickly leapt into a waiting sedan, which sped off noisily down the busy street and made a sharp turn at the nearest corner.

Officer Paul Lao was still moving even as he lay dying, and a massive puddle of blood pooled around his head. In his hand that was still shaking, was the same gun that took the life of the young man, Adrian Gates.

***

"Tragedy struck in Harlem late this afternoon when 23-year-old Officer Paul Lao was gunned down in front of Island Delights Restaurant. Officer Lao was only recently placed back on active duty after the shooting of 28-year-old Adrian Gates, in a Brooklyn Housing project just two months prior. Police are not sure whether this shooting was an act of retaliation for that death, but all avenues are being explored. Witnesses in the area reported that a shorter male dressed in black from head to toe, with his face covered by a skull-shaped mask, walked up to Lao and fired a single shot to his head, then fled the scene in a waiting vehicle. Officers found that vehicle, an early model 1000 Impala, abandoned only a few blocks from the crime scene. Lao's parents said that he was so proud to be

a police officer and just wanted to put everything behind him and get back to work."

Detective Sean Coughlin sat at the table and watched the news broadcast on the small, flat screen with his wife on the other side. Danielle hated when he watched television in the kitchen, but he didn't really like eating in the living room. He wasn't on duty until later in the day, and he was still in his bathrobe. He didn't mind being back on Homicide, but it removed any chance of bringing down Wakefield, who wasn't wanted for any murders, as far as he knew. Besides, he no longer had his partner. Matthew requested and was granted a voluntary leave of absence, which he had yet to return from. Danielle took the day off. He also contemplated calling out as well, for an opportunity for them to do something together.

"They're only saying that not to cause a panic," Sean said to the television. "Of course it's related. Who would just blow *that* cop's brains out in broad daylight for no reason?"

Danielle shook her head. "It's called karma," she said flatly.

"What?"

"Karma. The idea that his actions determined his destiny," Danielle explained. "He murdered someone innocent, and it came back to him."

Sean's brow furrowed instantly.

"So what you're saying is that what happened to that officer in Brooklyn was part of some cosmic scale of justice, and *not* because some jerk blew his brains out?"

"What I'm saying is he brought that upon himself. Yes, somebody did it to him, but he deserved it," Danielle said decidedly.

"Wow," Sean said excitedly, standing up. "So what you're saying is, it's okay to kill cops? What if someone decided to kill me? By your standard, they'd be justified. We're out there risking our lives protecting people, but if the public has a grievance, they can gun us down in the streets like dogs?"

Danielle shrugged her shoulders. "Your people don't seem to have a problem with it, but you're outraged! You weren't that outraged about the kid you shot, or any of the others for that matter. So I guess what you're saying is black lives don't matter as much as cops' lives to you. That point is clear."

Sean threw his glass of orange juice toward the wall and it shattered noisily. Danielle jumped and the juice dripped rapidly down the wall. He was boiling inside. This whole thing took everything out of him. He wasn't even sure he wanted to be a cop anymore. He had innocent blood on his hands. He couldn't go anywhere now and everyone recognized his face from the news and the coverage of the trial. Now, his own wife hated him... or at the very least, everything he stood for.

"You know, Dani, you can really be stupid sometimes," Sean spat. "You have no idea what we face every day. All my years on the force... I never thought in a million years that I'd see so many kids with guns and gangbangers shooting infants in the head by mistake! An officer's life is on the line every time they approach one of these guys. We do what we have to do."

"By killing young, black men – unarmed, young black men? *My* people!" Danielle yelled, clutching her chest.

"It's your people doing all the killing," Sean said calmly. "Killing each other. I see it every day."

Danielle shook her head and tears came to her eyes.

"There was a time when I really thought I knew you, Sean," she said. "I mean, I always knew that you were a cop. I never liked it, but you were different. You weren't one of them." She exhaled deeply. "In case you haven't noticed, I'm *black*, and your people are killing my people. That could be *me* one day, but you've chosen a side already, and it's not mine. I mean... don't you see that? Don't you care?" Danielle pleaded.

Sean didn't answer for a moment. He went over to her and gently grabbed both of her arms in his hands.

"I would never let anyone hurt you, Dani," he said.

She pulled away from him and looked down at the floor.

"You've already hurt me," Danielle said. She turned around and walked upstairs. Sean just watched after her until she was out of his view. He heard the bathroom door close as he looked at the pieces of broken glass on the kitchen floor. Once again, in that moment, he knew that his life would change forever and realized that some things could not be put back together.

∗∗∗

As weeks and months passed, there were incidents and demonstrations, but there were more murders. Men and women of all races and creeds took to the streets in every borough of New York City and marched with their hands up in a gesture of surrender, much like the posture assumed by many innocent men of color who died. Some lay quietly on the ground, while others loudly protested behind steel barricades – replicas of the bars they found themselves behind before the night's end. Every one of them were passionate and united by their disgust for a police force that was granted the authority to take the lives of minorities with impunity.

There was a turning point, however, a definitive incident that stopped everyone in their tracks. Officer Donnie Patrucci was found strangled, naked in his bathtub as he prepared to take a shower. His blue skin contrasted with the red rope marks around his throat. His eyes were wide and bugged and he stared off into eternity while the hot water still ran down his pale, wrinkled body. His fellow officers and friends discovered him that way. They forced their way into his apartment after he failed to show up to work for a few days. The irony of his dying by strangulation was not foreign to them. Just a few weeks prior, he was exonerated in the death of a 45-year-old black man, Eddie Gadson, who suffocated under the weight of his baton. Mr. Gadson was guilty of ticket scalping – selling tickets to a well-known Broadway show on the street – but he was unarmed. Patrucci and four of his fellow officers held him down. He struggled to breathe and pleaded for mercy while horrified bystanders looked on. A video of the arrest went viral, but the brutal reality of its contents was not enough to get him indicted on murder charges. Now, he was dead.

Many people on television, social media outlets, and engaged in everyday conversation speculated that it was suicide. They deduced that Officer Patrucci was overcome by guilt for the Gadson incident and took his own life, but there was no rope found at the scene. This small, yet significant fact was not revealed to the press. It was deliberately hidden in an effort to avert panic, while the search continued for anyone connected to the crime – anyone who possibly had a reason to kill the young officer.

Officers and detectives had other theories about what took place, but kept those to themselves. The fact of the matter was there was no proof, but something happened, and what that was became evident on the evening of December 11th. Jimmy Rozyczka and Shane Morrissey – two of the officers who accompanied Patrucci on the day of the Gadson arrest, that resulted in his death, were coming out of a coffee shop on the Lower East Side of Manhattan. It was a relatively easy day and one without incident, but it wasn't quite over yet. In the remaining hours, the officers went for coffee and a few pastries.

It was an icy, December evening. The snowfall from earlier that day dusted lightly across the concrete like confectioner's sugar tossed on a kitchen counter. Jimmy looked up at the night sky. It was clear but pitch black. He drew in a cold breath of fresh air. It was almost Christmas time. He didn't particularly care for the holiday, but his daughter did. He already bought her gift and became annoyed again as he recalled the frustration involved with his efforts. Then, a sad thought crept into his mind when he remembered how fond Donnie Patrucci was of the holiday season. He always talked about what he planned to do with his family and shared memories of what he did growing up. He even bought presents for him and a couple of the other guys who worked with him. Donnie really was a nice guy, and he missed him.

"Was that guy crazy or what?" Officer Morrissey yelled. "Talking about getting rid of Eli. The man gave them two rings!"

Jimmy shook his head. "I know, but it's over for them. They haven't had a win in how long?" he inquired.

He was just about to continue his rant when he noticed a bundle of some sort next to their car. A beat-up shopping cart was overturned and empty soda cans were strewn all over the ground like the contents of a busted piñata. A figure was positioned in front of the cart, covered in a raggedy blanket or cloak-type garment. The body appeared to have collapsed and from beneath the blanket they heard mumbling and crying.

"It's a drunk," Morrissey said sarcastically.

Rozyczka placed his hand on the weapon in his holster and walked over slowly. The person under that blanket was definitely sobbing.

"Alright, what happened?" he said authoritatively. "You can't be out here intoxicated. You gotta move."

The figure beneath the cloak grumbled a response, but Rozyczka couldn't make out what was said.

"What'd he say?" Morrissey asked.

The person coughed violently, then began choking.

Officer Rozyczka leaned closer to the figure. "You okay, buddy?" he asked. He slowly lifted the blanket and revealed the upper portion of the individual dressed in a black hooded sweatshirt. "What are you saying?"

The figure grabbed him by the back of his neck and quickly jabbed a small knife into his throat. A white skull mask with sunken, black eyeholes stared back at him.

The figure spoke in a raspy tone. *"I can't breathe..."*

Rozyczka's eyes widened as he fell backwards into the snow. Blood dripped slowly from beneath the handle of the knife. He gasped and choked as bubbles of blood forced their way to the top of his throat.

"Holy..." Morrissey screamed. "Jimmy!"

The masked figure raised its right hand and pointed a chrome and black handgun at Officer Morrissey's head. He grabbed at his holster, but before he could retrieve his weapon, the figure fired four times. Two of the bullets struck him in the neck, and one between the eyes. He fell over noisily and landed just a few feet away from his partner. He died instantly, but Rozyczka barely held on. He couldn't move and the hooded, masked figure stood over him and watched as his life slipped away. The figure waited until he was gone, then dropped the gun between them, ran down the block and disappeared into the darkness.

***

Sean sat at his desk and looked around quickly as he poured some Jamison into his coffee cup from a little flask. He phoned in for the last few days. Things were not the same since his fight with Danielle. She left the house that morning and never returned. He knew she was safe because she called from her parent's house and spoke with Danny, but she had no words for him. He tried to keep his mind busy and work the case involving the body of a teenager found in the projects about a week ago, who was shot three times, but his thoughts were preoccupied. He sat and wondered how things between him and Danielle had gone so far. Why couldn't she understand? Why couldn't she see that he did not intend to kill that boy?

Suddenly, the phone at his desk rang.

"Coughlin, Homicide," he said groggily.

"Detective Coughlin?" the upbeat voice at the other end of the receiver inquired. *"My name's Welsh, from the Seventh."*

Sean thought a moment. "The Lower East Side? What can I do for you, Detective Welsh?"

"Did you hear about the two officers who were killed earlier this evening – Rozyczka and Morrissey?"

"Yeah. Damn shame," Sean said apologetically.

"Well, we got a break in the case. The killer left the murder weapon this time – a nine-millimeter Walther. Turns out the slugs that killed them matched the one pulled from Officer Paul Lao's skull. Same gun was used for all three murders," Welsh said.

It wasn't his case. Hell, it wasn't even his precinct, but finding a cop killer's murder weapon? That tidbit was enough to wake him up out of his funk. "It's a series. That's a hell of a break, Detective," he said. "Prints might be too much to hope for, huh?"

"Why do you think I'm calling you – to exchange pleasantries?" There was a laugh on the other end of the phone. *"When we ran the prints and identified the suspect, you came up as the primary. Get your coat, Detective, you're gonna want to ride along for this one."*

***

The atmosphere at the Rock Steady nightclub was a bit subdued, but then again, it was relatively early. The music was thumping, and echoed in response to the emptiness of the place. There were a few patrons, however. Some were longtime regulars who came to see their favorite girls and

153

waited for things to really get underway. They wouldn't have to wait very long; it was Friday night. Charles Wakefield slowly walked through the club, dependent heavily on his cane for support. He nodded and greeted a few people, then stopped to look at the stage. He gave over a bit of his attention to one of the dancers. He didn't usually fraternize with his employees, but this girl, Tammy, was new, and he liked her style. She had bouncy, tightly curled hair and her shape was awesome. He held off from speaking with her on a personal level; there was no rush. He had no problem getting with the ladies. He just wanted to make sure the girl could be discreet and keep her mouth shut.

Wakefield stopped at the bar and poured himself a white Russian and then he sat at his booth facing the doorway. There was potential for some business that night, but in the meantime he just wanted to check up on things. He spent less and less time at the club after the night his cousin was killed. When he became aware that certain agencies were gunning for him, he realized he was more exposed than he thought. It was unclear if someone he dealt with was responsible. He wasn't sure. They took care of that snitch, Sviala. He started everything in the first place, but there may have been others. Nevertheless, he decided to be more careful. Chance was around somewhere and a few other guys he had under his command, but Wakefield carried his own piece – a nickel-plated .357 Bulldog. He loved that gun. It was big and hefty, like him, and he appreciated the power. It was easy to conceal, but would annihilate anything in front of him. He usually liked his nine-millimeter, but he couldn't find it for some reason. He usually refrained from carrying in the club in case the cops ran down on him, but Fridays were known to get a little crazy. He wore a gold, Jesus pendant on a long, gold chain with diamonds that shined and reflected from the club's bouncing lights. He felt confident in his cream sweater and new cream boots as he sat and surveyed the club's scene.

Even though he thought about Tammy, Wakefield hoped someone new came in that night. He didn't really have a girl, but he spent a great deal of time with Joanna. He convinced her not to return to school in Florida and spend the rest of her vacation with him in New York. He put her up in a hotel since she didn't want to go back to her mother's house in the projects. He didn't blame her. They talked about a lot over the past few months, and he really respected that she came to visit him in the hospital. He figured it was the right thing to do – to look after her in light of his cousin's memory, but it was frustrating. He began to like her more and more. They really had a lot in common, but it wasn't proper to pursue her so soon after Eric's death; maybe later, after some time elapsed. After all, E was gone and she had to live on, right? he thought to himself. In the meantime, they talked a lot, shared personal stories and visited a variety of places together. The shooting range was one of the most memorable. He taught her to shoot, although as a beginner, she didn't seem to catch on as much as he hoped. What impressed him, however, was her interest in his business – what he did, how it ran – everything. He usually refrained from divulging personal information to a woman, but there was something about her that encouraged him to open up.

Chance ran in from outside. Wakefield hadn't even realized he was gone. It was rare to witness a worried expression on that face of his, but there it was. Wakefield stood up as quickly as he could, which wasn't fast at all, and leaned most of his weight on the booth's table.

"What happened?" he asked.

Chance gestured toward the door, and almost immediately Wakefield saw the reflection of flashing red and blue lights through the glass and heard sirens.

"Put your hammer behind the bar and sit down," Wakefield whispered in his ear. "I don't want you getting locked up. I might need you."

Promptly, Chance handed his gun to the bartender and signaled him to pour a drink. Wakefield thought about getting rid of his gun, but as soon as he reached for it, uniformed officers and detectives entered the club. The first in was a familiar face and Wakefield recognized him immediately. It was Detective Sean Coughlin and he was grinning.

"I didn't think I'd see you again so soon, Sean," Wakefield said, smiling. "I've still got some of your bullets in me." He raised his hands halfway in the air.

"Yo, C-Rock, how you doin', homie?" Sean mocked. "You know, this isn't even my case, but when I heard you were involved, I just *had* to come down myself." He walked up on Wakefield with his right hand on the gun in his holster, and with his left hand, he reached behind his back and pulled out a pair of handcuffs.

"What is it *now*? Your partner again?"

Sean took one of his wrists, turned him around and bent him over the booth's table.

"No, but these were my partner's cuffs." He patted him down and shook his head when he found the large revolver in a leather holster clipped to the back of his pants. He took it out and handed it to Detective Welsh, who was a big, burly man almost the same size as Wakefield. "Nice gun," Sean said admiringly.

He placed the cuffs on his wrists, clicking one slowly, then the other.

"You've made a little career out of killing cops, Charles, but you messed up this time."

"Yo, this guy needs a serious psych eval. I never killed no cops," Wakefield said.

"So why do we have the gun that killed three officers with your prints all over it?" Sean asked. "You're under arrest, Charles Wakefield, for the murder of Officers Paul Lao, Jimmy Rozyczka and Shane Morrissey. You have the right to remain silent – anything you say can be used against you in a court of law. You have the right to an attorney..."

"I do have an attorney, and you have nothing," Wakefield said defiantly.

"You know, one thing I can't figure. Patrucci's death doesn't fit the M.O. of the other three, but I know you had something to do with it," Sean added. "I'm sure we'll find a way to link you to it."

He looked toward the bar as they led him away. "Call Arenburg and tell him to get down there and get me out. These cops are bugging."

"Call whoever you want," Sean said. "But I promise you one thing – you're never getting out."

He led Wakefield out of the door. A few startled patrons watched and the music was still thumping in the background.

***

The door buzzed loudly as Melvin Arenburg, Wakefield's attorney, entered into the visitor's room. He was in his late forties, but his hair was already pretty much gone at the top and the brown and gray remnants on the sides were slicked down with gel. His navy blue, pinstripe suit was immaculate paired with a blue and silver tie and his light brown satchel matched his shoes. It was a good thing he didn't have to wait for regular visiting days. He knew Wakefield would be pissed if he had to be in lockup for even a few days. Hell, most of his clients became agitated when they had to spend a couple *hours* in jail, although they should be used to it, he laughed to himself. In addition to a couple of guys like Wakefield, he represented quite a few rappers who were always getting locked up for one thing or another. Most of the time, it was for petty crimes – things that could be worked out. This, on the other hand, was a serious situation.

He sat down at one of the booths in front of the plexiglass. There were many aligned in the visitor's room and all of them were available. He was permitted to see his client alone, but Melvin could have done without the trip to Riker's Island. He noticed just how quickly they arraigned him and moved him. After a few minutes, he heard the sound of chains and slow, shuffling footsteps. Suddenly, Wakefield appeared in an ill-fitted, dark green uniform. He was visibly beaten up. The left side of his face was swollen and his eye was blackened. He also had gauze on top of his head that poorly covered an obviously fresh wound hidden beneath. Walking seemed to cause him pain, but he tried his best to hide it. The guard who escorted him barely fit into his own uniform. He unlocked Wakefield's handcuffs and foot shackles with disdain and then disappeared as quickly as he came. Wakefield winced a little as he sat down carefully on the metal stool in front of him.

Arenburg picked up the receiver that hung on the panel next to him, and Wakefield did the same – but a lot slower.

"Geez...what did they do to you, Charles?" he asked.

Wakefield smiled slightly through clenched teeth. "It was the C.O.'s," he mumbled. "They jumped me. I gave 'em a hard time with it, though." His eyes turned to steel. "You know this is bull. I didn't kill any cops."

"I know, Charles." He opened his briefcase and pulled out some papers. "The description from the eyewitness in Officer Lao's murder described a man of small stature in all black clothing. Besides, I'm sure you have an alibi for that night, correct?"

"I do," he said forcefully.

"However," Arenburg continued, "They do have a gun with your prints on it. They're trying to say that either you were driving the getaway car, or that you provided the weapon and gave the orders to carry out those murders."

"They didn't even give me bail, Melvin," he said. "And they arraigned me fast as hell – with this flimsy evidence? That's some B.S. too."

"Murder one – three counts. This case is too volatile. At this point, in light of what happened to you and your cousin, and all the other cases involving officers thereafter, the NYPD needs a win. The whole city – hell, the whole world is about to explode over this police thing, and if they can say that they've caught the killer, then they can distract everyone and put a lot of fears to rest." Arenburg paused, shaking his head. "How the hell does a gun with your fingerprints end up at the scene?"

"How do I know?!" Wakefield yelled, flinching. "That thing could have come from anywhere." He stopped. His mind raced – visibly. "What kind of gun was it?"

"I couldn't find out yet. I haven't seen it." He shuffled some more papers around and then selected one. "The gun they found on you, however, the .357 was clean – never been used in any homicides. That's a good thing," he said in an assuring tone.

Wakefield didn't speak for a while. He closed his eyes and was deep in thought.

"They can't tape this, right?" he asked.

Arenburg shook his head.

"Talk to Chance. Tell him to get in contact with Joanna. She can take over for me until all this gets cleared up. I already know you gonna eat them alive, but tell him to tell her never to come and see me. I don't want them to start looking at her funny."

"I understand," Arenburg replied. "I just don't want you to get caught doing anything stupid. Odds are, this will get knocked way down. Are you sure she's trustworthy?"

Wakefield nodded. "Trust me – she's smart as hell, and if we do go to trial, and you wanna keep getting paid, business can't stop. She can help Chance keep the club open and everything else." He made a gesture with his fingers. "But neither one of them comes here. Everything goes through you, understand?"

Arenburg stood up. "I got it. I'll come back when I have something. In the meantime, I'll call about these abuses and see if we can get you moved."

He hung up the receiver and walked toward the door. After a few seconds it buzzed, then clicked open, and he walked out.

$$***$$

There was a thump, then a high-pitched whine over the speakers as Commissioner Robert Kavanaugh tapped on the microphone in front of him. It was a bright, cold morning and a brisk wind whipped through the air. The sky was an undefined white color, like tea with too much milk. A group of about thirty reporters gathered outside the offices and awaited his statement. Once again, he was called upon to make a speech and to do his duty, but he called for this press conference himself. Sure, there were a million subordinates who could have given the public this information, but this thing was now political. Somebody declared war on the police – and with four of his officers dead, he had to let the public know that they had the situation under control. They had a criminal in custody, with motive and a smoking gun to boot.

He was bothered by how easily this thing was wrapped up – in only a few months. Sure, he thought to himself, criminals were dumb sometimes – especially murderers, but he checked on this Charles Wakefield, and he wasn't the brainless type. He had a couple of possession busts when he was a kid, but nothing since. Obviously, the kid was dirty, he thought to himself. He owned a nightclub at twenty-four, but whatever he was doing he had not been caught. He knew about the allegations of gun trafficking and the murder of Detective Sean Coughlin's partner when he was a rookie, but that was only a theory without so much as a shred of evidence to back it up. Coughlin didn't help his case by pumping the guy full of holes. Just thinking about that case again gave him a headache. It was nothing short of a miracle that they all didn't go to jail for killing that college kid on his wedding night. He lost weeks of sleep, but had no choice but to stand behind his troops and a light spanking was all he could afford politically.

In any event, presumably, the Wakefield kid moved in silence all these years, and then suddenly, out of the clear blue sky, he killed three cops and left a gun with his prints on it at the scene? He hoped to God one of his officers wasn't stupid enough to try and frame this man, but he did have a motive – the cops killed his cousin and crippled him. Maybe he just messed up. Kavanaugh wasn't sure about anything anymore. For now, he would make his speech, and hopefully, it would bring calm to both the police and the public... for now.

"On Friday, at about 8:13 pm, officers from the Seventh Precinct on the Lower East Side arrived at the Rock Steady club in Harlem and arrested one Charles Henry Wakefield on three counts of murder in the first degree. He is being charged for the deaths of Officer Paul Lao, Officer James Rozyczka and Officer Shane Morrissey. He was also found in possession of an unregistered handgun. That gun was not used in the murders of the officers or any others, as far as we know, but the gun found at the scene of the last two murders did have his finger-prints on it," Kavanaugh said. *"As of right now, Mr. Wakefield is being held without bail at Riker's Island Correctional Facility while he awaits trial. I will open up for a few questions, but bear in mind that is all the information we have at this time."*

He pointed at the young, brown-haired woman closest to him, *"Yes, you first."*

"Thank you, Commissioner," she replied. "Isn't it true that preliminary eyewitness accounts of both shootings describe the killer as a small man, while Mr. Wakefield is rather large?"

"We're still comparing the different accounts," Kavanaugh shot back, smoothing down his charcoal gray suit. *"There are conflicting stories."* He looked around and set his eyes on an older man. *"Next question?"*

"What about the strangulation death of Officer Patrucci? Was that a suicide? Are all of these connected?" he asked.

"That death was ruled a homicide by the medical examiner. We are not sure if it was connected, but we are certainly not ruling it out."

"In light of the recent officer-involved shootings over the past few months, has somebody declared war on the police?" a voice shouted from the crowd.

Officer Juan Pichardo, Kavanaugh's bodyguard and personal driver, stepped in front of the microphone.

"Thank you, ladies and gentlemen," he said. "The commissioner has a very busy schedule. Thank you."

The crowd of reporters erupted into noisy babble as he led the commissioner away, followed by at least a half dozen other uniformed officers. They surrounded him as he retreated back into the building, protecting him from stray reporters who found their way behind the barricade. They walked across the charcoal-colored, marble floor to the elevators in the back. All of them faced the elevators without saying a word.

"Thanks Juan," he said. "I was starting to feel like the kid who didn't do his homework out there."

"I don't know how they get their information," an officer said. "They're so sneaky."

"That's *how* they get their information," another one said.

The elevator opened up, and they all got on. Commissioner Kavanaugh took out a small key and turned it inside the slot to the top floor.

"I need to see those files again, Juan," he said. "All of those cases."

"Yes sir," Juan said. "Right away."

"I'll be in my office," Kavanaugh said.

He broke away from the group and walked through the glass doors of his office that proudly displayed his name in bold black letters trimmed in gold. The office had a lovely view and the ceiling-to-floor windows overlooked downtown Manhattan. He often took in this view when he was stressed and really in need of calm. This was one of those occasions. Even though they had Wakefield in custody, the idea that the killer was still running around or that he was part of a larger conspiracy haunted him. He decided to have another talk with all of those officers again. He didn't want to be out of the loop on any of the details. It was still possible that one of his officers had set this up, and if that was true, he needed to find out way before anyone else did. He took off his coat and hung it on the rack in the corner. He planned to check his e-mail and take another look at those files to see if he missed anything, then he would have a drink. He deserved it.

Kavanaugh turned on the computer and typed in his password, Periwinkle, the name of his cat. There was a 7" x 9" photograph of his family on his desk, but only his family knew he owned a cat. It was one of the easier things to remember. He could hardly keep track of all the passwords in his life nowadays. As he clicked onto his desktop, he went into his mail and spotted a couple of new notifications. A couple of them were from the mayor, and he didn't feel like reading them at that moment, but there was one entitled "The Beginning." He clicked on it and found a link to a site that played videos, and he clicked on the play button symbol in the middle of the small screen.

The first thing that appeared was a bright, burning flame that crackled and danced as its brightness blinded the camera ever so often. Soft, relaxing, classical music played in the background as photographs of young, black men flashed across the screen in slideshow fashion. Some of them Kavanaugh vaguely remembered. Others he didn't recognize at all, but the last two photos were of Adrian Gates and Eddie Gadson, and those he knew quite well.

Then, a voice spoke – a raspy, gravelly voice.

"Each of these men were special – unique in their own way. Each of these men were fathers or husbands, brothers and sons, but they are no longer with us. They are gone forever from this earth, leaving broken families and crushed hearts behind to mourn their passing. But one must ask, why? Why were these men taken from us so violently? What crime did they commit that they deserved this?"

A figure appeared in front of the screen – the face looked like a skull covered by a black cloak with a large hood– but it wasn't a mask. The glow of the flames from the fireplace shined on the side of the skull, simultaneously creating dark shadows that made it even more ominous. Kavanaugh put his face closer to the screen in a vain effort to get a closer look, but he could not assess any more about what was displayed in front of him. The eye sockets were pitch black and sunken in. The jawbone was slightly open, but just slightly and revealed nothing than more blackness. The mouth didn't move, but somehow the words seemed to emanate from its very being, from deep within.

"The NYPD has declared war on our community, on the Black Man. They have declared war on those they think powerless. Well now, Commissioner, they have power. There will be more deaths – countless deaths, and they will be on your head. As long as innocent men die in the streets, so too will your people die. As long as the cries of their families remain unanswered, so will the families of your people know their pain. You have drawn first blood. You have oppressed us. You have ignored us. Now feel our wrath."

"Retribution is at hand."

The screen went black momentarily, and Commissioner Kavanaugh stared at it incredulously as he tried to process the gravity of the message he just witnessed. Just then, an insignia of a bright orange-reddish flame came on the screen – and stayed there. Kavanaugh exhaled.

The war had begun.

CHAPTER FIVE

Retribution is at Hand

It was warm and toasty inside the Castobell home as Frederick pasted up the last of the faux-autumn leaves over the fireplace. His wife, Connie, was big on decorations around the holidays. He appreciated the ambiance, but preferred to pass on participating. Reaching around and climbing up on top of chairs only reminded him that he was getting up in years. God forbid his son, Freddy Jr., would get off his behind and offer some assistance. He was probably in front of the computer. He grimaced as he bent backwards and stretched; then he admired the fireplace as the flames crackled and danced in front of him. The house smelled wonderful; scents of cinnamon, nutmeg and stuffing, and all of the wonderful dishes on the holiday menu. The food wasn't the only contributor to Frederick's excitement. Thanksgiving dinner was a long-time family tradition; yet one slightly marred by their oldest daughter, Elaine, who went away to college.

What a waste! he thought to himself. She was supposed to become a doctor. Now, instead of making a real living, she chose to fly all over the world helping endangered species or some related nonsense. However, tonight she was on her way and due any minute. Frederick pulled at the neck of his tight knit sweater. He was in and out of the house all day. It was a bit breezy, but now it was heating up inside.

While he looked forward to Elaine coming, there was also a bit of trepidation. About seven years ago, after the shooting at the Rock Steady, more than a few discussions took place in their home about the abuses – as she referred to them – of the NYPD toward the African-American race. She was disgusted by them and by his defense of what they were doing. Castobell shook his head. He didn't understand his daughter or her generation, for that matter. How did she turn out the way she did? She grew up in his home and was indoctrinated with his family values. As she got older, Elaine associated with more and more people of color, especially when she went away to school and explored other places. What benefit was there from all the races fraternizing and mixing together? Castobell thought to himself. In his opinion, white kids, like her, were losing their identities. In any event, during her last visit from college, she voiced very strong views about the case, and things got heated. There was a lot of screaming, and they hadn't spoken a word since. That was a few years ago. She called every once in a while, but only spoke to her mother. When the holidays rolled around she never came to the house. He figured she was all wound up because she was probably dating some black guy, but he had no proof. In any case, he looked forward to seeing her again and to restoring some degree of "normalcy."

Things were very different during the years following the verdict – well, technically, even before the verdict – when the FTF was disbanded. Castobell was reassigned to the Robbery Division, where he was stationed before the task force was formed. He really didn't mind Robbery, but, to him, it was like a fall from grace after that promotion; especially now, with all the negative publicity. On top of that, there wasn't much action. Every so often you might have to chase a guy down, but in the FTF they did the heavy lifting – searched for and confiscated guns, kicked down doors – real police work. He missed it. Hell, in his opinion, that's why guys joined the force. Although no one admitted it, becoming a cop, especially in the current day, had little or nothing to do with wanting to be a hero. They did it to bust heads. Now that the old crew was broken up, things were definitely different around the station, and things only got stranger after the trial.

Velez wouldn't even look at him. They used to be partners and went back a ways. Why the hell did her opinion matter? he thought to himself disdainfully. She was probably an undercover lesbian. And Haines? He barely spoke now. True, he was black, but he always bled blue. As far as he was concerned, Haines was one of the good niggers, but he had some nerve! All those years in Narcotics, he had to be a little dirty, Castobell thought. God only knew what was going on with Matthew. He didn't even show up for work half the time, and when he did, he was on another planet. It was their fearless leader, Coughlin, who surprised him the most. If he hadn't cornered him one day and brought light to the situation, he wouldn't have known there was an issue. He came up to him and blasted him about how he was a disgrace and put them all at risk by lying on the witness stand. This generation was so touchy-feely. In his day, there was no question whether or not you stood up for your brothers in blue – no matter whatever it took. It shouldn't have surprised him. After all, Coughlin was a nigger-lover, with his black wife and mulatto son, he thought. He heard through the grapevine that the happy couple was now divorced. After that, he left the two-five and transferred out here to the Bronx.

The truth was, it didn't matter where you went nowadays. The city had descended into hell. It was as if the city exploded after the death of those two officers downtown and the arrest of Charles Wakefield. There were all kinds of protests; some peaceful, but a lot of them turned violent, with plenty of injuries and even a few deaths. With the increase of attacks on police officers and more of their fellow officers dying on the street, the NYPD realized they had a bigger problem than just some gunrunning nightclub owner (even though Wakefield was later convicted and sentenced to life in prison). Random searches that weren't so random were initiated, and more innocent people died at their hands – some shot and others beaten to death. Castobell had not shed a tear. True, they were there to protect and serve the public, but sometimes you had to put your foot on the public's neck and warn them that at any time, you could bring the war. It kept them in line. That's what they did in the old days and it was happening again. After a few months, the craziness died down, and there was relative peace in New York City, but every time there was an unjustified officer-involved shooting, that officer later died under mysterious circumstances, and there were no suspects. This year, the killer had returned.

"Connie!" Castobell called out.

He didn't hear any response, but the water was running. He walked over to the kitchen, leaned in the doorway for a moment and looked at all the delicious things – some prepared and some unprepared. Connie was rinsing string beans in the sink. She was still beautiful with her soft blue eyes and warm smile. Even though she routinely dyed her hair blond to cover up the gray, she still had a slim figure. Thank God for that, he thought. He looked down and patted his belly. Goodness knows he hadn't kept up with his.

"Connie!" he called again.

She looked up and turned around from the sink.

"What is it, Fred?" she answered.

"Did Lainey mention if she was bringing someone up here with her?"

Connie shook her head and turned her attention back to the sink. "She didn't say anything to me, but there is a boy – I think," she added.

Castobell shrugged. "She's a grown woman. What do I care if she has a boyfriend? As long as it ain't a *girlfriend* or a smoke," he concluded.

Connie sighed. Sometimes the things that came out of her husband's mouth made her wonder what she was thinking all those years ago. It was true, she came from the same place and time, but they shared very different viewpoints; especially now. As she got older, she learned to avoid a lot of conversations, but she had no intention of letting him ruin another Thanksgiving.

"Listen," she said firmly. "I don't want you going off on any of your rants tonight. We don't want a repeat of the last incident, do we? I want to keep seeing my daughter around this house."

"So you *do* blame me for her not coming around or calling," he said gruffly.

"I didn't say that," Connie replied softly. She immediately tried to change the tone of the conversation before it became another argument. Fred was so grumpy sometimes. It had definitely gotten worse over the last year or so.

"But it doesn't endear her to us if she gets in a fight every time she comes over, she continued. "Besides, you say such awful things sometimes – things you shouldn't say to anyone," she added.

Suddenly, the doorbell rang.

"Speak of the devil," he said as he walked toward the front door. "Listen, Connie. This is *my* house, and I'm not changing my opinions for anyone; especially my daughter. Let her live as long as we have. She'll see."

He opened the door, and there was a young, Caucasian man dressed in a delivery service uniform, with a small, brown package under his arm. He had bright blond hair that was cut neatly and parted. He smiled warmly.

"Mister Frederick Castobell?" he asked in an upbeat voice.

He responded, "Yeah, that's me."

"I've got a package for you."

He handed him the box, made a gesture that resembled a salute, and walked away.

"Don't I gotta sign something?" Castobell inquired after him.

He looked at the box, held it up to his ear and shook it. It was about the size of a dictionary, wrapped in plain brown paper, and tied with twine.

"I thought it was Elaine," Connie exclaimed as she walked over.

"I know," he replied. "I did too."

"Good thing it wasn't. That bird isn't nearly finished. I think I got a larger one than last year."

She looked curiously at the box in his hand. "Who's the parcel from?"

He shrugged and walked over to the dinner table and sat down. "There's no address," he said, looking it over. "It could be a bomb."

Connie shook her head. "Now why do you say things like that?"

Castobell untied the twine and tore off the wrapping paper, exposing a small wooden chest. It had a fine, glossy shine, with a golden hook latch in the front.

"It's a music box or something," he said excitedly.

"Who would've sent you that?" Connie asked.

He shrugged again. "Maybe it's Elaine – a peace offering of some kind," he said hopefully.

When he unhooked the latch and lifted the top, he heard a metallic ping. He opened it and revealed red satin inside. Pinned to the top, affixed with a screw, was a wallet-sized photo of a smiling Eric Harland. Attached to the screw was a short wire, and on its end was the pin to the grenade fastened to the bottom of the box. The safety pin and latch were lying next to it. He had just enough time to see Eric's eyes before it exploded.

"Holy..." he whispered.

***

Detective Sean Coughlin flinched as he struggled to get out of the passenger's side of his cruiser. His belt scraped him on the bottom of his belly. He put on a little bit of weight, but he had to admit that not all of it came from eating. He grabbed the roof of the car and pulled himself up. His partner, a younger detective named Aquila, was in the driver's seat. Their partnership was relatively new, only a few months, but who knew how long that would last. Lately, he went through partners like candy. Aquila was a health nut and he was already banned from smoking in the car. He missed Matt, but he never saw him anymore.

The scene was already crawling with blues and other emergency personnel. Yellow tape stretched from the tree on the neighbor's property to the large trunk on the Castobell's lawn and beyond. As he approached, Sean already saw the outline of a body under a white sheet on the grass, surrounded by shards of shattered glass and a couple of plainclothes officers. He ducked under the tape and removed his badge from his back pocket. He flashed it at the first uniform he saw, then walked over to join the detectives who were already standing over the body.

"Hey Sean," the detective said, shaking his hand. Bobby Antonacci was one of those Italians that looked and talked like a street guy, but, by the grace of God, just happened to be a cop. He had jet-black hair and almost bushy eyebrows. His maroon tie was loosened over a striped shirt, and he wore a brown leather jacket. He gestured with his thumb to the man on his right – a pale man in a long coat. "This is my partner, Frank."

Sean nodded. "Thanks for calling me, Bobby." He shook his head as he looked down at the sheet and pulled a pack of cigarettes from inside his coat. He reached for his green lighter, lit one and took a drag. "I can't believe it. Freddy's dead, huh?"

"I know. It's un-freakin'-believable," Bobby replied somberly. "He was a legend – a freakin' animal on the street. My father used to talk about him all the time."

"Mine too, and he used to be in my unit. We kicked down plenty of doors together."

"I *know*. That's why I called you, 'cause I know you guys had that thing together with the kid in Harlem. I thought you'd want to know," Bobby added.

Sean walked over to the body and knelt down. He looked up at the shattered bay window and then down at the body again. Rays of amber and red flashed over them ever so often from the lights of the nearby ambulance parked partially on the lawn.

"So what happened here, Bobby?" he asked.

"It was a bomb – something small. The squad is still trying to determine what."

He gestured for Sean to follow him, and they both entered the home through the front door. EMS workers, who were already inside, lifted Mrs. Castobell onto a stretcher and fitted her with a mask. Photographers milled about and took pictures of the demolished kitchen. The walls were blackened heavily, and what was once a proud chestnut table was in splinters amidst the shattered remains of china plates and Thanksgiving dinner. They made small crunching sounds as they approached and tried not to walk too heavily and disturb any evidence. Sean looked at the fallen chair as Bobby positioned himself near the open window frame. The lights from the ambulance outside shined on them and the siren wailed violently against the night's stillness as it pulled off down the street. Both of their partners lingered at the kitchen entrance and looked on.

Bobby began, "Freddy was sittin' here at the table, and he was blown out of the window behind him. He lost both his hands, and there was major damage to his face and chest cavity. Looked like some shrapnel. Most likely, he was dead instantly."

"What about Connie?" Sean asked, genuinely concerned. "What's her condition?"

"She was still alive, but unconscious when she was found. Neighbors made the call and reported a booming noise. She's probably got internal damage... no way to tell yet."

Sean grabbed Bobby around the shoulders and led him out of the kitchen and out of the house. He exhaled the smoke from his cigarette and threw the butt into the street.

"Let me ask you something," he whispered into Bobby's ear. "You think Freddy was dirty?"

"What?" Bobby said. "What do you mean, *dirty*? What are you talking about?"

"He was holding a bomb in both hands when he died. I mean, Freddy was stupid," Sean said smiling, "But not *that* stupid. Somebody sent it to him. Now, who would want to kill Freddy so bad that they'd send a bomb to him personally?" he added.

With that, his phone rang. It was Danielle. Funny, he thought to himself, he heard from her more now than he did when they were together. Things were on the rocks after the shooting, but when the incident about the two boys in the restaurant came to light, he almost lost his job over that one and that was the last straw for her. To her credit, she wasn't sticking it to him financially, but he had better exchanges with perps in interrogation.

"Hello, Danielle. What can I do for you?" he said mock-pleasantly.

"*I need you to take Danny this weekend,*" she replied abruptly. "*I have to see my parents.*"

"I can't. I told you, during the week is better."

"This is what pisses me off, Sean," Danielle shot back. *"You complain about not seeing Danny enough, but when I ask you, you've always got something more important to do."*

Sean dug the pack of cigarettes out of his coat again and lit another. "I resent the way you make it seem like a conspiracy – like I don't wanna see my son," he replied. "I just got a case. One of the guys from my old team just got blown up in his kitchen. He's dead," Sean added.

"Oh my God," Danielle said.

"See? There are bigger problems in the world than your parents." Sean exhaled. "I'll call you back."

He hung up the phone and shared his look of annoyance with Bobby.

"Sorry... my ex-wife," he explained.

Bobby shook his head. "That's just why I never did it," he said.

"Listen, there's something more to this. Go back and look at his files – recent cases. Start there. I'll go back and do the same at my house and see what he was working on that might be relevant." Sean motioned for his partner to follow him.

Just then, a taxi pulled up in front of the home, and a young girl carrying a small duffel bag with shoulder-length blond hair and a bright smile got out. Her eyes widened with shock and horror as they took in the yellow tape, news vans, and sirens of the police cars. She ran through the tape, and instantly, a uniformed officer grabbed her before she could reach the house.

"Oh my God!" the woman screamed. "What happened? Where's my mother?" She laid eyes on the body under the sheet, and immediately became hysterical. "No…"

Bobby looked at her disdainfully. "Who is that?"

"Mother of God… that's Elaine," Sean said regretfully. "Freddy's daughter. I haven't seen her since the trial." He walked over to her briskly and gave the officer a signal that it was okay to let her go. He embraced her and held her tightly as she cried in his arms. "Elaine," he said quietly.

"Oh Sean… No…"

He held her even tighter as she twisted around and tried to get to the sheet on the ground.

"I'm sorry Elaine," Sean said somberly. "We're still trying to figure out what happened. They took your mom to the hospital… I don't know how she is." He exhaled deeply. It was going to be one of *those* nights. "Come on, I'll take you to the station. When we find out about your mom, I'll take you to see her."

"I want to see him…" Elaine sobbed.

"Come on," he said, leading her to the car. "Bobby, you call me at the station when you get that explosive. I want to know what it is; along with anything else you find."

"No problem." He looked at Elaine. "I'm sorry, honey," he said to her. "Your dad was a great freakin' cop."

✳✳✳

Sean arrived at the precinct with Elaine in tow. Some of the officers gave him somber looks and knowing nods as he walked in. He sat her down in the chair next to his desk that was usually reserved for perpetrators, and grabbed one of the officers passing by.

"Hey Chuckie, could you bring her some coffee?" he asked. "Matter of fact, bring me one too if you don't mind."

The officer nodded and walked off. Sean ran his fingers through his hair and rubbed his temples. He tried to think of something comforting to say to Elaine, but his own head was spinning. Frankly, the last time he saw her father, they called each other all kinds of names. Even now he wasn't exactly sure how he felt about him, but he was one of them. He watched his back and they kicked in doors together, and now, he was gone. Fortunately, at that moment, his partner walked up with his eyes glued to his smartphone. He had to admit, he kind of liked Aquila. He was always dressed sharp in colorful, complimentary shirt-and-tie combinations, while Sean lived in a hooded sweatshirt. Aquila looked at them.

"You're not watching it?" he said incredulously. "What are you doing?"

"Watching what?"

He turned his phone toward Sean. "The killer called the news station claiming responsibility for tonight," he said. His eyes darted quickly to Elaine who was seated in the chair.

Sean shook his head. "People do that all the time; mostly crazies who just want attention."

"He posted a video online. It's already gone viral, and he sent it to the news stations. They're playing it in a few minutes – at ten." He continued walking. "Everybody's going to the breakroom."

Elaine stood up. "What's he saying? The killer turned himself in?" she asked excitedly.

Sean doubted that. "I don't know," he replied.

The breakroom was clamoring. Dozens of detectives and plainclothes officers stood around and spoke excitedly about what transpired that evening, while they looked up at the television in the corner overhead. The opening music for the nightly news came on as the camera opened up on the two newswomen. One was a middle-aged Caucasian and the other was a younger African-American woman with somber expressions. In the upper right-hand corner a graphic flashed with the bold words, "Officer Slain," with a gun and two shell casings surrounding it. Sean looked over at Elaine nervously.

One of the officers snickered to another, "These news reporters are jerk-offs. He wasn't even shot – he was blown up."

Sean shot him a look. "Maybe I should take you into one of the interrogation rooms," Sean said. "I don't want you to be upset any more tonight."

"I'm fine," Elaine sniffled. "I need to hear what they have to say."

"A city is in mourning tonight as another New York City police officer is killed," the first newswoman said. *"51-year-old Frederick Castobell suffered fatal injuries after an explosion at his home in Monticello. His wife, 47-year-old Constance Castobell, is in critical condition at an area hospital with undisclosed injuries. In related news, a video went viral on social media earlier tonight from the person claiming to be*

responsible for this bombing, and a host of other unsolved murders of police officers. We are about to air this video now. We must warn you – some of these images are quite graphic and the words are disturbing. Viewer discretion is advised."

The screen opened up to a crackling fireplace. Flashes of black and white images appeared on the screen. Naked black men hung from trees with their eyes bulging, while a group of smiling white spectators looked on and burned crosses. There were also groups of men covered in hooded white sheets. The video continued with police officers striking blacks with sticks, chasing them with snarling German shepherds, and spraying them with water hoses as they writhed under the water's pressure. Classical music played in the background as the images changed from black and white to color. Modern day police officers beating a black man mercilessly with batons, faces of crying family members and officers standing with guns drawn around the lifeless body of Eddie Gadson now played out on the screen. A white officer punched a woman repeatedly in the face. An officer shot an unarmed man in the back in a train station as he lay facedown on the ground, and the smiling faces of recently murdered African-American men during happier times began to flash rapidly. Then the screen went black.

A deep quivering voice emitted from the screen, *"The NYPD continues in their proud tradition of murdering innocent black men, women – even children. This corrupt and evil organization has been allowed to continue in its state, leaving those guilty among them unpunished. I, Taberah, have risen to mete out that punishment."*

The camera came back on and a horrifying image of a skull face in a bright-red, pope costume sitting at a desk appeared with the crackling fire behind him.

"Who the hell is this guy?" an officer shouted.

"I'm sure we are all saddened by the death of that murderous pig, Detective Frederick Castobell," the gravely voice continued. *"Yes, I am the one responsible, but I am not to blame! The blood of the officers that have been slain rests on the hands of Commissioner Kavanaugh. Seven years ago, I warned him that he had started a war. I gave him an opportunity to end it peacefully, and that offer still stands. He was advised to remove those officers guilty of murder, convict them and put them behind bars. Obviously, he has refused. The war will continue. You have an army, but so do I, and it grows stronger every day. Citizens of New York, convince your leaders to turn in their guilty or wear my symbol and join me in serving justice."*

"Come... and see the blood in the streets."

The screen went black again momentarily and then the symbol of a bright, orange flame appeared. The room went quiet for a few moments while everyone considered the gravity of the message.

"Jesus," Sean said.

"He's a monster," Elaine whispered. "You have to stop him."

Sean's phone rang and saved him once again from having to reply to an impossible request. The display revealed that it was Bobby.

"Might have some new information on your dad. Gimme a sec." Sean stepped out of the break room and put the phone to his ear.

"Did you see the video on the news?" Sean asked.

"Yeah," Bobby replied. *"Some crazy stuff."*

"What'd you find out?"

"The M.E. said Freddy died of a concussion. In addition to the damage to his internal organs, there were pieces of shrapnel stuck in his chest and face; get this... from a grenade," Bobby said. *"It was sent to him, rigged in some sort of wooden box.* They found fragments of it partially burned in the rubble." He paused. *"I'm over with Connie Castobell at Montefiore. It doesn't look good."*

"Yeah," Sean said, looking across the room at Elaine. "I should take her daughter over there in case something happens. She shouldn't be here." He exhaled heavily. "Anything else?"

"Actually... Yeah," Bobby continued. *"The killer left behind a little souvenir, message job. Meet me here and I'll give it to you."*

$$***$$

Sean was a little nervous the following morning as he sat outside of the commissioner's office. The truth was, after what he saw and heard last night, he planned to call Kavanaugh anyway, but the man beat him to it. Kavanaugh called him personally early that morning. He tapped his feet nervously. He was anxious to tell him what he had and share his theory on who was responsible. This was his first visit to the commissioner's office. The entire place was practically made of glass. What struck him the most was just how much light came through the place. It was a pretty sunny day, however, the blinds were down in the commissioner's office. Suddenly, the glass door to the office opened, and a uniformed officer beckoned him.

"Come in, Detective," the officer said.

Sean walked into the office and was surprised to see Chief Lannom seated in front of the desk in his dress blues and hat in hand. He looked at him with an indiscernible expression and then looked away. He was immediately concerned about going over his chief's head, especially since Lannom always went to bat for him. He was convinced that nobody was going to connect the dots on this like he would. He walked over and stood in front of the desk where Commissioner Kavanaugh was seated. He was wearing a navy blue suit and appeared preoccupied. He thought about sitting down, but kept standing instead. Kavanaugh let him remain as he was for a while without saying a word. Suddenly, he looked up. The uniformed officer left the room without a word, as if he knew he would be dismissed and spared his superior the trouble.

"So, what can you tell me about this, uh... *Taberah*?" he asked. "I've already spoken to your chief and he doesn't know anything. I was hoping you could do better."

They looked at each other briefly.

Sean sat down. "I did find something." He pulled a piece of paper out of his coat pocket and unraveled it. "The name Taberah is actually not a name at all. I looked it up. It's a Hebrew word that means *burning*. On top of that, it's his symbol. This guy has a thing for fire."

"I got that Detective," Kavanaugh said, looking over his glasses. "I hope you have more. Like who this perp is, and what he's planning."

"I think he's working for Wakefield."

Kavanaugh exhaled noisily. "Coughlin, you're a good cop, but you have to let it go with this guy. I mean," he said standing up, "Enough is enough. You've already got the guy doing forever on three cop murders. He's done. This is just some other maniac out there trying to cash in on his reputation."

Sean calmly reached into his pocket and retrieved a small portion of a photograph that was singed around the edges. He handed it to the commissioner.

"With all due respect, sir. Freddy Castobell was killed by a rigged, military grenade hand-delivered to his house in a wooden box. This photograph was along with it," Sean added.

Kavanaugh studied it. Even though the photograph was badly burned, somehow he was still able to make an identification.

"Eric Harland," he said decidedly. "The kid from your case; Wakefield's cousin."

"That's correct," Sean nodded. "I think he has a vendetta against the force, and he's not gonna stop until he kills as many police as possible – especially officers connected with that case."

"The Harland case?" Lannom asked, shifting in his chair. "So you think he'll be after the others in your squad?"

Sean nodded.

"If you're right," Kavanaugh said, "That means you're in danger too." He paused for a moment and looked out of his window at the city. "So, what do you need from me?"

"I'd like my old team back." Sean looked at Lannom and then at the commissioner and tried to gauge his reaction. He knew he had to go over everybody's head for that request, but he gave away nothing.

"I'll also need everything on all the police shootings for the last ten years to see if any of them match the M.O. of these Taberah killings. I also need to speak to Wakefield, but there's someone I need to find first."

"More important than Wakefield?" Kavanaugh exclaimed, turning around. "Who's that?"

"It's just a hunch, Commissioner, just a hunch," Sean replied. It might have been a little too early to reveal that tidbit to the commissioner, but he *did* have a suspect in mind. That is, if they *could* be found.

He had to find Joanna Harland.

As he left, Chief Lannom sat up in his seat.

"I notice you didn't tell him about the message you received. Very convenient, Bobby," he said. "He shouldn't know the full extent of what he's dealing with? You want him to solve this, he needs *all* the evidence."

Kavanaugh sighed. "I would love to, but I can't afford to have this floating around the station or even shown to other cops. If it got out that I knew about this nut seven years ago and didn't let the public know... They would crucify me – cops and the families of the fallen especially." He pointed a serious finger at him. "The only reason *you* know is out of respect for your position – and our friendship, but no one else can know."

"Why didn't you tell the public in the first place?" Lannom asked.

"Are you kidding me?" he said. "Let New Yorkers know there is a costumed psychopath picking off police officers? No way. On top of that, it's still not even clear if he's working alone. It would have caused mass panic."

"It already has. Everyone is on edge in this city now, and it's only gonna get worse," Lannom added.

"Well then, let's pray that your man's crazy theories have some merit and lead him in the right direction. You give him what he needs and support him. Anything new he finds, I want to know about it," Kavanaugh said. "The cops of this city and the people of New York need to know we're making progress."

Lannom stood up, put on his hat and straightened his uniform.

"Yes sir," he replied. "By the way, how are things going with the mayor?" he asked smiling.

Kavanaugh shook his head. That was another ordeal altogether.

"Get outta here," the commissioner said.

***

"I'm telling you, son, this is gonna get bad out here," Tre exclaimed. "They gon' be poppin' on us like crazy."

Treshon Wilkes, better known as "Tre Pound," moved excitedly and gestured with animated movements around the park bench where he and the rest of his friends were sitting. He was sporting a bright red, leather jacket with a matching knit baseball hat, acid-washed jeans and bright red and white sneakers. He lived in the projects – Taft Houses – on the East

Side of Harlem all of his life, but he wasn't a little kid anymore. He was a somebody – an important man in that tenement. At 30, he was finally making some real money and had a team of about ten guys. Most of them were seated out there with him, held down the fort, and were ready to protect their young leader. This was their territory, and Tre, for all intents and purposes, was their captain.

"That was dumb – whoever killed that cop," replied Black, a slightly older, dark-skinned man who ironically, was dressed in all black. "That just makes it harder on everybody. The boys will really be buggin' now."

"I'm saying," a young thin boy chimed in. "They deserved that though. All those cops killing whoever. They been getting off."

"You right!" Tre exclaimed. "But what dudes don't think about is, now it's harder to do things. They start the raids and searches early in the morning, and can't nobody get no money. Not saying I wouldn't push a few myself, but at the end of the day, there's mad police."

"That's what bugs me out, though." J listened quietly from his seat on the bench. He was in his twenties and from Taft Houses as well, but he had a tendency to think a little differently than his peers.

"All these dudes out here always talkin' about how they put work in, but most of them would never shoot no cops. With all the guns that's in the hood, they couldn't take us all at once. We got way more numbers and way more firepower. We should be killing them – but instead, we be killing each other," he said.

Everyone was silent for a while as they let J's words sink in.

"Yo, you right. You always be sayin' that smart stuff," Tre replied. "But if the boys came up in here right now, how many homies would *really* start lettin' off?"

Everyone was quiet for a moment.

"Whoever made that tape and put it online is about that, though," J answered. "They crazy as hell, but at least they official. They already doing it."

"I bet they ain't black, though. Black people don't have no unity," another boy said.

Suddenly, the sounds of wheels squeaking disrupted their attention. A short deliveryman in a brown UPS uniform was wheeling a rather large cardboard box on a dolly through the courtyard. The box was oversized and it was almost comical to watch the small man moving it. He had a matching hat, but beneath, his face was horribly scarred. The group turned their attention back to each other and continued their conversation, that is, until the man stopped right in front of them. He unloaded the box right at the feet of the group.

"Yo – what you doing?" Black barked.

"Chill," Tre said, looking down at the box. "Maybe he don't speak English." He looked at him. He didn't exactly look foreign, but he wasn't sure. "You don't have an address?"

"How could he work for UPS, if he don't speak English?" the young boy said.

"This is a gift," the man said. "From Taberah."

The man turned around and walked back the way he came.

"*Taberah?*" he said. "Who's that?"

"Y'all don't pay attention to the news?" Tre said sharply. "That's the one with the mask that's killin' them cops."

He took out a small knife and began cutting the brown tape on the box.

"That sound like that chick that come through from the fourth floor," Black laughed.

They all crowded around, bent over the box and looked inside. There were a bunch of white, rubber, skull masks and black t-shirts folded neatly into rows. Tre pulled one out and unfolded it. On the front was the flame insignia displayed boldly in reddish-orange print against the pitch-black background. He turned the shirt around and a sentence was inscribed on the back in the same fiery color.

"Retribution is at hand," he read.

As the other guys pulled out more than a dozen shirts, he saw something else underneath.

"Yo, look!" the young boy shouted.

Inside were dozens upon dozens of guns – Beretta and Sig Sauer nine-millimeters, Colt Forty-Fives and small machine pistols. There were also many boxes of ammunition.

"Hell yeah," the young boy said. "But I got some of these already."

***

"Our boy was always a good kid – a peaceful kid," Sharlene Tavares whimpered as the cameras flashed. She dabbed a tissue to her eyes and smeared them with mascara. She was

a dark-skinned woman of about forty years, with beautiful dark eyes.

"But he was shot in the park – playing with a toy – a toy gun; an instrument of violence." Her husband grabbed her by the shoulders stoically as she broke down in tears.

"This should be a lesson that violence only triggers more violence. So whoever is doing this; responsible for these killings, we ask that you please stop. We do not support any crimes against the police. There should be justice for our boy, but this will only make things worse. More of our young men will be killed…"

Sean listened to the press conference on the radio as he pulled onto the Freeman campus. The news kept him alert; he needed it after this early morning flight from New York to Florida. It was unexpected, the trip, but he wasn't exactly complaining. Between the weather and the politics, it felt good to get out of New York for a couple of days. He never met the parents of Raymond Tavares – the eleven-year-old boy who was shot and killed by an officer while playing the park – but they seemed like very caring and respectful people. The kid was playing with a toy pistol that looked like a Colt .45. He still didn't understand why they made toys like that. They served no good purpose. It still surprised him, especially with all that had happened in the recent past. As he made the right turn onto the grounds, he took in the calmness and beauty of the campus scene and observed the soft rays of light casting long shadows as the trees sported their newly changing leaves.

This was the very same university in Florida Joanna Harland attended before her husband was killed; when she was still Joanna Mosley. A visit to Estelle's house, Joanna's mother, set him on the right path, although she couldn't tell him anything about what she was studying or who she associated with. Oddly enough, however, he did remember that she was strung out back in the days, but she appeared to have gotten herself straight; Estelle looked clean and well put together. She did inform him that Joanna had long since returned to school to continue her education, shortly after the demonstration where she was arrested. Then she apparently disappeared from campus without a trace nearly seven years ago.

He slightly recalled hearing something about the case when it happened, but he also remembered not giving it much thought. He surmised that maybe the woman whose life was turned upside down and forced into the public eye just needed a vacation. With every subsequent year that followed, it became obvious that something happened to her and she wasn't coming back. The local police had no leads, and campus security offered no comfort. Joanna was not given to partying or any of the myriads of things college girls were usually into. So he drove up to see if he could learn anything new that would help him track her down. Sean had a couple of theories rattling around in his head about her disappearance, but they were in the early stages. At the very least, if he could find out some things unknown to the general public, they might help him find her. He hated to think that there was foul play but also hated to think that Joanna was involved. He had to tread lightly and handle that theory very carefully. She was now a national and beloved figure and a widow. If he was wrong, he would be accused of persecuting the wife of the man he murdered, and his job would definitely be in jeopardy. He needed to keep his speculations secret, at least, until he obtained proof that supported his suspicions.

He parked his rental, a tan Ford Fiesta, in the faculty parking lot close to the admissions office, grabbed the baseball cap off the passenger's seat and pulled it down on his head.

As he got out of the car, he caught a reflection of himself in the car window and smiled at his relaxed look complete with jeans, a hooded sweatshirt and baseball jacket – one of the many benefits of being single, he thought to himself. As he walked through the entrance, he saw flyers on the bulletin boards and was reminded and even briefly saddened that he didn't attend college. Immediately he noticed the girl at the admission's desk who had a bit of a moon face and was more than on the heavy side. She had that I'd-rather-be-anywhere-but-here look and her demeanor dared anyone to disturb her while she went through her phone. Sean walked right up to her and placed his badge on the desk. That got her attention. Her eyes shot up immediately through the oversized frames.

"Good afternoon, miss. I'm Detective Sean Coughlin," he said in the most pleasant voice he could muster. "I was wondering if you could pull up some old records for me and print them out." He had no intention of letting this little girl give him a hard time or make him lose it.

The meeting with the commissioner earlier that day left him slightly annoyed. The overtone was of the old man holding him personally responsible for the killings, as if this Taberah character was a case he left unsolved and was now out of hand. It was obvious that the commissioner wanted him to solve it and do it quickly. At least Sean respected him. He always stood behind his men. The mayor, pansy that he was, left the entire force holding the bag in the press. As a result, he lost the respect of the troops and the city was deteriorating.

"What exactly are you looking for?" the girl responded in a bored and dismissive voice. Even in this case, it seemed the respect for the badge had worn off.

"I would like the class schedule and room assignments for a Joanna Harland."

The girl hit the keys rapidly.

"There are a couple. Do you have a specific year?" she asked.

"2008 and maybe even a little bit before," Sean said decidedly.

The young woman hit the keys a few more times, then spun around on her chair to the nearby printer as it churned out the sheets. She tore them off and spun back around in one fluid motion and handed the printouts to him without even looking up. She then turned her attention back to her phone.

"Have a nice day, Detective," the young lady said as he walked away.

Sean's original plan was to find some of Joanna's old roommates, interview them, and inquire about her state of mind, until he realized that most of them were probably well on to their careers by now. Anyhow, he could track them down, if necessary. He took a look at the classes listed on her schedule. Criminal Law, which was to be expected, as well as Business and African-American Studies. He had to admire her; she was a pretty studious girl. It was a shame he couldn't interview her, or better yet, one of her roommates. What he could do was talk with instructors. Sean looked at his watch. It was still pretty early – not quite time for the teachers to get off. He wondered if he should wait or get something to eat; the day got away from him so quickly.

Just then, his phone rang. He answered, "Coughlin here."

"Hey buddy – it's Bobby," the voice on the other end responded. *"Just called to let you know – Connie Castobell died a few minutes ago."*

***

Chance drove the black Yukon steadily as he kept his eyes on the dirty white delivery truck a car length in front of him. It was a busy day. He made deliveries of used guns and t-shirts to different hoods around the city dressed in uniform. He hated the uniform part, but admired the way Taberah thought – the way he brought the war to the cops was unlike anything he had ever seen – and they were just getting started. Sure, in his time he ran across a few dudes who didn't mind taking a shot at police, but nothing like this. Strategic. Brutal. Taberah was also a better businessman than Wakefield. He was making way more money than before and was allowed to open a franchise of his own as long as he got the merchandise from his boss. He even got to keep a percentage of loads from new clients he brought in. The load in front of him, though, was a big shipment to one of their regulars. It was always dropped off at one of the furniture stores on the payroll, who in turn sent a driver with their truck to the destination that Chance provided.

He then followed on without their knowledge to make sure the load arrived at the appointed destination. It was a very smooth operation; they made lots of money, and there were never any problems. He didn't always go to these types of jobs, but from time to time he popped up just to make his presence known and show face to their clients. Even though he wasn't riding with the merchandise, he didn't particularly like the idea of being on such big shipments. They didn't like to keep guns hanging around – it was the one thing Taberah and Charles seemed to agree on. He rubbed his chin and looked at the zig-zagged scars on his face in the rearview mirror. Most would think he got them in jail or in some sort of street fight, and that assumption proved to his benefit over the years, but the truth was quite different.

His real name was Gary, but beyond his name and his scars there was nothing from his past that he carried with him. Charles Wakefield, or C-Rock, as he knew him, was the only person with whom he shared his story while they stayed in the same group home all those years ago, but not even he knew the whole truth.

His mother was a well-known prostitute in the neighborhood, and he was the fruit of one of her clients, but who remained unknown. To add to that, she was a horrible drunk, and because of that she very rarely cleaned or kept any food in the house. Young Gary roamed the neighborhood half the time starving and looking like a vagrant. Ever so often, men who weren't clients came around and stayed with his mother for a little while. Some of them treated him with a tolerable indifference, but most abused him with their fists whenever they felt the need. In the early days of his development, he ran to his mother for comfort, hoping she would make it stop. What he got was screamed on or beaten some more for his trouble. After a while, he stopped trying. When he was about 14, his mother took on a more permanent lover – a man named Tim, who shared his mother's indulgence for liquor. He also introduced her to something else – heroin – and it turned her crazy. They both took turns beating and putting their cigarettes out on him.

One fateful night, a starving Gary was caught going into his mother's purse – and paid dearly. She held him down and cut him several times across the face with the straight razor she kept for protection. After shooting up that night with Tim, the two of them fell asleep, and Gary found his .38 and shot them both in the head. The police chalked it up to a heroin deal gone bad and didn't even bother to look for the kid. After being picked up at the hospital by social services and a few unsuccessful stints in foster homes, Gary was placed in the Lost Boys foster home in East Harlem. As fate would have it, he ended a bunkie to a young Charles Wakefield, who was a couple years older than him. They spent two years together having each other's back and swapping stories about their lives. When Wakefield aged out, he told Chance to look him up and he would put him to work, so he did. He tried his hand at drugs, but he discovered early in his career that he preferred robbery and shooting people. So they both carved out a living robbing stores and houses. When Charles started to branch out for territory, Chance did the shooting.

One day, in particular, bonded them forever. There was a block where Charles wanted to open a new spot and the young kid running things didn't care to negotiate. Words were exchanged, then gunfire, and a rookie and his partner showed up just as they were fleeing the scene. One got out of his car, and in a blink of an eye, Charles took him down. He had no intention of going to jail that day, and they got away scot-free. The officer that survived was now Detective Sean Coughlin. After that incident, Chance remained loyal to Wakefield and had always taken care of him. He was always good to work for, but this new arrangement wasn't half bad.

Of course, there were differences working for the two of them. Taberah, for one, was a lot more mysterious than Charles – and a bit weird. The mask, the voice and the crazy costumes were all a little strange to Chance. Every time he arrived to get his orders, the guy was liable to be dressed as some new character. What remained the same was skull as his face – which looked disturbingly real. As long as Charles was happy and the money stayed green and frequent – to each his own. Charles preferred to have things sort of out in the open – flashiness, jewelry, the club. Although they never did any business out of Rock Steady and the cops never got him on anything they were doing, he ended up being put away on a triple murder. Chance didn't see it as ironic. In his opinion, the cops set him up. He thought to himself, no way C-Rock did those killings. That wasn't his style – at least, not anymore.

When C-Rock got arrested, Chance figured most of their operations were shut down, even though he had that girl Joanna running the club for a while – which she knew nothing about. Although it was crazy about her husband, he didn't trust her one bit and was glad when she went back to wherever she came from. Chance became worried for the first time when she disappeared after Charles got sentenced. He was always close to Charles and carried out his orders to a tee, but he also realized there were many aspects of his operation that he knew nothing about. Without his longtime friend and boss on the street, he might have had to go back to contract murder to make a living. When he received orders from Wakefield through the lawyer, Arenburg, to drive out to a deserted area in the farther end of Queens, he did as he was told. He still remembered that day clearly, although it was nearly six years ago. Since then, the team was making money, although he had to get used to some new people, which included a crazy white boy who was somewhat of an army brat. However, nobody was in danger, and they were about to take this war to the next level. That also told him something about his old friend and boss who he knew for many years; yet he never heard Taberah's name. Obviously, it was someone he trusted. It was apparent that Charles also knew how to keep secrets.

The delivery truck finally pulled in front of a building as Chance watched from behind the tinted windows of his truck from the next block over. A short Hispanic man got out of the passenger's seat, went up to the building, and rang a bell. When the buzzer rang, the man propped the door open while the other driver, a taller white man, got out of the truck and opened the back. The back of the truck was filled with furniture – bureaus, dressers, and even a few mattresses – items that would be delivered later to their rightful owners. The men, one at each end, grabbed a long heavy leather trunk and hoisted it from the back of the truck. Just then, a pair of Russian men in drab-looking leather jackets came down to meet them. Chance popped the glove compartment and retrieved an Ingram MAC-11 machine pistol. He popped in a long magazine and tucked it inside his coat. He pulled a P90 Ruger from his waistband, checked the chamber and then put it back in place. Usually the .45 caliber handgun was enough, but he liked to bring the machine pistol whenever there were large money exchanges, like today. The room could easily contain four or five people, and in a case like that, you needed quantity in addition to caliber. He pulled his hat down low, got out of the truck, and followed the men as they moved the trunk up the stairs. When they reached the third floor they set the trunk down, and one of the Russians walked into an apartment with an already open door. Chance handed the white guy a folded stack of money.

"Go make your deliveries," Chance said.

The two movers disappeared down the stairs, and the Russian who remained turned to him. His hair was shaved close on the sides, and the top was slicked down with gel. He had a low brow and a strong, serious jaw line.

"You are Chance, no?" he said in a thick accent.

Chance nodded. His eyes were on the doorway and his hand on the pistol in his pocket. The other man returned, who looked like a larger version of the first, and proceeded to slide the trunk into the open apartment. The man's face brightened up and he waved.

"I am Arkady. Come, come," he said. "Inside."

He walked inside the small apartment and scanned the room as quickly as he could. Instantly he heard the sound of yelling and machine gunfire on a television. The man led him to the living room where two other Russian men, who looked slightly younger, were engrossed in some military shooting game. The shorter man opened the trunk revealing several AR-15 rifles. The men all began to grab rifles – mock aiming, checking their weight and chambers.

"You have ammo?" one of the younger ones asked.

"No shells. We'll do that on a separate buy." Chance turned to the first man. "You've got the money?"

The man gestured to the smaller gentleman to go in one of the back rooms, and Chance put his hand in his pocket again. He couldn't take any chances on what was coming out of that back room, but the short man returned momentarily with a black duffel bag. He was less friendly than the larger one, but that actually put him more at ease. He held it in his arms like a baby, while the other one unzipped it. Chance looked inside. There was a dozen or so bundles of bills.

"Two hundred thousand, yes?" the man asked confidently.

Chance nodded, while he took the bag and zipped it up. He then in turn pointed at the trunk of rifles.

"You could kill a few cops with those, if the opportunity comes."

They all laughed with genuine enjoyment.

"Of course. This is nothing," Arkady replied. "We do this for fun."

$$***$$

Chance looked around cautiously as he walked to the back of the Yukon, opened the doors and threw the duffel bag in the back. He got in the front seat, pulled the MAC-11 from his coat and placed it back in the glove box, but he laid the Ruger on the seat next to him. He thought about how C always kept his in a stash box. Chance didn't believe in that. He would rather get locked up on a gun charge than not be able to get to his weapon when he needed it. He saw too many people killed in his day. Besides, he could do a bid – no big deal at all. Hell, he thought to himself, he'd done them before. He hated driving this far out to Brooklyn, especially when he had to make that long drive out to Taberah to deliver the money. He hadn't even eaten, but he was the boss, and he didn't want to keep him waiting. Maybe he could grab some drive-thru on the way. He started up the truck and pulled off.

Chance pulled up to the gate of the warehouse, munching violently on the last of some White Castle fries; the burgers were long since devoured. The warehouse was a two-story brown brick building that appeared to be in good structural shape, but by the condition of the property was clearly abandoned. There was junk in the yard; abandoned tires, balls and an assortment of things people had thrown in over the years. All the windows were bricked in. A bent-up sign hung on the second story, making promises of a sale if anyone was to inquire. No one ever did, and even if they tried, they would find that the number was disconnected. A couple of dingy-looking pit bulls roamed the dirt yard; their coats the same color as the dirt they played in. They barked at the Yukon as it strolled through the yard. In addition to the drive itself, another reason Chance hated taking that trip, was that he had to drive around an extra twenty minutes to make sure he wasn't followed. A little over the top, he thought, but again, they were his orders. He supposed it worked – he was never followed and the warehouse was never raided – not that he knew in the slightest what else went on, and quite frankly he didn't want to know.

He rolled down the window to look into the camera, but he didn't have to. As always, his presence was already known, the gate opened automatically, and he continued the drive up the road. He reflected back to the first time he came there, all those years ago. He came into the building, which was still basically abandoned, and found a small room which looked like an interrogation room at the precinct. It was a room comprised entirely of gray brick, with one chair facing a smoky mirror and a single, solitary light hung by a wire from the ceiling. He pulled up to the corrugated garage door, which also opened on its own, and entered the dark corridor. A few seconds after the garage door was completely down and he was totally encased in darkness, blinding lights from overhead flashed on. It was a moderately-sized garage, occupied by a few delivery vans from various companies – all stolen, of course. Chance had not stolen them, but he hardly thought Fed Ex operated out of this broken-down warehouse. He used one of the delivery vans himself earlier on to deliver a package to some gang members. He couldn't wait to see how Taberah orchestrated that plan – just another example of how his new boss thought, he thought to himself. That thought made him think of Charles again. He never wanted Chance to write or visit; in fact, he received specific instructions not to, so that he wasn't linked to anything in the future. True, the police were on him for a while after Charles went away, but not for long. So, his old boss wasn't exactly lacking in the cleverness department, either.

There was a single steel door embedded in the brick wall of the garage that opened by key card. Chance retrieved his – a shiny black one with a bright reddish-orange flame imprinted on the front. He slid it into the slot; a green light came on and the door clicked open. This gained him access to a narrow stairwell; he descended. When he came to the gray painted door at the bottom, he opened it. Inside was the chair where he sat for several years whenever he needed to receive orders on everything from deliveries and pick-ups to the murders of police officers. The space was about the size of an average living room, and in the far-right corner was another steel door. In front of the chair was a steel table and on it was a large manila envelope. Chance placed the duffel bag on the table and sat down in the chair, keeping his eyes on the reflective glass of the two-way mirror.

A bright white light suddenly illuminated behind the glass, shining harshly over the top of the skull and casting shadows over the hollows of the eyes, making them seem eternally deep. A black hood draped around it framing the skull in a lazy way. Chance saw the image of the grim reaper hundreds of times in his life on pictures and cartoons, but there was something terrifying about seeing it in person. He kept reminding himself that it was obviously a mask. Even still, it was unnerving to talk to a person wearing it, and it made him wonder exactly what kind of person was beneath the disguise.

"Chance," Taberah bellowed, his already deep voice amplified by the hollowness and the speaker in the room where Chance was seated.

"There were no problems, right?"

He shook his head. "Everything was good." He pointed at the bag on the table. "Two hundred, just like you said."

"I have something for you," Taberah continued. *"There was a shooting in Newark not too long ago; perhaps you heard of it. A man named Redding was killed by the police, leaving behind a six-month-old baby. The cries of his widow have reached me, and we are to avenge his death. The names of the officers responsible are in that envelope along with a little incentive."*

Chance opened the manila envelope slowly and found a couple of files. He opened one, which revealed a picture of a black man in uniform named Brogan Dias. He returned the file and opened the other and found the identity of a white officer named Randy Wooley. He placed that file back inside also, then pulled out a stack of money with a ten-thousand-dollar seal on it. He flipped through it quickly; then returned it.

"No problem, but I thought you wanted me to finish off the officers from the Harland case."

"I have something special in mind," Taberah responded. *"Besides, we will need to move quickly. Once another officer from that case dies they will have caught on – if they haven't already, and they will be on guard; but I have anticipated this."*

"All due respect, but why are we interfering with Jersey?" Chance asked. "That's a whole 'nother state."

"Yes," he hissed. *"But we are meant to inspire, not just New York City, but each state – the entire country to follow*

our lead and very soon, they will. We must lead first by example," he paused. *"Take the bus there; do not drive. The officers' precincts, shifts, and addresses are inside, and the number of a contact for your hardware. You should leave tonight,"* he added.

Chance nodded, stood up, and retrieved the envelope.

"One more thing," Taberah said.

"Yeah?" Chance replied.

"This is a message we are sending. Overstate it," he said firmly.

Chance smiled. "Done."

***

The priest sat inside the confessional booth. His head was leaned against the wood and his eyes were shut. He wasn't exactly sleeping on the job, but the day was a slow day for confessions and he was getting tired. He figured he'd just rest his eyes for a moment. Usually, he was in a pretty peaceful state. He dedicated his life to serving God some years ago, leaving behind a very stressful career and regrettable past, and now, he was truly doing the work he was supposed to do. His life was simple, and there was no one to make him tremble... until now. The recent news of the death of a man he knew, Freddy Castobell, brought his past flooding back to him in a very major way. Freddy was never really much of a friend to anybody, and as a person, was no great loss to the planet. However, he knew him and worked with him, and just to know that someone took his life in such a violent and gruesome manner had him on edge. The priest was never a violent man in his own opinion, and his life now definitely reflected that he renounced all those things. Now it came back to him, just as he always feared it would, but not in the way he expected. The person who killed Freddy came to his church and confessed in that very booth.

As much as he wanted to, he couldn't tell a soul. Not only did he not know what the murderer looked like, but it was made abundantly clear to him that his whole family would be killed if he breathed a word of what he knew – including his precious Erin. Even though he was no longer with her, he still cared for her very much. He breathed a deep sigh. If no one came in soon, he would clean up and retreat upstairs to his living quarters, as he did every night. He very rarely left there, and he didn't long for the outside world in the slightest. He knew exactly what it had to offer – sin and death for all those who were willing to wallow in its filth. No, he was happy here in the cathedral with its somber statues of Mary and the saints looking down upon him and the high, majestic ceilings that suggested the heaven we all aspire to. He was at peace.

Suddenly, the creaking of the wooden bench and the shutting of the door indicated that someone sat down in the booth beside him. The priest rubbed his face in order to wake himself. He then slid open the lattice.

"Have you come to make confession, my son?" he asked.

"Yeah sure," a familiar voice said. "I'm a piece-of-crap divorced Irish cop."

"Sean?" the priest whispered excitedly. "What are you doing here? How'd you know where to find me?"

"You know your mother can't keep nothin' from me. I've known for years you were a priest. I left you alone until now because you seemed like you didn't want to be found and I understood that," Sean added.

"So why the intrusion now?"

"To be honest, I came to make sure my friend was still alive," Sean said seriously. "I know you heard about Freddy. This Taberah has declared war on all police – especially us. You're in danger, Matt."

"Why *especially* us?" Matthew asked. "Just what do you mean?"

"I think it's Wakefield. He wants revenge for his cousin, and he's using his crew to do it. You need to get somewhere safe," Sean insisted.

"I think I'm plenty safe right here. After all, this is a house of God," Matthew said. "How are Danielle and Danny?"

Sean sighed. "Me and Danielle got divorced a few years ago. I don't really see Danny that much."

"I'm sorry Sean," Matthew replied forlornly. "She was a great woman, but that's what I mean about the job – it's too much for a marriage in my opinion. That's part of the reason I got out."

"So you're really happy here? You don't miss being a cop?" Sean asked.

"Not in the least. Look, I appreciate you coming by, but I feel confident he won't be coming for me. I've repented of my sins."

"Oh, I see, and I should?" Sean said belligerently. "Is that what you're telling me?"

Matthew shook his head. "I can't tell you what to do, Sean. I never could."

Sean exhaled heavily and stood up.

"Well, I hope you really are tight with the man upstairs because this guy is coming for all of us. You'll be at the funeral tomorrow, right?"

"I'll be there," Matthew said. "Goodnight Sean."

"Yeah," Sean replied dejectedly. "Take it easy, Father."

***

It was a cold, but brightly-lit November morning the next day at Mount Saint Mary Cemetery, as the groundskeeper sat in the grass on the hill and watched the procession of limousines continue to come in. He watched them all day, but these particular limos were late. The service for Detective Frederick Castobell and his wife, Constance already began. He listened intently to the bagpipes as they played a somber version of "Amazing Grace" about fifty or so feet away. He watched everyone arrive and looked on while the six officers in their dress blues carried the casket from the hearse – Detective Rosemary Velez, Detective Donnell Haines, and Detective Sean Coughlin were among them. Elaine Castobell, the surviving daughter, wore black with a pillbox hat and a veil atop her head. She cried uncontrollably onto the folded flag she was given only moments earlier. The groundskeeper, a young blond boy in his late twenties, reached into the open grave beside him and removed the green tarp inside. Beneath it was a camouflaged M24A2 rifle. It was almost show time. He already delivered the fatal bomb that killed him days ago, and now at the same man's funeral, he was preparing for his next target. The groundskeeper was not a groundskeeper at all, but rather, an expert marksman and a cold-blooded killer.

About five years ago, there was a young man named Jacob Paul Anderson who was a soldier and sniper in the United States Army. He was trained with guns as a young boy, and when he was eighteen, enlisted to serve his country in order to earn money for college. He met another soldier in his unit, the only one close to him, who was a magnificent shot. When he finished his tour, he returned home to Nebraska only to be contacted years later by this very same soldier, who told him that there might be some work using his unique set of skills. He agreed, flew to New York to find that the work in question was becoming an assassin for the secret Flame Syndicate, headed by Taberah.

He laid flat on the grass, just behind a wide tombstone, pulling the grass-colored tarp over his body while he cradled the rifle under his arms. He silently wondered why he couldn't take out as many as possible. He knew he could kill at least ten policemen before they even found his position, but he received strict orders from Taberah to kill only one officer in particular. Even though he had no idea who it was, he admired this guy's merciless attitude. He was instructed to fire a headshot. From this range the exit wound would be tremendous, to say the least; pretty nasty. His boss provided the rifle, and he was pleased with his selection. The A2 was his favorite piece of weaponry. Jacob had no love for the police either. He came from a family that believed in very little government control, but believed in protecting themselves by the right to bear arms.

The priest gave the eulogy and a line of seven officers stood ready and raised their rifles for the twenty-one-gun salute. He took the cap off of the scope and adjusted its range.

"READY...FIRE!!" the officer shouted.

The first round of shots rang out and echoed through the November air. Jacob pulled the bolt back, filled the chamber with a 7.62 cartridge, then closed it.

"READY...FIRE!!" the officer shouted once more, then the second round of shots rang out.

"NOOOOOO!!!" a woman screamed.

The head of Detective Donnell Haines jerked back suddenly. A mass of blood and brain matter splattered on the face of the man who stood behind him. His wife, Justine, continued to scream. It took a few seconds for the rest of the policemen to realize what happened, even with half of their fellow officer's head hanging off. The third round of shots went off before the majority of them heard her screams and realized something was horribly wrong. What was left of Detective Haines' head pointed toward the sky; his eyes were buggy and wide. Sean spun around sharply and drew his gun from his side as he got a glimpse of his fallen friend. His eyes darted about in all directions as he ran over to his body. The funeral broke into chaos. The women started screaming; cops were half-ducking and looking around and some of the men were ducking down. They did not expect a simple service to erupt into bedlam. Sean continued to pour his eyes over his surroundings, but all he saw were rows and rows of tombstones.

"Donnie!" Sean yelled. "Oh God..." He pointed his gun in the air, spinning back and forth in all directions. "Where are you...you son of a bitch?!"

The other officers looked around as well, pulling their guns and keeping them half-raised while they looked for any sign of someone suspicious. Jacob picked the perfect spot – behind a tombstone set on a hill. He crawled back over it in the opposite direction, wrapped the rifle in the green tarp, and by the time the third round of shots were fired, he had already made his way over to a waiting van. He drove off and took the weapon with him. Justine Haines hung onto the legs of her husband as she bawled his name, "Donnie… Donnie…" Velez, with her gun by her side, walked over and stood next to Sean while the noise began to die down.

"Jesus," she said, swallowing hard. "I didn't see a damn thing."

"It's him," Sean said, breathing heavily. "It's Taberah."

***

Chance followed a few feet behind the black and white patrol car. He navigated along the wide streets of Newark, watching intently from beneath his yellow hard hat. The navy-colored van was stolen, and his Kalashnikov that rested in the passenger's seat was fully loaded. He trailed them for a half hour or so and watched as they made their rounds. He was hoping they passed through the block where the man Redding was killed. It wasn't necessary, but he worked with his boss long enough to know what moved him; it was just that type of attention to detail that pleased Taberah. It took incredible skill to follow them all this time undetected. Fortunately, for Chance, they made plenty of stops, but they had not come to one person's aid in the last few hours. The car between his navy-colored van and the officer's patrol vehicle turned right. Now he was directly behind them, but still kept a safe distance. The traffic light up ahead changed to red, and the officers' cruiser slowed down and stopped. Chance, whose hands were covered with workman's gloves, turned the steering wheel slowly and pulled up beside them. He reached over and rolled down his window.

"Excuse me, officers!" he yelled out.

Officer Wooley, who was behind the wheel, turned his head slightly in his direction and frowned. It was near the end of his shift, and he was in no mood.

"What is it?" he said sharply.

Chance stuck the AK-47 out of the window and squeezed the trigger. The report echoed rapidly and loudly through the wide, empty street. The sparks from the muzzle illuminated the darkness with bright streaks of yellow lightning. In a matter of seconds, the squad car was filled with dozens upon dozens of holes while the ground between them became filled with spent shell casings. Dias' and Wooley's bodies danced and jumped around inside the car as if they were being shocked by volts of electricity. Their blood splattered, painting the inside of the car with wild patterns. Chance dropped the gun inside the car, reached behind him, and retrieved a gas can. He dispensed gasoline quickly all over the van, then took out a book of matches from his pocket and struck one. The van instantly erupted into a bright ball of orange flames while Chance took off his hat and coat and threw them inside. He then disappeared down an adjacent street.

***

The squad in the 25th precinct sat around the television in the breakroom and watched the videotape of Taberah's latest message released online hours earlier. The news stations aired the story at six. Sean spent the better part of his day trying to calm down Elaine Castobell *and* Justine Haines, both surviving members of the fallen traumatized by recent events. He was exhausted. He hadn't even had a chance to change his clothes. He managed to grab a department-issued sweatshirt, but there was still blood on his pants – Donnell's blood. He spent the previous day interviewing Joanna's former professors, and even though he learned some interesting things, he was still no closer to finding her. His only decent lead was to go and talk to Wakefield; perhaps he could offer him some sort of deal as an incentive. He was planning to make the trip after the funeral, and now this. The press was no help either. They were camped out in front of the station all day, and it didn't make them look great that their officers were getting killed with impunity. It was a little later now – around eleven at night, and they went after Chief Lannom who finally gave them a brief statement. Even though the phones were ringing off the hook with reporters' inquiries and false tips, the station was relatively quiet.

Everybody was stunned. Feelings from the sting of Freddy's death were still fresh among the men in the department, and now, they had to mourn all over again. Velez' hands were shaking as she held them tightly together, while a muscular detective Mariota, who had a face like an eagle held her around the shoulders and rubbed them gently. Aquila, Sean's partner, sat still over in a corner. Nobody knew what to say; they only looked down at the ground. They didn't want to look at each other because even though they knew there was really nothing they could have done, internally everyone blamed themselves... and each other.

"I just can't believe it," Diane said regretfully. Diane Kahn was a young female detective who transferred from out of state a few months before, and now worked in the Criminal Investigations Division. She was sharp, tough and definitely hot. She seemed to notice Sean and made little off-color comments; playful banter, but that was it. Diane was flirting, without a doubt, but she had not gotten physical with him at all, which struck Sean as odd. Diane didn't exactly seem like one of those "good" girls. There was a darkness there, he thought, but he liked it. He was in no rush; he could wait.

"What I mean is," she continued, "I was just getting to know him... and now he's gone."

Detective Hugh Daly, one of the senior detectives from Major Crimes, shook his head as he stood over in the corner with his crossed arms resting atop his large belly.

"You know, I've been on the force for a long time," he said tiredly. "I've been through all kinds of eras. Mafia, crack, pimps, gangs – you name it, but this... this is different. This feels like 'Nam."

He looked over at the usually polished Chief Lannom, who seemed a little flushed. "I mean, what are we gonna do here, Chief? This bastard has declared war on us, and we're losing. We look like a bunch of sitting ducks out there," he added.

"There was another shooting somewhere in Jersey tonight," another officer added.

Lannom pointed at the television. "Play it again," he instructed.

Sean reached over and pressed the button.

Black and white images of Klansman in white pointed hoods riding horses flashed across the screen as they rode through old towns, dragging blacks behind, chasing and shooting at people. Those images were suddenly replaced with black and white images of black men laid out in the streets, bleeding to death while smiling white officers looked on. The scene continued – riots broke out in the streets, fires raged in store windows, citizens ran in and out of stores looting, policemen repeatedly beat people over the head with batons and punched and kicked helpless people on the ground.

The images then changed and displayed policemen in the present day punching and kicking Blacks and Hispanics who were already subdued, handcuffed and on the ground, followed by multiple videos of black men with their hands up being fired upon by officers. Then the screen faded to black.

Next, the crackling fireplace appeared as "Ode to Joy" by Beethoven played in the background. A figure sat down in front of the camera, dressed in some sort of uniform that was hard to make out. As he came into the light, they saw that he was wearing a police uniform. The hat sat perfectly atop Taberah's skull as he folded his hands, clad in ceremonial white gloves, on top of a table. The black holes of the sockets bore into the camera screen with a deep intensity; the jaw full of long, bony teeth was undisturbed even as words pour out through them.

"Yes, Commissioner Kavanaugh – the death of another New York City police officer is on your hands. Did you get the flowers?" Taberah laughed throatily. *"You seem intent to protect your guilty, but I remind you today that you can't protect them. Deliver up your guilty. Show the city that you care more about justice than protecting your flock, and I will cease this bloodshed."* He paused. *"But maybe you're not convinced. Maybe you've heard about the shooting of two officers tonight in New Jersey. I have avenged the blood of the innocent in our neighboring state as well. Perhaps their citizens will soon follow my example, as the citizens of New York already have. The next move is yours Commissioner... and time is running out."*

"Oh, and to the brave officers of the 25th precinct," Taberah added, *"I think we know who is next... don't we?"*

The screen went black, then the symbol of the flame appeared and remained, as if to mock everyone who saw it by its perpetual burning. Once again, the room was silent. Velez looked at Sean; her eyes were filled with helplessness and guilt.

"We gotta do something, Chief," Mariota said authoritatively.

Just then, a uniformed officer entered the room.

"Chief Lannom, you have a call on your line," he said quickly. "It's Commissioner Kavanaugh."

The chief's face turned to stone as he thought of the impending conversation, but he kept silent as he exited the breakroom.

"What about those kids they caught shooting at cops on the East Side wearing this guy's symbol on their t-shirts?" Aquila inquired. "There's gotta be something there."

Sean shook his head. "I think the 23rd has that, and they're not giving us anything. Gang Unit got involved and it's a mess. Besides, they could've made those t-shirts themselves; doesn't mean they know anything."

"I don't wanna die," she said as her voice quivered.

Sean went over to her and patted Mariota on the hand. "Let me talk to her a minute," he said.

Velez nodded in agreement as Sean replaced Mariota's arms with his own, wrapping them around her shoulders. Mariota wondered what he could possibly say to her that was more comforting than his rubbing her shoulders repeatedly. He led her out of the breakroom into the main area and pulled her into a corner. Tears began to well up in her eyes as she looked at him.

"Jesus, Sarge," Velez said. "He's going to kill us."

Sean shook his head. "We are gonna be fine, Rosie. Nothing is gonna happen to you. We're gonna catch him."

She looked at him with an expression of skepticism. "How can you say that to me? With Donnie and Freddy lying down there?" She exhaled. "You know, I ain't never been scared on the streets. I kinda got a reputation for it over the years, and I guess in some ways I was proud of it. It meant to me that I could really play with the big boys, but this is different. This isn't like being afraid of being shot in the line of duty. This is like *punishment.*" She looked him in the eyes again. "We were wrong that night with the Harland kid. That's why this is happening to us."

"This is happening to us because some sicko out there is playing vigilante, and that's all," Sean said reassuringly. "We did nothing that night except our jobs. The kid's death was a tragedy yes, but we don't deserve to die." He swept back her hair, smiling slightly. "Listen to me. I'm working on this, and you know I'm gonna find him. Now go to the bathroom and clean your face," he said. "The Rosemary I know doesn't know how to cry."

"Okay Sarge," she said, sniffling.

"And stop calling me Sarge," he said smiling. "Even as much as I wanted it, I never made it. Probably never will."

"You did make it," Velez replied. "You *were* the sarge to us. Just catch this guy – that's all you gotta do."

She turned and walked away from him and into the ladies' room. Diane came out of the breakroom and walked over to him.

"Is she okay?" Diane asked.

"I just need to catch this guy," he stated. "Did you work the scene today?"

Diane nodded. "But there was nothing to find – no prints, no weapon – not even a casing. We know it was a rifle but that's about all. We're waiting on the body...," she paused. "I'm sorry. I know he was your friend."

"Yeah."

"Look, you wanna get a drink?" Diane asked. "All due respect, you really look like you could use one. I know I could use one."

Sean looked at her, wondering if she was serious. He wasn't exactly at his best nowadays, and he hadn't gone out – really gone out with a lady in quite some time. Diane was an attractive woman; she was on the petite side, but had an athletic shape. She also had the most beautiful light-brown skin, and her eyes seemed familiar, but made him nervous at the same time. She turned him on. It was difficult to tell exactly what she was though; not that it mattered in the least, he quietly reassured himself, but he wondered.

"Coughlin!" Chief Lannom shouted from the doorway of his office. "I need to speak with you."

"Right away, Chief." He laughed, turning his attention back to Diane. After the last few days, a couple drinks with a woman was exactly what he needed. "Sure, why not. After this meeting, who knows? I might have all the free time in the world."

She laughed.

"Okay, cool. Meet me at the Ace of Spades in about an hour," she said. "We'll play some pool, eat something, whatever. You know where it is?"

"Of course – I love that place." He looked at his watch. "I'll see you there."

He walked into the chief's office, where he sat at his desk, rubbing his temples. Sean looked around quickly. The office wasn't the least bit cleaner from the first time he stepped in.

"Sit down Sean," he said.

Sean sat and put his hands up in defense. "Look Chief – I know what you're gonna say – I'm on it, believe me. I was at Freeman University tracking down Joanna Harland's teachers. I'll be close to finding her..."

Lannom held up a hand, cutting him off.

"I'm taking you off the case. I just got a call from the commissioner. That last video by this character sent him over the edge," he said.

"I need time. This thing is moving so fast... but you know I'm gonna catch him, Chief. I need to talk to Wakefield. He'll tell me what I need to know. You just gotta give me a little more time," Sean pleaded.

"This is not a punishment, Coughlin," Lannom said reassuringly. "I'm doing this for your own protection. See, this Taberah guy has put the ball in the commissioner's court. Even though he's the one doing the killing, in the court of public opinion,

Kavanaugh's gonna be held responsible. I can already see him positioning himself to shift the blame on this department," he said, pointing a finger straight at Sean, "And whatever officer is investigating – and not to mention how the Harland case ties in. You're too close to this, and it won't be long before the families start to blame you – if they haven't already."

Sean exhaled heavily.

"So what do you want me to do?" Sean asked.

"Officially," Lannom said, leaning back in his chair, "You're suspended. You find out what you can, but do it quietly. To everybody else, though, you're suspended until further notice." He shook his head and furrowed his brow. "I'll put Daly on it. He's almost outta here, and he can stand the heat. Give whatever you have to him."

Sean stood up. "Alright, Chief."

"Listen to me," Lannom said seriously. "Get some rest. Get out of town for a while. Obviously this guy has it in for you. Find out what you can from Wakefield. I'll back whatever you try to do for him, within reason. Get lost until we can find this guy. I'm telling Velez the same thing. I don't want to lose any more of my officers to this maniac."

"I hear you, Chief," Sean said. "Thanks a lot. I'll let you know as soon as I get something new."

He walked out of the chief's office, went to his desk to grab his coat, and saw Mariota.

"Hey Gino," Sean said. "I'm on my way out. Tell Rosie the chief wants to see her."

"Alright Sean," he replied without looking up.

With that, he grabbed his coat and walked out of the station.

***

Father Stone took his place in the confessional that night, just as he did every night, but a bit more shaken. He spent most of the evening in prayer, asking God for the courage to continue on in his pastoral duties and to protect him from Taberah. He agreed not only to attend the service for the Castobells, but also to perform the mass at the church and the prayer at the burial. Seeing Haines' head hanging off like that... He was so many years removed from violent scenes like the one that happened today, with the gunshots and the screaming. It shook him to his very core. On top of this, it was now obvious that Taberah was going down the list of officers from the night of the Harland shooting, and he never knew when his day would come. Today, he lit three candles; one for Freddy, one for Donnell, and one for himself.

"Have you come to make confession?" Stone asked.

"And they will serve as a refuge for you," Taberah said, *"from the avenger of blood."*

"Joshua 20:3," Stone said decidedly. He swallowed hard. "What are you doing here?" he whispered. "I've kept my mouth shut, as you asked. Have you come for my life now?"

Taberah laughed terribly.

"A man of the cloth? I'm not a monster, Matthew. I only kill murderers."

"So why are you here?"

"I came tonight to make you a deal, but there is a time limit on this offer. Convince your friend to turn himself in… and confess that he murdered Eric Harland in cold blood. His sacrifice will inspire others to do the same. If he does this," Taberah added, *"he may live."*

"You must stop this," Stone pleaded. "This city will be filled with blood, and it will be innocent people that die because of it."

"For once, Matthew, we are in agreement. Erin is as beautiful as ever, and young Caitlin is growing up to be a fine young woman."

"Please…"

"Save your friend, Father," Taberah continued, *"And save those you love."*

Father Matthew Stone closed his eyes and prayed as the figure in a dark coat and hood walked out of the booth and into the cold November night.

***

Diane leaned over the pool table at a perfect right degree angle, lining the pool stick up with the orange ball on the far right of the table. Sean looked around at all of the young people drinking and laughing, and even though he wasn't much older than they were, he felt a bit out of place. The Ace of Spades was one of those new trendy bars – not exactly what he was accustomed to, but it was an okay place. They played some of that new thumping music that he hated. Sean showed up at the bar a little late; he went home to change, but she didn't mind. He noticed that she changed her clothes from what she wore earlier and put on some lipstick – magenta, he thought to be the color. The powder blue sweater she wore had a thick collar that rolled under itself but had a plunging neckline that revealed just the slightest hint of a black bra. The blue denim jeans clung to her figure like spandex, and the black boots that gave her a few inches stopped mid-calf.

Sean tried his best not to look like a creep as he stared at her butt. However, the pose was just too good to pass up. He didn't know why he just noticed her now; she was there for a few months. Then again, she never looked that good at work, at least not that he ever remembered. She ran her hand quickly through her short, brown hair, tucking it behind her left ear in one swift motion. Then she repositioned herself for the shot.

"Five – side pocket," she announced.

Diane tapped the cue ball swiftly and it shot forward, making a clicking sound as it connected with the five ball and sent it spinning into the middle pocket on the left side. Sean took another sip of his whiskey.

"I'm getting killed over here," he laughed.

Diane walked around the table and positioned herself for another shot. "What, you didn't expect me to be good?"

"Yes, that's it," Sean said. "I thought because you were a woman, you would suck at the game of pool."

"Wow, a cop and a chauvinist? You're blowing me away," Diane said sarcastically. She took a drink from her own glass, then set it back down on the side of the pool table. "So how you holding up?"

Sean shook his head, then downed the rest of his whiskey. "I'm not. I mean, I don't even know what the hell is going on here. Somebody is killing my friends, and I can't find him."

Diane nodded. "It's really crazy." She put down the stick. "You have any leads?"

"I have one. I'm just hoping it pans out." Sean looked around trying to find one of the waitresses, but he didn't see her. "I think I need another drink. You want another?"

"I'm fine. So tell me about yourself, Sean. You married?" she asked.

"I was, but I'm divorced. We have a son, Danny. He's thirteen now," Sean said. "He lives with her though." He paused. "You got a family?"

Diane's eyes went hard. "I was married once," she said firmly. "But it didn't work out."

Sean nodded. There was an uneasy silence for a while, but being the man that he was, he wouldn't make an attempt at levity.

"Well, I hope you're not looking at me as a possible replacement," he said nonchalantly. "I'm a drunk, and I wasn't a very good husband. I'm not really a great father. The only thing I've ever been good at is being a cop, and now I'm even failing at that."

Diane motioned with her fingers as if testing the quality of some fabric; then she frowned.

"Was that the part where I was supposed to feel sorry for you?" she said suddenly, looking him straight in the eye.

"The first thing you need to do is cut out the pity party. You're supposed to be a man, right?"

Sean just stared at her. He had no idea what was going on. Here he was pouring his heart out, and this woman he barely knew, who had invited *him* out by the way, was making him feel like crap. He nodded.

"Well then, act like one. Grow a pair," she said, "And accept responsibility for what you've done."

Diane walked over to him and came so close that their faces were almost touching. She never took her eyes off of him.

"And what you haven't done," she added.

"Why did you ask me to come here?" Sean asked. The truth was, he hadn't the slightest idea, but he liked it.

"You looked like you could use a break," Diane replied.

"Well, I got that. Lannom put me on leave," he exhaled. "Too many people dying around me, I guess."

Diane nodded.

"So I guess you don't have to get up early, do you?" she said, smiling.

"Nope, I guess not," Sean replied sheepishly.

"Another whiskey?" she asked. "It's my treat."

***

Suddenly, Chief Lannom stuck his head out of his office, looking around the station with his oversized frames. There weren't many officers around at that late hour, but it was just as well. Daly and Mariota were at their desks as well as Angela, the desk clerk.

"Has anybody seen Velez?" Lannom shouted.

Mariota looked up, and shook his head. "Not since the meeting, Chief, but she was pretty upset – she might've taken off," he said.

Angela, who was a bleach-blond in her early fifties, was at the station so long that she was regarded as an old painting or a plant – something you got so used to that you barely realized it was there. Even though they ignored her, she knew everything that went on in that station – or at least, everything she could know.

"Last time I saw her," she said without looking up, "She was headed into the bathroom."

The chief sighed. "Well, can somebody go check? If she's still here, I need to see her – now."

He went back into his office and slammed the door shut. Angela stared at Mariota, and he stared right back. Finally, she rolled her eyes, let out a heavy sigh and got up from her chair. She strolled over to the bathroom while Mariota mumbled under his breath about her work ethic, when suddenly; there was a blood-chilling scream. Daly frowned as he looked up from his paperwork and Chief Lannom flung his door open again to see what all the fuss was about. Mariota jumped up from his seat, grabbing his gun from his holster and rushed into the ladies' room. He found Angela standing up against the wall, holding her hands to her mouth as she looked wide-eyed into the stall directly in front of her. Mariota, with his gun raised, came around slowly and his eyes shifted from Angela to the stall...

Inside was Detective Rosemary Velez, staring up at the ceiling as a small stream of blood leaked down her face.

She had been shot right between the eyes.

***

Diane took out her car keys as they walked down the block toward where she was parked. Sean was a few paces behind her. He tried to walk as straight as possible, but with very little success. He used the brick wall to steady himself.

"You're not going anywhere like this," she laughed.

"I know this is gonna sound lame," Sean said, slurring his words slightly, "But this usually never happens."

"I'm sure," Diane said. "Well, I can take you home, or we can go to my place – your choice."

Sean's face turned to a mask of confusion. "Wait, you're driving? How are you not drunk?" he asked.

"Because I only had ginger ale."

He held up a knowing finger, wagging it and smiling as he stumbled toward her.

"Clever girl..." he said smiling. "Well, I guess it would be better if..."

Suddenly, his phone rang. It took him a minute to find out where it was as he fumbled around. He clicked the button and took a minute to compose himself, trying not to sound drunk.

"Coughlin," he said.

"*Sean,*" the voice on the phone whispered. "*It's Lannom. Rosemary's been shot... She's dead.*"

"*What?!*" Sean exclaimed. "Where?"

"*Here – at the station,*" Lannom explained. "*I don't know... This is a nightmare. Listen to me. Get out of town, Sean, and don't tell anyone where you're going.*"

"What are you talking about?" Sean yelled. "We gotta come in..."

"*Just do it, boy,*" Lannom said firmly.

With that, he hung up.

"What's going on?" Diane asked.

Tears welled up in Sean's eyes as his mouth tightened in anger.

"It's Rosie," he said. "They found her at the station. She's dead. He killed her!"

"Oh my God," Diane gasped. "That's horrible."

"Listen, I gotta go," Sean said, turning around. "I'll call you, alright?"

"Where are you going?" she asked.

"I gotta go to the station. I have to find out what happened."

Diane waved a hand. "Come on, I'll drive you."

"No! Go home, Diane," Sean said firmly. "If this guy's after me, I don't want you to get hurt. I'll call you later when I know what's happened."

He waved a hand, then turned around and walked down the street as Diane watched him leave.

***

When Sean walked into the station, he immediately felt the tension and anxiety. Everybody was on edge. The place was crawling with Criminal Investigations and Forensics as well as the Homicide detectives. Two of their own died tonight, and one right in their own precinct – right under their noses. Fortunately, no one was dumb enough to call the press on this, Sean thought to himself. They didn't know yet, but when they found out it would be terrible for the NYPD – and even worse for the 25th. They lost three officers in one week, and the significance was not foreign to him. Sean knew his number was up. If he didn't find Taberah before then, he would probably end up dead.

He walked toward the bathroom, where the photographers were taking shots of the crime scene, and caught a glimpse of Mariota in the corner being consoled by some counselor. He always knew there was something between him and Velez, but they didn't parade it around. He braced himself to see Rosemary's lifeless face, but fortunately for him, they had already taken her out. As he walked under the tape and into the bathroom, he saw his partner, Aquila, who caught sight of him as well. The look wasn't friendly, and Sean knew why. True, he was ditching him, but he was going through a lot right now and he really didn't want to converse, which was Aquila's specialty. Tonight with Diane was the most he talked to anyone in a long time. It looked like the kid was working the scene; maybe deferring to him would soften things a bit.

"So what did you find?" Sean asked as he walked over.

Aquila was bent over in the stall, dusting the walls with a small brush. "Where did you go?" he asked.

"The chief sent me home. What did you find?"

Aquila stood up, shaking his head. "She was shot once in the head – right between the eyes. There was scorched bone and skin, so she was shot at close range. The bullet hole was small too – .22, maybe a .25, but there was no casing," he added.

"I was just here a couple hours ago!" Sean exclaimed. "What's the time of death?"

"About that time." He looked at Sean nervously. "That means you were probably here when it happened. It also means..."

"How could nobody hear anything?!" he yelled out, spinning around. A couple of people turned their heads. "This is a police station for God's sake!"

"Sean," Aquila said. "That's what I was gonna say, but it was probably a silencer."

"I gotta go," Sean said. "I don't want Lannom to see me, but I'll track you down. I want to know what you know." He patted him on the shoulder. "I'll be in touch."

He left the bathroom as quickly as he could, but when he rounded the corner his eyes locked on to the chief's through the glass. Sean actually saw his face fill up with rage. Lannom flung open the door of his office; his hair was askew and his tie loosened.

"Crap," Sean whispered.

"Coughlin!" He came straight towards him. "I told you to get lost for a reason," Lannom whispered. "Not just to save your miserable life, but to keep you out of trouble." He made a sniffing noise. "Jesus, I can smell the Jamison. Are you out of your mind? If they catch you like this, you're done."

"Trouble? What are you talking about?"

"IA is on their way down here," Lannom said excitedly. "They want everybody's gun. Now this is starting to look like an inside job, and they're trying to spin the whole thing that way."

Sean took his gun out of his holster and handed it to the chief.

"Take it, I've got nothing to hide," he said. "But whoever's doing this is not gonna stop; you should see that by now. I've got to find him."

"I told them you were on leave, not suspended, in case you have to use a weapon. You got a backup?" the chief asked.

Sean nodded. "It's in the car."

"Alright. Get somewhere safe. I'll put a unit on your family's house. Go," he said. "Stay out of sight."

"Thanks Chief," Sean said.

It was close to one o'clock in morning, and he was exhausted. Sean got into his car, put the key in and started it up. He reached under the seat and retrieved a Beretta 92FS.

He checked the magazine, found it full, and placed it on the seat next to him. The engine roared through the silent street as he pulled off. He grabbed his phone and dialed Danielle's cell phone. It rang a couple times, then three. Finally, he heard her voice on the other end.

"Dani?" he yelled. "Where are you?"

"*Sean?*" Danielle answered. *"What's going on? Why do you sound like that?"*

The engine roared louder as he shifted gears.

"Listen, they killed Rosie at the station today. I want you to get out of the house and get somewhere safe," he shouted. "I'm getting out of town."

"Oh my God – that's horrible," she said. *"And Donnell. We're at my father's house Sean – I don't know…"*

Sean's eye caught the shape of a large SUV pull onto the street a few feet behind him.

"That's good," he said. "Just stay there. Don't go back to the house... At least not for a few days."

The SUV behind him sped up just slightly. There were a few cars around, but this one was behind him consistently for a few blocks. Sean took a left on 125th Street and Park, keeping his eyes on the rearview. The dark truck made a left as well.

"Sean? Sean?" Danielle shouted through the receiver. *"What's going on? You're scaring me…"*

"I'll call you back. Take care of Danny."

He hung up the phone, pressed down on the accelerator and sped up. The truck did as well; he was definitely being followed. He planned to go home and grab a few things, but he couldn't now. Whoever it was had probably been on him since the precinct. He went across town, toward the West Side. Sean thought hard. If he grabbed this guy, maybe he could scare him into telling him who sent him – and who he worked for. He might even get an address. Sean kept driving all the way toward the Hudson River, then made a right turn, as if he was about to get onto the West Side Highway. The Yukon was right on his tail. Sean clicked on his seatbelt.

"I got something for you, you son of bitch," he muttered.

He slammed on the breaks and the SUV crunched into his rear fender, sending him rocketing forward into the seatbelt, then yanking him back. That was smart, he thought to himself. The effects of the evening's alcohol hadn't fully worn off yet, and now, his whole body hurt. Sean grabbed the Beretta off the seat and never took his eyes off of the rearview. The windows were dark and tinted all the way; he couldn't see a thing. He got out of the car and kept the gun aimed at the windshield while he took a look at the damage. The back was totaled. *Sherona...* he thought. Now he was really pissed.

"Get out of the car!" Sean yelled. But there was no movement – only the hissing of the SUV's radiator smoking into the night air. The grille was dented slightly and the bumper was bent, but other than that, there was no visible damage. That made him even angrier.

"Put your hands out of the window, now!"

The SUV's engine grumbled, then revved. Sean heard the grinding of metal as the two intertwined bumpers struggled to pull themselves apart. The SUV threw itself in reverse and its tires spun furiously against the asphalt.

"Freeze!!!" Sean yelled, but the truck continued to move.

Sean stepped up and fired four rounds into the windshield on the driver's side of the vehicle. The Yukon swerved to the right, backing into a steel support beam that held up the overpass and created a racket of crunched metal and broken glass. Sean advanced slowly toward the truck with his sights trained on the windshield. Suddenly the door flung open, and out stumbled a short man in a black suit and tie, clutching his chest and coughing as bright red blood spilled out. Chance looked to his right and caught a glimpse of Sean. There was a black Ruger in his hands, and he smiled as he raised it.

"For the movement," Chance gasped.

Sean fired twice, struck him in the chest, and he collapsed. He walked over to him, keeping his gun trained on him as he was taught, but Chance was not breathing. He was gone. Even though he was covered with blood, he still recognized the scarred face of the man he met so long ago. He looked around; the view of the lights of New Jersey twinkled across the water. A few cars with wide-eyed passengers zipped by, but nobody dared stop. He bent down near the body and checked his pockets. There were a few thousand dollars in one pocket and a soft black alligator wallet in the other, but no identification; only a black card with a flame insignia raised and shining. He took the card, but left the rest. He couldn't call this in. He wasn't even supposed to be on duty, much less involved in another shooting. He searched around inside the crumpled Yukon – under the seats and in the back. He opened the glove compartment and found the MAC-11. He grabbed that and took it with him. He knew he couldn't turn it in, at least not now, but he didn't want some other person to find the automatic pistol. He took the other gun out of Chance's right hand, walked back to his car and left Chance's bleeding body on the pavement. He put the MAC-11 and the Ruger in his glove box, where they would remain safe until he had further evidence.

He thought about continuing home, but honestly, he didn't feel like going home. He thought about going to get his family, but if there were others tailing him, he didn't want to risk leading them to his family. Sean got into the car, turned on the ignition, and made a horrible noise as he ripped his rear fender from the front of the Yukon. He made a violent U-turn and got on the highway. He would drive around and make sure he wasn't followed again, then he would get some sleep because tomorrow he had someplace to go. He was going to get answers.

***

CHAPTER SIX

Taberah

Detective Sean Coughlin sat at the visitor's table early that morning and looked exactly like he felt – a disaster. He just killed a man a few hours earlier and left him on the street. He hadn't even been home to shower or shave and still had a tremendous hangover. The room usually reserved for lawyer visits was empty and cold and gave him a clear listen to the sound of officers laughing and telling crude stories which were probably all lies. The table where he sat was a dull, matte gray over steel, with a plexiglass divider that stood only a few inches high. Sean had a delightful thought that it wouldn't stop him from tearing Wakefield's head off. He derived even more mental pleasure when he heard the sound of shackles clinking together at a slow pace.

The door opened, and there he was – Charles Henry Wakefield, clad in the black boots and the dark forest green of Sing Sing Correctional Facility. He seemed much bigger than the last time he laid eyes on him – in muscle mass, anyway. Two sets of wrist shackles were necessary to keep his hands bound, and those long chains hung all the way down to his feet, which were connected by a shorter chain. The officer that walked in behind him resembled an MMA fighter. He had a strong, set jaw and bulky muscles that threatened to rip apart the cauliflower-colored blue uniform. All of his hair was shaved off with the exception of a small tuft of brown hair spiked toward the sky. He didn't even acknowledge Sean as he entered, but sat Wakefield down in the adjacent chair, then knelt down and unlocked the foot shackle and fastened it to a small metal rung in the floor, which in turn brought Wakefield's wrists down near his knees. He then gave it a firm shake and made sure it was secure.

The C.O. gave Sean the smallest of nods, then promptly left the room, slamming the thick steel door shut behind him. Sean stared at the man and focused all of his hatred into his eyes, making sure that he felt it.

"Where's Taberah?" Sean hissed.

Wakefield appeared unfazed by his intensity. His head was still clean-shaven, but his beard was intact – close and well-groomed. He spent almost seven long years inside, getting jumped by groups of officers whenever they felt the inkling, and beat most of them senseless on numerous occasions. He took his share of losses too, but they were hard to come by. He had no issues with any inmate or gangs, even though he wasn't a part of one, he had the money on his books to live like he wanted. Even still, he waited for the day he would finally be found innocent and get out of there. Until then, he would stand firm. He no longer wore his classic smirk; instead it was replaced by a look of all-knowing defiance.

"What makes you think I know that?" Wakefield replied sharply.

"I know you think things can't get any worse for you," Sean said. "You've already got life – and that appeal you keep thinking about...? We both know that is never gonna happen. I know you're not scared of this place; in fact, I hear you live like a king – like a *boss*." Sean got up, walked over to Wakefield slowly, and put his face close to his. "You don't have any family or children I can threaten, but what if I just killed you?"

Wakefield turned and looked at Sean with a shocked expression – but only for a second. Then he smiled, nodding up toward the ceiling.

"You ain't killing nobody," he said. "There's cameras in here."

"Oh, not right now, but what about tonight?" Sean asked. "In your cell? Or in the shower? At mess? Huh? Wherever. All I'd have to do is tell the C.O.'s that you're definitely the man responsible for killing all these cops... and that Taberah is working for you." Sean returned to his seat, letting what he just said sink in. "It would just be a matter of time."

Wakefield's expression didn't change.

"You know, as soon as I met you I knew you were dumb as hell," he responded. "How can Taberah be working for me when he's the one that set me up?"

Sean leaned forward.

"What are you talking about?" he said.

"At first," Wakefield continued, "I thought it was one of your boys or you, but that didn't make sense. You wouldn't kill a few of your own just to get me behind bars. You could have done that with the burner by itself. Whoever did this to me wanted me out of the way, permanently – and at the same time, had no problem shooting cops," he added.

"Joanna Harland," Sean replied.

"You killed her husband – my cousin," Wakefield shot back, his eyes narrowing. "A good dude – for no reason at all. She had a motive, but I know Joanna. I took her to the range and she could barely shoot. On top of that, everything with her was about non-violence, because that's what Eric would have wanted. She couldn't do this. She wouldn't destroy his name like that."

"So who, then?"

"A couple weeks after Joanna goes missing, I get a letter. Now when I went in, I gave instructions through my lawyer to have Joanna look after my businesses like the club and some other things – legitimate stuff. The letter said that this person had Joanna, and if I didn't give up my connections and control of everything, he would kill her. So I sent my lawyer with the info, but she still never turned up. He probably killed her anyway."

"You still have the letter?" Sean asked.

Wakefield nodded.

Sean leaned forward. "Listen, Charles," he continued. "If what you say is true and you give me what you have and I can get Taberah, we can prove your innocence. You can get out of here! Who do you think it is?"

Wakefield looked him straight in the eye. "There are only two people that had access to my gun to plant it – Joanna and Chance," he said. "Nobody else would have known how to get to it."

"Chance," Sean said thoughtfully. "Chance is dead."

"What?" Wakefield shouted. "What you talking about?"

"He was shot late last night...there were no witnesses."

There was a silence between them as those words hung in the air.

"Where'd they find him?" Wakefield asked.

"Harlem." Sean paused again. "Is the lawyer in the same place?"

"I got a new one now. Haven't heard from him for years," Wakefield said.

Sean got up and knocked on the door twice. As the C.O. came and opened the door, he turned back to Wakefield.

"I hope you told me everything you know," Sean said. "And I hope you didn't lie because I'm gonna find out."

"Just do your job for once," Wakefield replied. "You're about seven years too late."

"Escort Mr. Wakefield back to his cell with me present. He has something for me."

***

"Last night, the police killed our fellow soldier, Chance," Taberah said. *"He gave his life in the struggle. I know the policeman responsible, but he is mine."*

The stone waiting room was occupied by the mercenary, Jacob, who sported his fatigues proudly, as well as about a dozen other killers who took care of jobs for Taberah in the past. Some of them wore masks of their own as they listened intently to the figure in the black cloak and hood that spoke through a skull face whose voice sounded like the cold breath of death. For all of them, it was the first time they saw their general in person, and for many of them it was an exhilarating moment. In their lifetime, they never found a leader so willing to take on the biggest gang in America – and with results. Many of the men who occupied the room, came from different cultural and economic backgrounds; some from poor neighborhoods, some from privileged families, some from military backgrounds, but they were all united in their shared hatred of the police, its abuse of power, excessive force, and the taking of human lives. After months of talking about these issues in a secure chat room, Taberah demanded that each person show their loyalty to the cause by taking the life of a specific police officer. After that officer was eliminated, those with the courage to make the kill became a part of the Flame Syndicate. The Flame Syndicate was the hidden army that was growing in the darkest corners of the city of New York and preparing for the day of an all-out assault. In most cases, Chance was the go-between for all of the other connections. Now that he was gone, Taberah summoned them all to the warehouse for the next phase of the war.

"The time has come for you, the Flame Syndicate, to show its face," Taberah said, pointing a thin, black-gloved finger. *"The NYPD will now know the true strength of our numbers. They have failed to right their wrongs, to take responsibility for the lives they've snuffed out, and now, they will pay in full."*

Jacob nodded, smiling. The others looked at each other pleased at the visions given to them, but also a bit worried. Nothing like this had ever been done in their young lives and time. This indeed was new ground.

"In a few days, there will be a ceremony for two of the fallen oppressors whose sins they have so quickly forgotten," Taberah continued. *"They will be naming a street after Officers Rozyczka and Morrissey. It is at that ceremony that we will strike next. More blood will be spilled. More families will mourn. Alert all of the soldiers – all of you."*

"It's time to turn it up."

✳✳✳

Chief Lannom sat outside the commissioner's office once again, in his dress blues – one, out of respect for the commissioner himself and – two, he wanted to retain some dignity when he walked out of there, since he fully expected to lose his job. There was a time when the tone between the two of them was nothing but playful. Nowadays, after he left him, it felt as he had been summoned to the principal's office – not that he could really blame him, though. Kavanaugh was under a tremendous amount of pressure; from the citizens themselves on how to properly train up-and-coming police officers, how to prevent unnecessary shootings, and how to hold officers accountable when they *did* happen. Then, there was pressure from his subordinates on how they should respond in dealing with the public, since every chief of police had their own unique examples of how they led and influenced their departments. However, the biggest pressure came from the NYPD's union president, Lyndon Patrick, who in the past few months influenced many officers in the NYPD to join in public displays of disobedience to Mayor Washington over his alleged non-support of the organization. Mayor William Washington, on the other hand – a black man – appointed Kavanaugh and was his champion and biggest supporter, and, in turn, Kavanaugh too was his. Now that relationship was strained as well.

The thing was, none of those monumental problems affected or included Chief Lannom directly. He always had a good relationship with the commissioner, even through the trial and coverage surrounding the Harland shooting. After the trial, the publicity that hounded their department started to die down. Now, these Taberah killings reopened old wounds for the public, brought attention to the Harland case once more, and thrust the 25th precinct back into the spotlight. Moreover, Taberah had publicly held the commissioner accountable, thereby placing responsibility for the killings directly in his lap. That responsibility, he foresaw, was about to trickle down to him. He lost three officers under his command, and if he didn't catch Taberah soon, he would lose even more. The door to the office opened and Kavanaugh appeared in the doorway.

"Come on in, Lannom," he said.

Lannom stepped into the office, closing the door behind him. Commissioner Kavanaugh sat down at his desk, leaned in, and folded his hands.

"You have to bring your boy in," he said pointedly.

"What boy?" Lannom asked. "What are you talking about, Bob?"

"Coughlin." The commissioner paused, leaning back in his seat. "Late last night officers found a truck on the West Side of Harlem all smashed up, like it had been in an accident. The driver was laid out beside the truck with three bullets in him. Guess whose license plate was at the scene and whose fingerprints were all over the guy's car and wallet?"

Lannom swallowed hard. "Dear God," he whispered. "Who was he?"

"His name was Gary Laurain, but on the streets he was known as Chance. He was at the scene the night of the Harland shooting and was believed to be working for Wakefield. He's got quite a jacket; well, he had quite a jacket."

Lannom was silent. There wasn't much he could say anyway, but his head was spinning. What the hell was Coughlin thinking about?

Kavanaugh stood up, walked over to his bar cart, grabbed the crystal decanter there, and poured himself a drink.

"Here's what I think happened," he continued. "Coughlin was so overcome by grief at what happened to Eric Harland that he couldn't take it. He snapped. He held himself responsible, but instead of killing himself, he took that anger out on other officers and cooked up this Taberah character. Splitting – I think that's what psychologists call it."

"Commissioner, come on," Lannom pleaded. "That's crazy."

Kavanaugh shrugged. "Or maybe he wanted Wakefield so bad for this that he really did frame him, killing two officers in the process. We both know he had a hard-on for him since forever."

"Robert, listen to me. I know the death of Velez looks bad, but ballistics tested his gun. It's *not* him, and it's not anybody in the department!" Lannom exclaimed.

"That doesn't prove a damn thing!" Kavanaugh barked. "Even a rookie would know enough not to use his service weapon in a murder. The bullet was a different caliber anyway. Somebody in your house is responsible. At the very least, they know something." He pointed a finger at him. "Listen to me, Lannom. I should shut you down – fire you. Out of respect for your record and our friendship, I'm gonna give you 72 hours to find Coughlin and he better have a damn good explanation for those fingerprints when you do. After that, I'm issuing a warrant for his arrest – for murder."

Lannom nodded, standing up. "I understand," he replied through tightened lips.

"Find Taberah *now*," he continued. "Because I'm not going down as the commissioner who let half his police force get taken out." He leaned in. "But if I do, *you'll* go down as the chief of the precinct where it started."

***

Sean drove his now battered black Corvette up Saw Mill Parkway, thinking about the story that Wakefield told him. It turned out that the letter was real; there it laid, right on the passenger's seat of his car. Interestingly, the lawyer, Arenburg, was nowhere to be found. Of course, he knew it could have all been bullcrap – something Wakefield cooked up just in case, or better yet for his appeal. Sean interviewed a thousand guys in his career, and he was sure that Wakefield wasn't lying. Either the lawyer disappeared when all the cops started to die, Sean thought, or he was dead himself. Nevertheless, he had to get out of the city now; he already pushed his luck by going to the prison, and that wouldn't take long to get around, and he had a body. He only noticed this morning that his license plate was missing. If he got stopped, he'd have to flash his badge and hope that was enough.

His plan was to get to a hotel somewhere in New Jersey or maybe upstate and lay low for a couple of days until he could regroup. He wished he could get a message to Matt. He was the only one he trusted to watch his family, but he was off the grid. He didn't even have a cell anymore. He shook his head as he thought of his former best friend. That shooting really affected him so much; he was never the same after that. Maybe Diane would do, he thought. They only had that one encounter, which in his opinion would have probably gone further if he weren't interrupted, yet he sensed something from her – an inner strength that he could trust. He looked through his cell phone – yes, he had her number. He decided to call her later, just to check in and see what was going on around the precinct.

As he sped along, watching the trees whip by outside his window, he thought about his family. When all this was over, he would have to try to reconcile with Danielle – build a friendship with her at least, for Danny's sake. He was really a mess over the last few years, and he had to be honest with himself – it wasn't the job. He always handled that just fine. He just didn't know how to get close to his son, and that pained him. His father was never close to him, and he had no idea how to bridge that gap. The disorder didn't make it any easier, but he had to find a way before it was too late and he lost him forever.

***

The next morning, Mayor William Washington smiled as he waved to the medium-sized crowd in front of him. His powder blue scarf lodged free for a moment to blow in the wind. Most of the people that stood there on that brisk morning in November clapped and cheered in support of the leader of their city, although this was his first year in office. He was the first African-American mayor in New York in nearly twenty years, which was especially significant in these times because of his wife, Charlene, who was also African-American, and his two children. Having grown up in New York, he knew all too well the perils of being black and dealing with the police, and he brought those experiences into his politics. Starting out as a political organizer in his youth, he fought bravely on the side of the disenfranchised – from affordable housing to immigration. Aiming to end the climate mistrust between the police and young black males, upon entering office, Washington put a stop to many unpopular policies such as the highly controversial "stop and frisk" policy that was instituted by the previous mayor. The policy brought the all-too entrenched practice of racial profiling to the forefront again, which in this new era of camera phones, was being recorded for the world to see. None of these things put him on the map or in the hot seat like the press conference a few months earlier. He expressed his difficulty of having to raise a black son in this city, where the harsh reality was that because of the color of his skin he had to train him on how to deal with the police – something he would not have had to do if his son were white. This was something *every* black family did at some point. His relationship with the NYPD was already strained; he instituted new sensitivity training and body cameras for many officers, but now, it was at an impasse.

The union president, Lyndon Patrick, used this remark to incite officers to cover their eyes with their hands anytime the mayor arrived. The first time was at Castobell's funeral, but the impact was overshadowed by the assassination of Detective Haines. Now today, at the unveiling of the street signs in honor of the two fallen officers, Rozyczka and Morrissey, they had another chance to show their disdain for the mayor. However inappropriate, they seized the opportunity. He arrived a few minutes ago with his family, and all of the officers promptly covered their eyes with their fingertips until he passed. Mayor Washington took it all in stride, taking his place behind the podium set up a few feet from where the slain officers had lain. An older Russian man in a black suit and tie stood to the right. He owned the coffee shop the officers came out of before they were gunned down. Commissioner Kavanaugh was to his right with his lackey, and Washington gave him a ceremonial nod, which he didn't return. Washington knew what that was about. He was getting pressure from Patrick to show the same support for the officers, but Kavanaugh didn't support abuses of power, which Washington respected.

However, he had the nerve to come to him and ask him to apologize for his comments at the press conference, to which he responded, "Hell no. I'll be mayor for a few more years, but I'll be black forever."

Since then, their relationship was never the same.

"Good morning, my fellow New Yorkers," Washington said, leaning into the microphone. "We are here on this cold November morning to honor the lives of two of New York's finest – Officers James Rozyczka and Shane Morrissey, who died on this street not so long ago. Today, we honor their memory and their service by renaming the street."

He gave a head nod to the officer with the thin golden rope in his hand, attached to a white satin covering. The officer pulled it, revealing two Kelly green street signs; one read, "Morrissey Street," and the other, "Rozyczka Way." The officers and the people behind them applauded simultaneously, and Washington leaned over to the commissioner.

"I see you still can't get your men to behave," he smirked, "Even at an occasion like this."

The commissioner leaned in as well.

"I'm surprised you could take your lips off the black voter's backsides to get down here," he replied.

Washington actually thought that was funny and was about to say something really clever when he felt something wet on the right side of his face. He touched his fingers to his face and looked down at them. They were covered in blood. He looked to his right and saw Commissioner Kavanaugh falling backwards with a quarter-sized hole in his forehead and his eyes rolling up. He smacked against the building behind him then slid down, leaving a streak of red on the tan bricks above him. Screams rang out from the crowd and the mayor ducked down behind the podium. His head of security grabbed him quickly and whisked him toward the caravan. As the officers drew their weapons and look around frantically, Jacob Anderson drew back the rifle and spoke into his mouthpiece.

"What about the mayor?" he asked.

"Leave him," the voice crackled through his earpiece. *"Your job is done. Bring it in."*

He broke down the rifle, put it in a small black case, then stood up, donning a policeman's hat to match his dark blue uniform. He opened the roof door that led to the staircase and descended the stairs.

While officers on the ground looked wildly up at the windows and rooftops, trying to get a glimpse of a possible assailant, a city bus came careening down the street that was just named Morrissey, causing officers and bystanders alike to flee in every direction. The bus came to a screeching halt and filled the air with the sound of its breaks. The doors flew open, and out piled dozens and dozens of young men and women – all clad in black t-shirts pulled over their clothes, bearing the flame insignia, and their faces covered by various skull masks. Their hands were filled with guns of every shape and size and they waved them frantically as they looked for targets. The first one to fire was Officer Juan Pichardo, the late commissioner's driver and bodyguard, as he sat on the ground holding Kavanaugh's bleeding head in his arm while trying to aim with the other. He hit one of the masked men in the chest three times, and he went down hard. As he took aim at another one, the man he hit stood again; the holes in his shirt were still smoking but he bore no blood. The masked man took aim, fired once, and struck Pichardo through the eye. He fell back awkwardly; dying next to the man he guarded for so long in life, and guarded his body in death. The streets were bombarded with the sounds of automatic gunfire as each of Taberah's soldiers took aim at the officer nearest to them. One masked man took an officer's shot right in the head, leaving bright red blood leaking through the skull mask. A young officer named Damien Wilson took cover behind the open door of his cruiser. He grabbed the radio with his right hand and fired his Glock 19 with his left between words.

"This is Wilson!" he screamed, firing twice as he crouched down. "We need SWAT down here, now!"

"What's your 20, Officer Wilson?" the radio responded back.

Just then, a figure with an AK-47 in his arms, the t-shirt with the symbol pulled over a hooded sweatshirt, and the hood pulled over a skull mask, ran up close to the car. He took aim and fired a dozen or so rounds. Wilson fell back onto the car dazed, looking down at the blood on his shirt. He tore open his police shirt, revealing a blood-soaked bulletproof vest. It stood no chance against the 7.62 rounds. He leaned back weakly, letting his eyes close as his breath left him.

"Officer Wilson?" the radio asked. "Wilson, come in..."

Some of the officers who got a move on early managed to line their cars side-by-side, making them function as a barrier, but a navy blue pick-up truck spun a U-turn, revealing a heavyset masked man holding an M60 machine gun in its back carriage. He let loose a volley, pinning them down, and put hundreds of holes in the cruiser's steel frames in a matter of minutes, killing six officers instantly. Brave officers traded shots with whom they could, but they took heavy losses. An older officer laid on the ground with the radio receiver next to his ear, yelling into it as he tried to avoid the bullets overhead.

"We're getting killed out here..."

***

"I want to see *every* case file since the Patrucci killing!" Chief Lannom barked. "Everything!"

The station was in turmoil as a result of the shootings earlier. Everyone felt shaken to the core; there was never an attack on the police like that in the history of the NYPD. They started to gain a little bit of ground when the SWAT team showed up, but they lost close to forty officers today. Lannom ordered Daly to bring him all of the case files to see if maybe there was something he could spot; that was overlooked. Daly was a little out of touch with the street, and Sean was in the wind. There was a little bit of relief that he felt guilty about – at least he didn't have to worry about the commissioner putting the screws to him, but he needed a break in the case.

Suddenly, one by one, officers and detectives stopped talking as they stared at the person entering the station. The priest was dressed in a black suit, with a black shirt complemented by the white collar. His dark brown hair that was receding just slightly in the front was parted and swept to the left side.

"Jesus Christ," Angela said. "Matty?"

Some of the officers nodded at their former fellow officer, Matthew Stone, as he approached the chief's office. He had a somber expression on his face. Daly came up to him and patted him strongly on the shoulder.

"So that's where you've been," he said.

"Yeah," said Matthew. "I need to speak to the chief."

Daly nodded, then knocked on the door. Lannom looked up, saw Matthew through the glass, and signaled for him to open the door.

"He wanted to see you Chief," Daly said.

Lannom waved at him, and he left them alone, closing the door.

"Sorry Father," Lannom explained. "But it's been a hell of a day. I don't have too much time."

Matthew smiled just slightly.

"Chief," he said. "It's me – Matthew Stone."

Lannom looked him over again and then shook his head.

"Jesus, boy – I didn't even recognize you!" he exclaimed. He cleared a stack of papers off the seat in front of his desk and gestured for him to take a seat.

"So you're in the priesthood now, huh? We didn't know what happened to you. Sit down, Stone. I'm sure you heard about the massacre today."

"I did, Chief. That's why I'm here," he said. "I'm only sorry I didn't come sooner. May the Lord forgive me."

The chief flopped down in his chair, exhaling deeply. He held up two hands, as if telling Stone to relax.

"Calm down, Matty boy," Chief Lannom said reassuringly. "Just tell me what you know."

***

Matthew held his arms up in his office while an officer taped a microphone to his recently shaved chest; it was irritating him already. Lannom was standing by along with Daly and Aquila, Sean's partner.

"You sure you want to do this?" Aquila said.

"He should've done it sooner," Daly snarled. "He might've saved a few dozen cops' lives."

"Shut up, Daly," Lannom said. He turned his attention to Matthew.

"So how can you be sure he will come tonight?" he asked.

Matthew buttoned up his black shirt over the mic. "I can't be sure, but usually after there was a killing, Taberah...or whoever, would come in for confession – either that night or the night after."

"*Usually?*" Daly said.

Lannom shot him a look, and he kept quiet.

"Listen to me, Matthew. We're gonna be right outside in the van. Try to get him to talk about what happened today if you can," Lannom said. "But get him to say that he killed officers. As soon as we hear that, we'll come right in."

"Okay," Matthew said, nodding. "Listen, Chief. I'm sorry I didn't come in sooner, but he promised he would kill my girls. Now I've been threatened a thousand times when I was on the streets, but after seeing what he could do..."

"But I don't understand that," Aquila interrupted. "Why would he risk coming in here all the time, just to talk to you? You could have been wired up at any time or had us waiting."

"It was to taunt me," Matthew said, shaking his head. "I was part of the team. Whatever connection he has, he holds me responsible for Harland's death, just like the rest."

Daly folded his arms. "So how come you're not dead yet?" he asked scornfully.

"God," Matthew replied.

The chief patted him on the shoulder.

"It's all right, kid. Just get this bastard on tape." He gestured to the other detectives to leave, and they began to file out. "We'll be right outside."

Daly and Aquila left the office, and Lannom followed.

***

A few hours passed and nothing happened. Chief Lannom, Daly and Aquila were in the back of the surveillance van, watching the front of the cathedral as they recorded the people coming and going. They were also listening to the bug they planted in the confessional booth, turning it off after a few seconds when they heard nothing about the shootings and then turning it back on again. A steady stream of people filed out now that evening mass was over, but none of the people looked like killers, Aquila thought, but they had no idea what they were looking for in the first place.

"You think this guy's really gonna show?" Daly asked. "I mean, he's gotta be a little squirrely after today."

"Stone said it was like clockwork. He'll show," Lannom said with finality.

A FedEx van pulled up slowly in front of them and double-parked in front of the cathedral. The deliveryman stepped down from the running board in his dark gray and purple uniform and matching cap pulled low on his head. He reached back in and pulled out a small package about the size of a lunch box. It was wrapped in brown paper and tied in triple twist twine.

"You know, I've never seen a delivery come to a church," Aquila said wistfully. "Isn't that funny?"

"It's a building," Daly said. "They get deliveries just like anybody. Or maybe he's just coming to make confession."

"Think that could be him – Taberah?" Aquila asked.

Lannom kept on listening intently to his headphones.

"If it is, we'll grab him when he comes out. He can't go anywhere," Lannom said.

***

Father Matthew Stone sat in the booth as still as he could, listening intently for the voice of the killer. There were a few confessions that night, but not many, and he thanked God for that. He couldn't have handled it; it was a miracle he got through mass. He hadn't said much to the ones that did come; only "go on, my son" and a few Hail Mary's. While he was in there, he started to rethink bringing the police in on this. Could they really protect him? He wondered. How? Taberah demonstrated a knack for finding anyone – anywhere. How did he manage to kill all those cops? The thoughts rattled around in his head like loose marbles. He closed his eyes and tried to focus as he said a silent prayer that his family would be safe, that they would catch Taberah, and that this nightmare would finally be over.

Suddenly, he heard the sound of the small wooden door squeaking and someone entering the confession booth next to him. He swallowed hard and stuck his finger between his white collar and his neck, trying to loosen it up.

"Are you here to make your confession?" he asked gingerly.

There was no answer – only a tearing sound, or what sounded like someone flipping through the newspaper. There were a few more indescribable sounds, then some clicking noises. He didn't look through the lattice, although he was dying to. Instead, he kept looking forward. He was still pretty paranoid about Taberah's ability to reach him, even if he *did* end up in custody that night.

"You don't have to be nervous, my son," Stone said. "It's only you, me and God."

There was still no reply from the person in the next booth, but rather a click then the sound of the door opening and closing again, as if the person was leaving. Father Stone thought about it, peeking out of the doorway, but he was still frightened. He didn't want to provoke this guy in any way.

"Lannom?" he said, speaking into his chest. "I think somebody was in here, but they didn't say anything."

Chief Lannom watched as the man in the uniform exited the cathedral quietly, but quickly, and got into his delivery van. The red lights flashed brightly as the engine was revved and the van pulled off.

"Maybe they just changed their mind," Aquila said.

"Hello, Father Matthew," Taberah said, the timbre of the deep ghoulish voice vibrating in the booth. *"I'm certain by now that you've heard about the massacre this morning – at least, what the press is calling a massacre. I prefer to call it justice."*

"It's him," Lannom whispered as he listened in. He grabbed his radio and pressed the button. "All units, standby. We're about to go." He grabbed his sidearm – a .38 Smith & Wesson and checked the chambers as the others tightened their bulletproof vests.

"I made your commissioner an offer – hold the guilty responsible, and there would be no further loss of life, but he refused," Taberah continued. *"So I had to take his life, and many others as well."*

"Let's go!" Lannom said. The doors on the back of the white van swung open as Daly, Aquila and Lannom jumped out. The uniformed officers who were stationed a block away in each direction came out of their cars, guns drawn and proceeded toward the cathedral. Other cruisers created a perimeter a few blocks out. Churchgoers gasped as they rushed inside and surrounded the booth; some of the less elderly ones began to make their way outside, all the while looking back to see exactly what the fuss was about.

"I made you an offer as well, Father. Convince your friend to turn himself in, in exchange for the life of your family, but it seems you made another deal with your true family."

"Taberah!" Chief Lannom yelled through the bullhorn. "This is Chief Aubrey Lannom of the NYPD. I want you to come out – now! The building is surrounded!"

"But then, I realized something," Taberah continued. *"This is about retribution. This is about the guilty and the innocent.*

Your family should remain safe. Your family is innocent but you, Matthew Stone, are guilty, and today I pass sentence."

"If you have any weapons, throw them out now and come out with your hands up! You've got ten seconds!" Lannom screamed. His .38 was trained firmly on the small wooden booth, as were the barrels of all the other officers there. The killings from this morning and the past week were fresh in their minds, and no one was taking any chances.

"It is you who shall have judgment Taberah," Matthew said nervously. "You'll never make it out of here alive."

"If I may borrow a line from the good book itself," Taberah continued. *"After all, God is the greatest killer there is."*

"Vengeance is mine," Taberah said. *"I will repay."*

The explosion was massive, shattering both of the confessional booths and blowing Chief Lannom and the other officers into the pews behind them. Those that were worshiping upfront screamed in terror as the blaring sound echoed through the high ceilings of the cathedral, and many ran toward the doors as the place filled with thick gray smoke. Chief Lannom was knocked unconscious, as were many other officers, under a few collapsed pews. A bloodied and bruised Aquila crawled around blindly on his hands and knees, searching for his gun and the chief.

"Chief Lannom?" Aquila shouted, coughing as he felt around with one hand. Suddenly, his hand plunged into something wet, warm and squishy. As the smoke began to clear, he brought his hands to his face, and they were covered with blood.

Under his hands, were the body and innards of the former detective, Matthew Stone.

CHAPTER SEVEN

Sean & Diane

Detective Sean Coughlin sat on the bed in his hotel room, watching with wide eyes as the scene unfolded on the news. Helicopters caught overhead footage of the shootout between Taberah's men and the officers at the ceremony. He watched in horror as policemen, who scattered for their lives, were chased and mowed down by assailant's bullets. Downtown was a war zone. There were so many casings that you could spot them on the concrete – even from overhead. He felt so helpless, and what was worse was he probably would have been closer to catching Taberah if he left Chance alive. Chance was his best lead at the moment – well – and Wakefield's claims. He couldn't corroborate a thing he told him, but Sean still believed him.

He was too slow to save the commissioner. On television, he saw that the officer was so pinned down that they weren't even been able to rescue the commissioner's body. When the SWAT team arrived, they killed more than a few of Taberah's army. With massive losses on both sides the point was made – with the right leadership and the right weapons, somebody could bring war to the NYPD's doorstep – and possibly win. Of course, it was just after ten at night, and this was the fourth time he watched the coverage since it happened. He made a mental note of that then grabbed the remote and promptly changed the channel to a comedy about a black family he liked. He looked at the empty bottle of whiskey on the nightstand and felt disappointed. There was no mini bar in that cheap spot, but it was all he could afford on such short notice, and there was nothing else in that remote area. He was extremely thirsty, though.

Sean got off the bed and ran his hands through his hair, which was really long as of late. As he got off the bed, he caught a glimpse of himself in the oval-shaped mirror on the wall; his pale stomach stuck out about a half inch from his gray t-shirt. He was aware that he had let himself go, in general, but he wasn't feeling too great about himself after letting all his friends die around him. Not to mention he hadn't seen his son, Danny, in quite a while; and even though they weren't together, he missed Danielle. It did no good to consider that; she had made it clear that she had moved on. There was a space though – a very small place in him that still believed. He grabbed his jeans off the floor and slipped them on. He decided to go down the hall to the machine and get himself a soda and maybe some water. He'd give Danielle a call when he got back. Suddenly, the phone rang, and he hoped it was his family. He was anxious all day about their safety; hoping and praying she took his advice to keep them out of the city.

He grabbed the phone off the nightstand and turned it on.

"Dani?" he said nervously. "You alright?"

"*It's Diane,*" the voice answered abruptly. "*Diane Khan.*"

He heard the chaos of sirens and people yelling in the background. He recognized the distinct horns that fire trucks employed, honking and wailing through the streets. It was pandemonium.

"Where are you?" he asked. "What's going on?"

"*I'm at the scene right now,*" she replied. "*It's a mess.*"

"What scene? What are you talking about?" Sean asked.

"*You haven't heard?*" Diane shot back. "*There was a bomb at your friend's church – Matthew. It's all over the news.*"

Silence filled the short pause, then she said, *"He's dead, Sean."*

Grief welled up in Sean's chest and shot through his body. He grabbed the remote and changed the channel back to the news; and sure enough, there it was. The camera was showing an overhead view of the cathedral with smoke still floating up from the doors. In addition to numerous police cruisers, two fire trucks were parked in front blaring, but there were no flames – only smoke. A few people, coughing from the smoke, were escorted out by uniforms. A young male reporter was now in front of the building, holding a microphone as he gestured behind him.

"Damn it, Matthew," Sean hissed, closing his eyes tightly. "I told him to get out of town. It was Taberah, wasn't it?"

"It's hard to get anything right now. All I know is that they were on some kind of stakeout here," Diane said. *"Lannom's in critical condition, and Daly and your partner are banged up pretty bad. They're being treated now at St. Vincent's. After I finish up here, I'll be heading down there."*

How did he know Matthew was there? He thought to himself.

"Listen to me, Diane. You call me as soon as you know something – you hear?" Sean stated. "I'm still on this case."

"I hear you," Diane said.

"And watch your back," Sean added. "Shoot first."

He hung up the phone, flopped down on the edge of the bed, and put his head in his hands. Visions of Matthew and him in school and at the academy flashed through his mind. He remembered the time they smeared toothpaste on the backs of everyone's combination locks and laughed themselves silly about it. He stood as his best man when he married Danielle and kept everyone laughing at the reception. He thought about them busting in doors together after the FTF was formed and the comfort he felt that his best friend had his back every time. He felt the hotness of the tears on his face and watched them fall down on to the cheap tan carpeting beneath him. After a few minutes, he got up and went to the bathroom and threw cold water on his face. He cleared his throat, sat back down on the bed and dialed Matthew's mother.

***

Mayor Washington stepped up to the podium slowly as the cameras flashed, straightening his claret striped tie and navy blue suit. He changed his clothing from earlier in the day because that suit had the commissioner's blood all over it. His personal security detail was increased by two more men, and each of them stood right behind him, scanning the crowd of reporters intently. This morning was a disaster, a tragedy – but what was even more of a tragedy was watching the deputy commissioner try to take over, he thought. He was a short man with wisps of flyaway gray hair and he always seemed to fumble over his words. It became clear immediately that he didn't have the slightest idea about how these killings were related to one another or about the killer himself. It was a good thing he spent so much time grilling Kavanaugh for answers, he thought to himself, or he might not even know. At any rate, thirty-eight police officers were killed in one day, three in the previous week, and now, a priest who was a former homicide detective was murdered. The press was already all over it, splashing the news and papers with headlines like "City Under Siege" and "Are We To Blame?" dousing an already inflammatory situation with the gasoline of emotion and reminding the public of the connection to the Harland killing.

This month was nothing short of a whirlwind. It seemed as if every time he visited a fallen officer's house to console the surviving family, he got a call about another one. Tonight was supposed to have been the night they caught the bastard. Chief Lannom called the mayor's office personally to update him on the new lead, and now he was in a coma. That was one of his many stops later that evening, after he was finished there. In times like this, the city needed real leadership and they needed solutions. That's what he was there to give.

"Thank you for coming ladies and gentlemen," Washington said somberly. *"There will be no questions this evening. This month has been tragic for the people of New York City, with the deaths of innocent citizens and police officers occurring seemingly without fail. We have been steeped in mourning and endless funerals. When will it end?"* he asked passionate-ly. *"The officer-involved shootings were unfortunate accidents, but the killings of these officers are being perpetrated by one man – a terrorist – who calls himself Taberah. This coward and his band of murderers are known as The Flame Syndicate – many were captured today wearing the symbol of their leader – a bright, burning flame. Well, I've come tonight to let him know that our city will not be set aflame by his terroristic acts or torn apart by division and violence. The good, decent people of this city maintain that violence is not the answer and do their utmost to attain peaceful relations with the police, as the police do with them. They wholeheartedly support the men and women who risk their lives daily to protect this city – and as mayor, so do I."*

There was a pause, which was quickly filled with flashing camera lights and clicking shutters.

"However," the mayor continued in a more serious tone, *"We cannot let this violence against our officers continue. In the interest of keeping the public safe and avoiding any escalation of these attacks, I am declaring a curfew in the city of New York. Citizens should return to their homes immediately. Anyone caught outside after 12 am will be arrested. Until further notice, there will be a seven o'clock curfew in the city. All persons are to remain in their homes until this person has been apprehended."* He paused again, letting that statement sink in response to the sound of low grumbles. *"Also,"* he continued, *"A special detail has been formed to police the streets, with the express task of capturing members of the Flame Syndicate. The officers used in this capacity will not interfere with any department's normal ability to police,"* he added. *"But this will be a separate task force, numbering at about four hundred men."* Just then, Washington looked into one of the cameras intently. *"Taberah,"* he continued, *"You will be caught – by any and all means necessary. That is all. Thank you, everyone,"* said the mayor. *"Goodnight."*

The room exploded with questions, flashing lights and more shouting as the mayor exited the stage lined with dark suits – his security detail.

* * *

Jacob drove along the dark, empty streets of downtown Manhattan at a steady pace, his light blue eyes steadily checking the rearview for actual police. After all, he was riding around in a stolen police cruiser wearing a stolen police uniform after the massacre on the NYPD that morning – but it was almost over. After the last piece of work that night, he could go back to his hometown of Joplin, Missouri for a little while. He missed his wife and little girl, Abilene, who was just about five years old. He also missed his grandma, Juju. They were all waiting for him to return, and with good reason. When he arrived home from his tour almost three years before, Jacob came back with severe nightmares. He would jump up in the middle of the night, hearing sounds of automatic gunfire and RPG's in his head with visions of explosions in his mind's eye. He remembered vividly the day his friend, Ross, was killed in the seat next to him and the gaping hole in his helmet as his eyes stared off into nothingness. Now they didn't only come when he was sleeping; any loud noise could set them off, which proved to be a problem on construction sites where he worked occasionally.

After a while, it became clear that he wouldn't be able to hold down any job – at least, not until he could get some help. The government took its own sweet time cutting him a check to see a therapist, and in the interim, he had to pay with what little savings he had. It wasn't long before they were broke. Grandma Juju was living with them as well, but she was getting old herself, and some of that money would have been of help to her. After a while, it looked like it was never going to come. He then got a call from an old friend in his unit, telling him there was a hundred grand in it for him if he would fly to New York and do some of what he did for the government while he served in the war. The irony was that every time he pulled the trigger on one of those rifles, he imagined that it was one of his superiors on the receiving end. He felt used – and forgotten – and this job made him feel useful again, so he was happy to help out an old friend. The money wasn't bad, either; it came right on time. It was amazing how things worked, but more than that Jacob felt he understood the cause of the oppressed and the voiceless. He was a soldier.

"I want you to go to St. Vincent's Hospital in Greenwich," Taberah said a few minutes earlier. *"The chief, Lannom, is*

still alive. He's guarded, but it shouldn't be anything you can't handle. Shoot him! I want the message to be clear, then you can return to your hotel. The remainder of your fee will be waiting."

Jacob grabbed the clear orange prescription bottle from his pocket, shook a few Prazosin into his hand and downed them. He actually looked forward to relaxing; being perched on that roof and the shootout earlier with the cops shook him up in a strange way and put him back in hype mode. His boss was a freaky dude, he had to admit, but he was serious about bringing it to them cops, Jacob thought. That voice – *Taberah's voice* – was almost like some ghoulish commander ordering him on an assignment of the damned. He felt he was on another mission, but this time he wasn't just a grunt – he was a hero. He was working for the oppressed and taking out yet another fascist regime rising up over the people. Maybe he'd finally get a medal.

The police cruiser pulled up fast around the back of the hospital, screeching just slightly as it stopped. On the drive to the hospital, he thought about the easiest way to get in – maybe take out a doctor and take their scrubs, but decided that was a bit too complicated. He didn't want to leave any bodies lying around unnecessarily. He marched through the double doors, the policeman's cap pulled low on his head. The lobby was buzzing with patients and doctors milling about, and he was about to ask the receptionist where to find the chief when he saw a couple of uniformed officers gathered together talking.

"Excuse me fellas," he said, trying to hide his Missouri accent. "Which room can I find the chief in? I wanna pay my respects."

The three of them turned around; Jacob was worried he was found out, but they didn't seem to pay him any special attention. A tall officer with a thick mustache pointed down the hall.

"You take one of those elevators up to six – trauma unit. He's unconscious, though," the officer said matter-of-factly. "He won't hear you."

Jacob nodded and smiled, giving a small salute. "I'll go up anyway."

The gift shop was just to the right, and he stopped in and bought a small bouquet of flowers and a card, which he didn't sign. He carried them to the elevators and took the car up to six. Immediately he saw what looked like detectives with pensive and worried expressions on their faces. He decided not to approach them, but walked up to the receptionist's desk on that floor instead.

"Excuse me," he said as charmingly as he could. "I'm looking for Chief Lannom's room."

She looked up momentarily, then back down. "Down the hall, room 326," she said.

Jacob continued down the hallway, flowers in hand, searching for the right door.

Detective Diane Khan was in the corner of the waiting room along with Daly, Aquila and a few other detectives. Almost every officer was talking about somebody they knew that died that day, but Diane stuck her head out of the huddle to get a good look at the officer walking toward the chief's room.

"Did you see that officer's pants?" she said. "They looked a little short to me."

Daly shook his head. "What are you talking about, Khan?" he said, annoyed.

Diane didn't respond. She proceeded slowly down the hall after the tall young officer with the ill-fitting uniform.

Jacob opened the door slowly. He knew how to be as quiet as possible, but it wasn't necessary. Chief Lannom was being kept alive, at least for the moment, by machines. It would have been easy to just pull the plug, but Taberah gave specific orders for him to be shot, which sent a very clear message that he had been finished off. He closed the door softly and pulled the silencer from his pocket. He pulled the Glock from its holster and screwed it onto the barrel. The thick-soled black boots squeaked slightly on the white and green tile as he approached the bed; the only other sound in the room was the rhythmic pumping of air from the respirator. Lannom looked peaceful. Jacob smiled as he put the cold cylinder to his temple.

"Freeze!" Diane shouted. "Drop that gun right now!"

Jacob did freeze, but he didn't drop the gun. He put his left hand in the air, but the right was still pointed at Lannom's temple.

"If you shoot me, he still dies," Jacob said.

"Drop that gun... and turn around," she repeated firmly.

There was a pause, then suddenly Jacob spun around, aiming the gun at her. For a fraction of a second, there was the slightest look of recognition.

She fired twice, striking him in the head. The police hat flew off as he fell and his body collapsed in a heap on top of Lannom. There was a rush of squeaking footsteps as detectives and officers stampeded toward the noise with their guns drawn. Surprisingly enough, Daly was the first one in, nearly knocking everyone else over with his size and intensity. His eyes went wide as he took in the scene – the silenced pistol on the floor and Jacob's bleeding body lying on top of the Chief's.

"Jesus," he whispered.

He looked at Diane, who, as if in a trance, kept her gun trained on the body. Her face was expressionless.

"You got him," Daly said.

***

Sean pushed the blinds to the side and looked intently out of the window of the hotel room. He had a craving for Moo Shoo Pork, but it had been over a half hour since he placed his order. He was on the phone with Danny. He finally broke down and called them. He couldn't help but be worried.

"So how are things going in school?" Sean asked.

Danny held the phone to his ear, listening but he didn't respond. His hair was a couple shades darker than his father's but still visibly red, and there were a number of scattered freckles across his pale face.

"Are those kids still picking on you?" Sean said. "I'll come down and speak to the principal again."

"Have you caught the killer yet?" Danny asked suddenly. *"I saw the shootings this morning."*

Sean exhaled heavily. He loved his son, but he hated the way he talked – flat and without emotion. It was hard for him to know what mood Danny was in at any given time, but it wasn't his fault. It was part of the disorder.

"Danny, I told you I don't want you following this stuff. The only things you should be focused on are your schoolwork and taking your medicine."

"I've been following the case. I made a scrapbook," Danny added. *"I can help you when we get home."*

"Wait a minute – *get home?"* Sean yelled excitedly. "What are you talking about?"

"Mom says we're coming home in a few days," he replied.

"Let me speak to your mother."

Sean heard nothing but silence for a full minute, then a rumbling exchange.

"Sean?" said Danielle. *"Are you alright?"*

"Yeah, I'm fine. I'm at a hotel. Listen," Sean said firmly. "What is this Danny says about you coming home? I thought I told you guys to stay up there."

"Sean, we don't have any clothes. Danny has to go to school in a couple of days, and I have to go to work." Danielle sighed. *"I'm sure we will be fine, and I'm really tired."*

"Danny told me he was following the shootings again," he added. "I don't want him watching that stuff. It'll upset him."

"Sean, he gets fixated on things – you know this. Now when he's with you, you do what you want, but he's in a pretty good mood today, so I'm not disturbing him," Danielle said. *"I'm getting ready to walk out the door."*

Before he could give her all the reasons why it was totally unnecessary to return to the city, his other line rang. The display read "Diane Khan".

"Dani, hold on a second – I got a call," Sean said. He clicked over to the other line and heard a lot of clamor in the background. "Diane? What's up?"

"Sorry to call so late," Diane said. *"I'm down at the hospital – somebody just tried to kill the chief. I got him, though,"* she added. *"It was crazy. The mayor was coming to visit Lannom; now he wants to give me a medal or something."*

"Whoa." Sean was shocked at the lengths this guy would go to see as many police dead as possible. But that was great for Diane, he thought. "What did this guy look like?"

"Tall, white with blond hair," Diane said. *"Young kid. This mean anything to you?"*

"Nah – nothing at all. How's the chief?" he asked.

"Still in a coma. He might not make it," she replied.

Sean exhaled loudly; he hadn't really meant to, but it was the built up frustration of this whole thing. He was exhausted.

"What's the matter?" she asked.

"It's just, I feel like a coward hiding out here while all my friends are dying. I mean," Sean added, "I don't know what to do. I mean, after Rosie... I feel like I can't trust anyone."

"Maybe you should come back then," she said. *"You won't feel right until you do something."*

There was silence for a moment, then she spoke again.

"You can trust me, you know," Diane said.

The statement made him feel really good for the first time in a long time and made him think of Danielle simultaneously who he left waiting on the other line. She said that to him once. Funny, he never recalled her making that statement until now.

"Oh!" Sean yelled out. "Diane, I'm sorry – I gotta call you back. I left somebody on the other line."

"I'll be around."

The phone hung up, and Sean tried his ex-wife again, but this time the call went straight to voicemail. He told himself not to get crazy; maybe it died or she left it someplace. He sat back against the pillows and felt a fullness in his chest that he hadn't felt for a long time – if ever. He thought about Danielle; there was so much history between them, and although some of it was good, most of it was marred by some sort of difficulty. As much as he wanted it, it didn't look like they would ever reconcile. Over the years, he saw other women here and there, but the truth was he never really let go of Danielle, even after the divorce was finalized. Maybe he was holding himself back from something good, he thought.

Now, here was Diane; even though he didn't know her well, there was a certain self-assuredness about her – a danger even – something exciting that he hadn't seen in other women. Usually if they were dangerous, they were crazy too, but Diane seemed to have her head on straight. She was a cop. She understood the drive, the excitement, the violence, and the sense of duty. In any case, he felt something that night at the sports bar; there was definitely a spark. She looked damn good too. He let himself think about her body a little bit more, then picked up his phone and dialed her back.

***

"Come on Danny! I'm ready to go!" Danielle shouted. "It's supposed to rain and I do *not* want to get caught in it!"

Danny Coughlin didn't hear her; he rarely ever did. The earphones were buried in his ears as he watched the coverage of the church bombing on his tablet. He received a notification as soon as it happened; he followed every news channel there was. Even though his mother didn't want him to know, he was well aware that these killings were connected. He didn't have all of the pieces, but he knew one thing – he was going to help his father solve them. A picture flashed on the small screen of a younger Matthew Stone smiling in his uniform, and Danny remembered the kind man that used to come over to the house and try to make him laugh. He also thought about the quarter he pretended to pull from behind his ear. Danny always thought it was stupid, but he did like the fact that Matthew tried to be nice to him. Usually adults ignored him altogether.

He set the tablet down and tied his shoe – first making a left bunny ear, then a right bunny ear, then looping them around each other. He repeated this six times, as he always did, but he wasn't aware of the number. Danny wasn't even aware that he straightened up the room where he was staying and alphabetized all of the books, but he knew he couldn't wait to return home, back to his room where everything was neat and familiar.

Danielle came storming into the room, a small red coat in her left hand and her trench coat flying. She pulled the earphone bud out of his right ear. "This is why you can't hear me – you got these things buried in your ears!" she said. She handed him the coat. "Put your coat on. We're leaving. Come and say goodbye to your grandfather."

Danny put on his coat – left arm first, then right. He zipped it and snapped the buttons from the bottom to the top. He put the ear bud back in and continued listening to the rest of the news report as he walked out of the room.

"Dad!" Danielle yelled from the bottom of the stairs. "We're leaving!"

Instead her father came from the living room, dragging his feet along the wooden floors in his dark gray slippers. His wild curly gray hair gave a youthful touch to his otherwise hardened face. He wasn't really as old as he appeared, but he moved that way – something that frustrated Danielle in her later years. Orrin Smalls had lost a bit of weight, but he was still a large man. Danny didn't like him much. He gave Danielle a big bear hug, which she sorely needed, then patted Danny on the head – a gesture he didn't acknowledge, but stared at him instead as if he were a strange animal.

"He keeps his head in those things, doesn't he?" Orrin asked.

"That's how they are nowadays, Dad," Danielle said. "We have to get going. I want to get home before it's too late." She tapped Danny on the shoulders. "Tell mom I love her."

"Why don't you tell her yourself?" he asked.

She smiled, gave her father a kiss on the cheek, grabbed Danny by the shoulders, and they walked out the door.

***

As she got off the highway and drove through the streets of Queens, Danielle could feel the desolation; as if the town had been evacuated in an instant. No longer were there crowds of young men in front of the Chinese restaurants and bodegas. Their presence was now replaced by ubiquitous crowds of officers who roamed the sidewalks with their hands poised atop their guns. Every few minutes, a cruiser whisked by, and she shook her head. She hated what she allowed that job to do to her family, but she felt strongly that she could no longer be married to Sean as long as he was a police officer. She looked in the rearview mirror at her son, who was in the back seat. Only God knew what the divorce did to him, on top of what he was already dealing with, she thought. Danielle knew from her research on his disorder that he had a problem connecting with people emotionally, and communicating socially. Now that he was older, he was even harder to reach – especially with his father gone.

They pulled up to the house where they all once lived as a family and parked in the driveway. When she got to the door, she barely got it open before Danny rushed past her, up the stairs, and into his room. Danielle just shook her head. What he *really* needed was some time with his father, she thought.

Danny closed the door to his room. He placed the tablet on his desk, aligning it with the edge of the table, then snatched his coat off hurriedly and hung it in his closet next to the other red things. He took off his sneakers and placed them on the floor in the closet – toes pointed out. He hung the book bag he was carrying on the back of his door and pulled out his composition notebook which was marked with the words "The Taberah Case" on the front in black pen. The room was in immaculate condition. His multicolored bedspread was neatly folded back just under the pillows, the clothes were put away in their proper places, and all the books around the room were in size order on their shelves. Most of them, except for those left over from his early childhood were about serial killers and famous criminals. Some were detective stories and true crime. Above his desk was a large piece of construction paper that was taped to the wall, also with the heading "The Taberah Case," but was littered with newspaper clippings of each murder – both of police officers and civilians. In the right-hand corner, a box was drawn containing the names of the detectives that were part of his father's unit, each with handwritten dates next to their newspaper photos. Each box had a straight line flowing from it to the left – connecting it to the newspaper clipping of Eric Harland. The names, pictures, and dates of other innocent African-Americans that had fallen were pasted under his. Danny stood up on his wooden chair with black magic marker in his hand, and wrote the name "Matthew Stone." Then he stood back, looking at it for a long time. He sat back down in his chair, grabbed his tablet and typed a name into the search engine – Eric Harland.

Neither Danielle nor her son was aware of the black van that was parked across the street or those in it – waiting for the moment they arrived.

✳✳✳

The sound of howling and frightened screams permeated the air around him. He couldn't recognize their voices, but somehow he knew them. The streets were dreary; the pavement slick with rain water, but shining in the spots that were illuminated with streetlights. He looked above him; the buildings that enclosed him had windows, but all of them were dark, with no one moving about behind them. Detective Sean Coughlin walked alone slowly – looking around and peering into every dark corner. He saw no one, but he felt their eyes on him. He couldn't remember exactly how he got there or even what he was looking for, but something told him to keep moving. He felt at his side for his gun, but there was nothing there. How could he have been so stupid to leave it back home? He thought.

Suddenly, there was a figure up ahead – small, hunched over and standing perfectly placid under one of the streetlamps. Its face couldn't be seen, but Sean got the sense that it was a woman. Steadily, he approached the form and found an elderly black woman with gray hair staring at him through a veil. She wore a plain black dress with her wrinkled hands folded in front of her. For a long time, she said nothing.

"What are you doing all alone out here?" Sean asked.

The woman said nothing. Instead, she turned and looked away.

"It's late," he added. "Let's get you home."

"You killed her," the woman said suddenly. Her abruptness startled him.

"Who? I didn't kill anyone," Sean said nervously.

The woman turned back to face him, and Sean could see tears in her eyes.

"My granddaughter... you killed her," the old woman continued. "She never did anything to anyone, just a little ol' thing..."

Sean was scared now, but he didn't know why. He didn't know this lady or what she was talking about, but he definitely wanted to leave – right now.

"I don't know what you're talking about," he replied. "It's not me."

The old woman's face turned into a skull – eyes into pitch black holes and the mouth opened wide, gaping at him...

Then just like that she disappeared, and he was alone again. In the next instant, he felt a sense of urgency, as if a great danger was about to come upon him. There was a rushing noise, and as he turned around he saw a great wall of water tumbling toward him – the front foaming. He turned and tried his best to run, but it was as if someone had pushed a slow-motion button on his movements, leaving them long and drawn out. The wave smashed into him, thrusting him forward and turning him upside down as the waters covered his head. Sean could feel himself beginning to drown ¬– the undeniable sense of doom that came with losing your breath; the indisputable feeling of dying. He noticed somehow in the midst of this panic that there were others in the water with him – bodies. Their eyes were open and stared into his as they floated underwater past him.

Sean recognized their faces – there was a young girl, who looked about eight, whose name was Asjai Jordan, but he couldn't remember how he knew that. There was a large man named Eddie Gadson and a boy who looked about twelve years old. They were all submerged along with him. Instead of drowning with them, however, he was instantly up in the air as if he was being carried. In fact, he was being carried. As he looked down, he saw green grass beneath him – and rows of tombstones. He was in a cemetery. Sean looked down at the fingers that were holding him. They were gleaming white bones – the fingers of a skeleton gripping his body. He didn't want to look in the other direction, but he couldn't stop himself. Sean turned slowly to his left, looking up and he saw the jawbone of the skeleton. The head looked down at him with huge hollowed eyes and a black hood draped just over the skull. Suddenly, it stopped moving, and Sean looked back to see where they were. He looked over... and there were three tombstones.

Danielle Coughlin. Daniel Coughlin. Sean Coughlin.

The grave was open in front of his tombstone, and it was then that he began to struggle, but the death-like figure dumped him in, and he fell for what felt like forever. When he finally collapsed in a heap at the bottom, he tried to claw against the sides, but instead his fingers were buried in the dirt's moistness. The hole began to fill up with dirt – rapidly. The drowning feeling was beginning to set in again...

Sean jumped up from his bed, gasping for air. He could practically taste the dirt in his throat. He looked around the dark hotel room, trying to get some indication of where he was, until he remembered. He laid back down on the pillow that was now damp with his own perspiration and stared at the ceiling.

If he didn't stop Taberah, he would kill him... and his family.

***

The black Corvette with the damaged trunk shot down the highway like an injured bat; tires spitting up a mist of water from the falling rain. Sean gripped the steering wheel tightly, zipping in and out between cars. He called Danielle's cell again, but got no answer; her father said she left hours ago. The Beretta was in the passenger's seat next to him, but he silently wished he had a shotgun. He would have to make do. He pulled off on Rockaway Blvd., only a few blocks from the home he and Danielle once shared. At the light, he chambered the first round. Sean's eyes darted in every direction as he turned right onto his street; he shifted the car into neutral to quiet the engine and let the car roll into the driveway – right behind Danielle's silver station wagon. So she *had* come home, he thought. All the windows in the whole house were dark except for one room on the top floor – the room he and Danielle once shared. More than likely, she and Danny were fine, he assured himself, but just in case he wouldn't go in through the front door. As he crept around toward the back, he got his keys out of his pocket. Even after the divorce, Danielle never demanded that he give her the house keys. True, he did still come by to pick up Danny, but to Sean this was one of the strongest indicators that they would one day reconcile.

He slid the key into the lock slowly, turned it ever so gently, and opened it. The lower level was quiet, but he could hear a television on in the room upstairs. He kept the gun in front of him, trying to focus his eyes in the darkness. He wanted to call out to them, but he couldn't take the risk of tipping off whoever might be in the house. He made the journey across the living room floor; the carpet helping him with his covert mission, and he began his journey up the stairs. Every step was agonizing as each one sounded a light creak, which Sean could only pray was overshadowed by the television. As he reached the last one, he peeked around the corner – and saw nothing – only the light from the bedroom. He closed his eyes, took a deep breath, and said a silent prayer. Then, he raised his gun and charged in.

"Danielle?" he said.

The bed was neatly covered with a floral print comforter. The perfume bottles on her dresser were neatly arranged. There didn't seem to be anything out of place, but she wasn't here.

Sean looked around the room, trying to sense any indication of intruders. He slid open the door to the closet with his left hand; the gun raised in his right, but there were only clothes. He walked over to the window next to her nightstand, and that's when he noticed the phone. Her cellphone was sitting on top, plugged into a charger. That was odd; she never went anywhere without her phone – even if she had to charge it in the car. He instinctively looked out of the window, as he always did when he lived there, peering into the dark street below.

The cloaked figure came up behind him slowly, drifting almost as if a vapor entered the room, and Sean felt an explosion go off in his brain. He went down hard. His head was ringing and his eyes blurry as pain shot through his neck. The last thing he saw was the blurry image of a pale white skeletal face looking down on him, with jet black eyes just like in the dream.

"Welcome home, Sean," Taberah said.

＊＊＊

Sean Coughlin awoke to an inundation of pain and discomfort. His head was throbbing, his eyes were stinging, his wrists and ankles ached sharply and the skin was chafed, as if it was being cut into. He was tied to the bed – handcuffed, he thought. As he started to regain consciousness, he realized he felt wet all over. He tried to move, fighting through the beginning feeling of nausea, but he was restrained. As he opened his eyes and tried to get a look at what had him bound, they only hurt more, as if they were on fire. The insides of his nostrils began to sting a little as well, and when he took a deep breath, they stung more immensely. He licked his lips, instantly tasting a pungent liquid, and as the smell became familiar he suddenly realized what was happening to him.

He was covered in gasoline.

"You should be familiar with the restraints around your wrists, Detective Coughlin," Taberah chuckled. *"After all, you've made a career out of slapping them on the arms of my people."*

Sean spat. "Only those who deserved it, and you're no different. Just a criminal... like all the rest," he said.

"Yes," Taberah hissed. *"I guess I am... a murderer, a terrorist, as they say. I wasn't always, but when every institution fails, the truly courageous have only one recourse – to take matters into our own hands."*

"You try to make yourself sound like some kind of a hero," Sean laughed. His eyes still burned, but he wanted to see his captor, so he fought through the pain and kept them open. It was becoming slightly more bearable. "Is that what you think? You're a *hero*? *Cops* are heroes. You're just another scumbag killer who destroyed a bunch of families..."

"And I suppose the hero is you, Detective? But your hands are not free of the stain of blood. The only difference is," Taberah stated, *"I've killed the guilty."*

"What about Connie Castobell?" Sean said, coughing. The fumes were getting to him. "What'd she ever do? What about all the wives of those officers? Their children?"

The skull shook back and forth forlornly inside the black hood. *"Collateral damage, but the victims by your hand have families too. This is a war, Detective. We didn't start it, but we certainly will finish it. Sometimes people get caught in the crossfire. You should know."*

"Who are you?!" Sean yelled. "Stop being a coward. Show your face – it's only me and you here!"

"I will show you a face," was the reply. *"It's the face of a man who was innocent once. Perhaps you will recognize it."*

The black-gloved hands pushed a small card of some sort near his face. As it got closer, Sean realized it was a picture, and even through the stinging in his eyes, he knew he recognized the person. It was a face that had come to him many nights in his dreams – the smiling face of Eric Harland.

"The significance of today – is it lost to you, Detective?" Taberah growled. *"It is the eighteenth of November – the same day that you hastened Eric's departure, and now on this same day, I shall hasten your own."*

Sean began to cry as he heard the distinct flick of a metal lighter. He cried for his great love Danielle, whom he would never see again. He cried for his son, Danny, whom he would never get to see grow up. There was so much he wanted to do now, so much he wanted to say. He would quit the force and convince Danielle that she was the most important thing in his life. He would devote more time to Danny and try and understand more about his disorder and what he was going through. In those final moments, he finally, for the first time understood what he had taken from Eric Harland when he shot him. He had taken his entire lifetime.

"I'm sorry," he cried. "I'm so sorry..."

The figure grabbed at its own head and pulled the mask of the skull from it, and Sean instantly recognized the face – the face of someone he came to trust. At first, he didn't understand, and he searched the face for the possible reasons, but found none. Nothing he came up with or that raced through his head made any sense. Then, he looked into the eyes. They were eyes he saw before – a long time ago, and he always knew he would see them again.

"Dear God," he whispered.

"*If you see him,*" Taberah replied, "*You can tell him yourself.*"

Taberah threw the lighter at the bed, and it immediately was enveloped in bright orange flames. They grabbed and snatched at his body, and he thrashed in pain, pulling violently against the bed frame as the fire ate away at his skin. Soon his screams were quieted as they were overpowered by the roar of the flames, and Detective Sean Coughlin gave yield to death.

***

Danielle and Danny struggled vigorously as they lay tied to each other in the back of the van; their sounds muffled by silver masking tape. Only a couple hours earlier, Danielle heard the doorbell ring while she was making dinner, and when she opened the door was instantly grabbed by two masked men in black. They covered her face, wrapped her in the tape and threw her in the back of a van parked across the street. A few seconds later, Danny was thrown in along with her, and they were tied together. She closed her eyes, silently praying that the death that was coming would be quick. It brought her no comfort that Sean was right to be worried about them; but the van never went anywhere. They weren't harmed in the least, and after a while she felt confident that they were safe – at least for now. They managed to shake the cloths from their faces, but it wasn't long before they saw the glow of the fire dancing in the windows of the van. Danny kept licking his lips and twitching his face back and forth until the tape fell off. He bent his head down and gnawed at the tape wrapped around his chest. It wasn't long before he freed himself, then tore the tape from his mother's mouth and face, freeing her. They burst out of the van and onto the street, immediately feeling the blaring heat on their faces. They stood in front of what used to be their home, watching helplessly as it disintegrated into a sea of flames before their eyes. Both of them were so engulfed that they failed to hear the sirens as the fire trucks pulled up or notice that Sean's car was in the driveway. Danielle felt someone grab her shoulder, pulling her back.

"Ma'am, step onto the sidewalk please," demanded a comforting voice. Danielle turned to find a young fireman in his full uniform and gear staring back at her, and for a second, she was concerned about her appearance.

"Is this your home?"

Danielle nodded, but nothing was really registering. A number of firemen donned their oxygen masks and some had already begun shooting streams of water onto the house. She just grabbed Danny close to her and held him as tight as she could. She looked down at him, but he hadn't said a word.

"You two are fortunate to have made it out," the fireman continued. "This is a really serious blaze." He paused for a minute, looking over the house.

The top half was completely roofless and spurting out wild flames into the cold night air, but it had already spread to the bottom, where they were beginning to fight it.

"Is there anyone else in the house?" he added.

Just then, Danny set his sights on the black Corvette in the driveway with the smashed-in trunk.

"Why is Dad's car here?" Danny asked.

At that moment, Danielle's heart sank.

***

CHAPTER EIGHT

His Father's Son

A bird drifted for a long time in a pocket of air as Danny watched from below. The sky was pewter-colored with the feeling of an impending downpour that had not yet arrived. Next to him, his mother, Danielle Coughlin, cried silently into her handkerchief, but Danny's eyes wandered – and so did his mind. He thought about the last funeral held there; where the assassination of Detective Donnell Haines occurred. He figured that Taberah would hardly strike the same way twice; he was way too clever for that, but it didn't deter Danny from focusing on every tombstone, looking for a sniper. Danny thought, if he chose to attack, this would be an ideal time – when literally tens of thousands of officers were present. An ocean of navy blue uniforms flooded the driveway and the green grass of the cemetery, just as they had filled the streets beforehand. This was the largest departmental funeral in the NYPD's history. Over forty officers were being laid to rest including Detectives Rosemary Velez and Sean Coughlin.

Danny was not unaware that most of the people were crying, but he was not. It wasn't that he didn't feel the somber mood of the occasion; he just didn't feel the need to shed tears. Indeed, he would miss his father, yet Danny always wished he knew more about what his father did, which was the reason the case became so important to him. He knew how important it was to his father – even more so now that he died for it. He listened closely to the things said about Sean. There were a number of people who had shining compliments for the man they barely knew, but Danny had a feeling that the ones who knew him best would be laying right beside him soon enough – all of them silenced at once, as well as their secrets. He met Chief Lannom a few times before. He wasn't in attendance, but he heard people talking. No one was sure if he would ever wake up from the coma. There were a few people, however, who he seemed likely to get answers from – Detective Reginald Aquila, who was his father's partner when he died, and Detective Diane Khan, who had some very nice things to say about him. She even read a poem at the church, but Danny couldn't remember the words.

The ocean of blue uniforms became speckled with white as all of the officers lifted their gloves in a salute. Two officers, stiff as statues, folded an American flag into a neat triangle and placed it in the trembling hands of Danielle, then saluted both of them. The seven officers that were lined up a few feet from them raised their rifles, taking aim at imaginary targets.

"READY... FIRE!" an officer commanded.

The air echoed with the shots fired from the twenty-one-gun salute, accompanied by the click-clack sound of their bolts and the smoking brass casings that fell onto the grass that was blowing. The command was repeated twice more, followed by two more volleys of gunfire and the whine of bagpipes that filled the air that November morning. Everyone got up and consoled one another with hugs and pats on the back. Danny looked over at his mother, who had sort of folded into herself, weeping silently behind her dark glasses as she gripped the flag for dear life. Danny got up; he had a distinct purpose in his mind. He walked briskly over to Detective Aquila, who served only moments ago as one of his father's pallbearers. Aquila saw him approaching and immediately bent down on his knees to his level and placed a concerned hand on his shoulder. He saw the boy once or twice, but never really spoke to him before. It must be horrible for him, he thought.

"Hey Danny," he said in a concerned tone. "How you doin'?"

"I'm fine," he replied.

"You know, I didn't know your father that well," he continued, "But he seemed like a really great guy. A lot of people liked him. We're gonna catch the person responsible – you know that, right?"

"I would like you to do something for me," Danny said.

"Okay... If I can do it, I will."

"Can you get me my father's property from the night he was found?" Danny asked. "Nobody has turned it over to us yet. His house keys should be among his belongings; I want to get into his apartment to collect some things."

"Oh." Aquila stood up. "Okay, Danny – I'll see what I can do."

"Thank you Detective." Danny shook his hand, turned, and walked away.

Aquila shook his head. All due respect for Sean, he thought, but that was a strange boy.

***

Danielle opened the door to the apartment gingerly, standing back as Danny walked in ahead of her. She convinced herself that she was ready to go in, but during the drive over realized she was wrong.

It was only a few days after the funeral, but earlier that morning Detective Aquila came to their home bearing Sean's keys and some of his personal belongings. His car, which had been repaired at the expense of the department as a future gift for Danny, accompanied him as well but his former partner also came bearing news. There were two guns found in Sean's car that were not his he explained, and even though they found Sean's fingerprints on them they also had the fingerprints of another man – Gary "Chance" Laurain, who was killed by Sean after an apparent collision. When ballistics ran the bullets, they found that they matched the ones that killed Officer Paul Lao earlier that month. It was obvious to them that this man not only worked for Taberah, but was also trying to kill Sean when he himself was shot. This cleared Sean of any suspected wrongdoing, but there was more. Aquila believed that Sean was close to finding out who this killer was when he died, and although he wasn't able to remove any files from the precinct, he was sure that Sean kept some evidence at his home. He agreed to keep that information between them, at least for the moment, giving young Danny the opportunity to look through his father's place before they did, provided he didn't remove anything. He handed her the keys with the assurance that if she needed anything else, she was to call him.

Almost as soon as he left, Danny demanded that she take him over right away. Danielle couldn't say she understood. He had not even seen him every month when he was alive, but she figured this might be some form of closure for him, and she didn't want to interfere, so she agreed to take him over. Now, they were there.

"You can leave me here," Danny said to her. "I want to be alone."

She was relieved. Danielle wasn't exactly thrilled about leaving her son in her dead ex-husband's apartment, but she would be even less thrilled if she had to stay. He brought his backpack with him along with his tablet that he never parted with. He also had a large piece of construction paper rolled up in a bag with him as well. She guessed it was all part of the process.

"Okay," she said. "I'll be downstairs in the car. Call me when you're ready to leave." She pulled him close, hugged him tightly for a long time, then kissed him on the forehead. "I love you. Be careful," she added. She waved and disappeared down the staircase.

Danny closed the door, locked all three locks and fastened the chain. He went straight into the kitchen, opened the freezer, and found some fudge ripple ice cream, which he ate promptly from the carton with a spoon. He unpacked his bag, pulled out his composition notebook and pen and placed them on the kitchen table. He unrolled the construction paper onto the floor, which was his collage of Taberah's carnage – a catalogue of killings. There was also a newspaper in his book bag, which he retrieved; the front page of which bore a smiling picture of his father. He found a pair of scissors, cut it out and taped it in the box of fallen officers. He also wrote the date next to it – November 18th, 2014.

He walked around the apartment, taking in different things – the furniture, pictures, and the way things were arranged. All the while, he had his headphones placed firmly in his ears as he listened to some of the news coverage of old protests from several years ago. Finally, he went into his dad's bedroom. The bed hadn't been made; the comforter and sheets were askew, and there were some clothes on top of it as well. Danny made the bed and put the clothing in the drawers. There was a shirt that needed to be hung up and he went to the closet to do so. When he opened it up, immediately he saw his dad's gun – the Colt 1911 – hanging from the pole in the cowhide holster. The nickel plating glistened in the overhead light, and Danny turned the gun from side to side, watching it shine. There was a box at his feet inside the closet. He dragged it out into the living room and set it next to his things. He opened the box and found dozens upon dozens of files, as well as loose papers. Danny sat down, cross-legged, and went through every one of them, making notes of appropriate information in his notebook. He realized his father had done a lot of work – probably more than anybody knew. He just didn't have a chance to finish it.

After he found everything there was to find here, Danny went back into the bedroom and opened the closet once more. He got out the cowhide holster, slipped both his arms into it, and fastened it tight. Then he closed the closet door and looked into the full-length mirror hung on the back. He took out the pistol and held it with both of his small hands. He never held a gun before; his father always kept them tightly locked up when he was alive. It looked mammoth compared to his tiny wrists, but he used all his strength to hold it up. He aimed it at the glass and looked into the barrel through the reflection. The blackness of the hole seemed eternal, yet fascinating.

"Bang bang," he whispered.

***

"Yes honey, mommy will be home soon," Diane said sweetly into the phone. "You listen to grandma until I get there, understand? Okay... Okay... Bye bye, honey."

Detective Diane Khan was exhausted. She jetted around her apartment quickly, navigating through the dozens of taped brown boxes that were scattered about the place. She gave an acceptance speech earlier that day at a ceremony where she was awarded for her role in saving Chief Lannom's life and killing the sniper responsible for the deaths of at least three officers. He was later found to have been a soldier who served in the United States Army. Mayor Washington and his family were there, and he himself praised her as a hero. She also used that forum to inform the city of New York that she would no longer be working there and of her plans to return to Florida. The truth was she had no intention of remaining a police officer. All she cared about right now was making it home for her daughter. Her flight was in less than two hours, and all this stuff needed to be ready so that the movers could pick it up. There was a knock at the door; she naturally assumed it was moving men. Instead, when she opened it, she found a young boy with a backpack standing in front of her, staring impassively.

"My name is Danny," he said immediately. "I'm Sean Coughlin's son. I mean... he was my father," he added.

Diane looked into the hallway, but there was no one behind him. She looked back at him and realized that this was indeed Sean's child; he bore the spitting image of his father.

"Yes, of course – Danny," she said somberly. "We finally met at the funeral. Again, I'm so sorry for your loss."

"Thank you. Can I come in?" Danny asked. "I just have some questions about my father, and I thought you could help me."

"Alright."

Danny walked into the apartment, looking around as if appraising items he was going to purchase. Diane followed the young boy, watching him curiously.

"Can I get you something to drink?" she asked.

Danny just sat down on the couch and was silent for a long time. He shook his head.

"You should have changed your voice," he said. "That's the thing. You should have changed your voice."

"What are you talking about?" Diane asked in a voice not quite her own. "You're not making any sense."

"My father knew. He knew other things as well, and he wrote them all down," Danny continued. "He went to Freeman to interview witnesses. You went to Freeman University, but you stuck out too much. Your English professor remembered you because you were the best at recalling poetry and quotes of the authors you loved. There was only one other person who loved the same ones you did, and both of you seemed to love all the same subjects – Classic Literature, Performing Arts, African-American History. That was another mistake."

Diane's eyes began to go wide and she swallowed hard.

"You did a lot of things right, like in some of the mystery novels. You had to know you would be a prime suspect, so you disappeared. You changed your name," Danny said. "You changed your appearance too. Your hair is different, which was easy, but your skin is also lighter now. Oh, and becoming a police officer? It was all brilliant." Danny stood up and looked around the house. "You're leaving, aren't you? You've killed everyone you wanted to kill, so now it's time to disappear again."

"Danny," Diane smiled. "I know that your father's death must be very hard on you but I think you're confused."

Danny took out his tablet and pressed on it a few times.

"I recorded your speech from earlier today," he said. "I don't really like poetry, but this one was nice." He pressed play, showing Diane the image of herself. "It's called 'Fire-caught' – I looked it up. It's by some guy named Langston Hughes."

"The gold moth did not love him,

So gorgeous, she flew away.

But the gray moth circled the flame

Until the break of day.

And then, with wings like a dead desire,

She fell, fire-caught, into the flame."

"It sounded just like another poem from a long time ago," Danny continued. He pressed on the tablet again, then turned it toward her once more. On it was a younger woman, dark-skinned with jet-black hair. She stood in front of a courthouse, by lawyer Albert Sampson and one Charles Wakefield.

"Tell the mourners mourn in red...'cause there ain't no sense in me bein' dead."

Diane smiled, but there was sadness in her eyes. "He was one of Eric's favorite poets," she said. She reached behind and pulled a small .380 from under her sweater. "Who else have you shown this to, Danny?"

"Detectives Aquila and Daly. They have all the evidence now," he said. "They're already outside."

"Nobody will believe you," Diane laughed. "It's just your word."

"There's no way you could have become a police officer without falsifying your records," Danny said. "When they run your real prints, your real name will come up – Joanna Harland.

You were arrested during that protest, and I know they always fingerprint during arrests."

Diane walked over to the window, looking down at the street. Dozens of detectives were quietly directing people off the streets, while many other officers had their guns trained on the building. The streets were taped off in both directions. There was no way out. She turned around quickly and found Danny pointing a Colt .45 at her. She was no longer smiling; her eyes had become callous, piercing into the young boy before her.

"Sean taught you well," she sneered. "But did he teach you how to kill? Did he pass on the family legacy before he left you?"

She walked toward him – slowly and steadily. The gun in her hand was straight and unmoving.

"Your father killed my husband, but he did more than that," she continued. "He stole a lifetime from me – a future that I can never have back! So he got what he deserved – to die screaming and begging for his life as the fire tore the flesh from his bones!"

Danny pulled the hammer back on the .45 with both hands, the ridges leaving rough scrapes on his thumb. He aimed it at her heart, but it was a heavy gun, and he was shaking. He wanted to pull the trigger, to kill her for what she'd done, but he couldn't. After a while, he lowered it. Diane made a face as if she pitied him and continued walking backwards toward the door. She put her hand on the knob and turned it. The gun was still trained on him.

"You're no killer," she said decidedly. "Not yet. But one day, you'll make a really good detective. I'm sure you'll make up for lost time. It's in your blood."

She whisked out of the door, leaving Danny alone in the apartment holding the gun in his hand.

***

As she reached the entrance of her building, Diane saw the rifles rise at attention quickly, but everything slowed down for her. Her mind flashed back to the long nights she spent on the phone with Eric while at college and the warm way he smiled at her when they were riding in that car on the way to the reception. She still saw his eyes in her mind and felt the warmth of his touch on her hand. Then, she saw his eyes again – this time, lifeless, staring off into the distance as the blood poured down his face. She remembered how her heart sank when she heard the gunshots outside of the Rock Steady and how she knew something terrible had happened – and the horrible confirmation when she ran outside and saw for herself. She pulled back the slide on the .380 while her eyes watched the eyes of the officers through the glass door.

"*Joanna Harland!*" boomed the sound from the loud speaker. "*Throw down your weapon, and put your hands above your head! Do it now!*"

There was no way she was surrendering. Her destiny was clear, but she had done what she set out to do. She had avenged him. She was at peace.

"I love you Eric," she whispered. "I'll see you soon."

She darted outside, firing blindly all around her. The officers shouted and screamed as they returned fire, decimating the building's brick frame behind her. The air around them filled with clouds of gun smoke. She fell to the ground and her once beautiful body filled with holes, now struggled to suck in her last few dying breaths. Waves of pain darted through her and tears filled her eyes as they rolled around blindly. She grabbed at the pavement, gripping at it with her fingernails. Then, the movement stopped. SWAT teams and uniformed officers approached slowly, creeping in with their guns trained on the petite young woman who had brought New York City to its knees. Now, she was gone. Joanna Harland, also known as Taberah, was dead.

***

For the next few weeks, the newspapers, blogs, and internet were filled with the amazing and almost unbelievable story of Joanna Harland – the woman whose husband, Eric Harland, was killed by the NYPD on their wedding night, who later transformed herself into *Taberah* – a phantom of bloodshed who brought terror to the hardened officers of that great city. Records were found in her house that proved that she had indeed altered her physical appearance with plastic surgery to disguise her identity and avoid the risk of being recognized while she attended college where she studied Criminal Psychology, among other things. This was a long-thought-out plan to get into the military as Diane Khan where she later met Jacob Anderson – a fact that was uncovered when the wife of the rogue sniper recognized her in pictures with his unit. It was there that she got her first taste for blood, living out her fantasies of killing on the battlefield and testing her mettle.

When she returned to the states, she soon joined the police force in the state of Florida, and after a few years, made detective. Even still, she bided her time. Having already framed Charles Wakefield for the murders of three police officers years ago, she assumed control of his gun-running operations, which gave her access to a wide variety of military-grade firearms, which she now knew how to use. The move also gave her control of his men and connections, which she later utilized to make even more money, while, at the same time, amassed an army right under the noses of the NYPD.

When Taberah first made an appearance and the killings started again, she simultaneously joined the 25th precinct, making it all too easy to find the homes and addresses of the officers on her list. She then picked them off – one by one. The .380 caliber pistol found on her was later linked to the death of Detective Rosemary Velez, in the bathroom of the very precinct where she worked. When her demands to convict guilty officers weren't met, she took the police to war in the bloodiest street battle New York had ever seen, leaving almost forty officers dead and many more wounded. The outcome of that battle left Commissioner Robert Kavanaugh murdered and Chief Aubrey Lannom in a coma. She then sent her friend and fellow soldier, Jacob, on a mission to finish off the still living Chief Lannom, only to kill him instead, in order to cut off one of the few remaining links to her origins.

After the plan succeeded and made her a hero, it also placed her above suspicion. She then used that advantage to take out her most important target of all – Detective Sean Coughlin. If it hadn't been for Danny, Joanna Harland would have been long gone by now and would have gotten away with dozens of murders. When they finally searched her apartment, they found a journal chronicling the details of her entire plan and vision for the future of New York City – a city where the Flame

Syndicate controlled everything through fear and replaced the police force with her own militia group. The evidence inside was used to set Charles Wakefield free, clearing him of the murder charges. If only Sean had been alive to see it.

Danny stood over the grave of his father and stared at the tombstone for a long time. He didn't know exactly what he was feeling; maybe he had wanted to be closer, but neither one of them really knew how. However, he liked the idea of being on a case. He already had a room full of his favorite genre – detective novels. Now, becoming a police officer would have so much more meaning for him than it did in the past. It would be his way to honor his father in death, the way he was never able to in life.

To this, Daniel Coughlin would devote his life. It would become his legacy.

Epilogue

It was a year later – on a breezy morning – November 18, 2015 in a Harlem cemetery that a large man approached the gravestones of two people he once knew in order to pay his respects. The long dark topcoat flapped in the wind as he climbed up the hill carrying a bouquet of flowers in his right hand. The man was Charles Wakefield. The cemetery was relatively empty; he hadn't expected many people to be here, but Eric's grandmother was still alive, so he came extra early so they wouldn't cross paths. Cora never had much use for him. As he came over the hill, he saw two figures standing in front of the place he was planning to visit and wondered who they were. There was a major turnout when Eric died; the entire city rallied and filled the streets over his tragedy. Now, eight years later – Eric Harland was just another young black man in a long line of others who lost their lives unjustly. Someone else besides him saw fit to visit.

Wakefield stood beside the two and placed the flowers on top of Eric's grave. The young girl looked up at him with big, wide dark-brown eyes. He could tell she was young – no more than eight or nine, but there was a maturity about her and an understanding beyond her years. She didn't exactly look sad, but her expression was severe. The girl was beautiful; her skin rich and dark and her jet-black hair twisted into two large braids on both sides. She wore a checkered red and black dress under her dark coat, with white stockings and shiny black shoes. When he saw her expression, Wakefield knew instantly who she was.

The woman by her side leaned over as she sensed his presence, and a slight smile came over her face. Wakefield nodded; he recognized her too, but was even more surprised to see her looking as well as she did. He laid the flowers on Eric's grave and then removed one rose and laid it on Joanna's.

"How you been, Estelle?" he asked.

She shrugged. "Taking it one day at a time. I'm still clean – gotta be for this little one. I got a second chance."

"That's what's up." He knelt down in front of the girl, facing her. "And how you doin'?"

The girl frowned. "I don't know you," she said. "Did you know my parents?"

"I like that," Charles replied, smiling. "Eric was my cousin, which makes us cousins, so I'll be watching out for you from now on." He looked over at the tombstones. "I'm sorry about your pops – that was my man, and your mom was an amazing lady. Fearless – she stood up for her people." He looked in her eyes. "So... what's your name?"

She looked at him with her mother's eyes.

"Erica," the girl said with a smile. "Erica Harland."

The End

Credits: Poems Fire-Caught and Wake by Langston Hughes

Coming Soon...
Nation of Flame